Ashleigh Bingham lives in Queensland where she writes full-time. A love of history and travel has taken her on journeys that provide the exotic settings of her novels. *Winds of Honour* was shortlisted for the RNA Romantic Novel of the Year 2006.

ECHOES OF A PROMISE

When Victoria Shelford runs away to sea in the name of love, her parents disown her, and she feels the pain of her father's rejection keenly. Nevertheless, Victoria's wandering spirit is not dampened, and she sets off to exotic Kashmir to find a new life. Here, she encounters the unpopular and grim-faced Andrew Wyndham, whose misspent youth has left him with empty pockets as well as a closely guarded secret. Victoria is intrigued by Wyndham, but the complications that beset his life mean that it is hard to get close to him. Can Victoria succeed where all others have failed?

Books by Ashleigh Bingham
Published by The House of Ulverscroft:

WINDS OF HONOUR
THE WAYWARD WIND

ASHLEIGH BINGHAM

ECHOES OF A PROMISE

Complete and Unabridged

ULVERSCROFT
Leicester

First published in Great Britain in 2010 by
Robert Hale Limited
London

First Large Print Edition
published 2010
by arrangement with
Robert Hale Limited
London

British Library CIP Data

Bingham, Ashleigh.
    Echoes of a promise.
    1. Fathers and daughters- -Fiction. 2. Kashmir (India)- -
Fiction. 3. Love stories. 4. Large type books.
    I. Title
    823.9′2–dc22

    ISBN 978–1–44480–479–9

Published by
F. A. Thorpe (Publishing)
Anstey, Leicestershire

Set by Words & Graphics Ltd.
Anstey, Leicestershire
Printed and bound in Great Britain by
T. J. International Ltd., Padstow, Cornwall

This book is printed on acid-free paper

1

London 1875

Victoria Shelford was in a sombre, reflective mood as she walked home from her day's work with the volunteers at the Bloomsbury Foundling Hospital.

This morning, for the first time, she'd accompanied a midwife on her call to a girl in labour and had stood by helplessly as a young woman died giving birth on the floor of a filthy, overcrowded East End tenement. The girl didn't live long enough to hear that she'd delivered a daughter into the world.

With the tiny, unwashed creature wrapped in a hospital towel, Victoria had carried it away, past the other occupants of the room who stood hovering like vultures in the doorway, waiting to snatch a few rags from the corpse before it was taken to the morgue. The dead girl's soiled linen petticoat still had remnants of fine lace on the hem.

The day's events hung heavily on her mind as she made the long walk home. What misfortune could have brought that poor young woman to her wretched end amongst strangers? No one in that house had even known her name. And what future would be waiting for her daughter? Would the baby still be alive when she went back to work at the hospital next Thursday?

The lump in her throat grew tighter. How very different that side of life was to the privileged upbringing that she and her sisters enjoyed. She hoped that her father would be at home when she arrived; he was the only one in the family she'd be able to talk to about today's tragedy.

'Oi! Watch where yer goin', miss!' The angry shout startled her as she was about to step into the path of a wagon trundling along Oxford Street.

'I'm sorry,' she mouthed up at the driver, as she pulled back.

But further ruminations were diverted the moment she turned the corner into Hanover Square and saw her mother's carriage pulling up at their house. The butler ran out to lower the steps and Emily, her younger sister, scrambled down, weeping into a handkerchief. Their mother, Lady Mary, needed assistance to alight, and even at a distance Victoria could tell that she was about to have one of her *turns*.

Obviously, Lady Marchant's tea party had not gone well today.

By the time Victoria swept through the front door, Emily had disappeared upstairs and their white-faced mother, leaning on the arm of her maid, was climbing unsteadily towards her bedroom.

'Ah, here you are at last, Victoria! Tell your father that I wish to see him immediately. What I've been forced to endure today is beyond description.' She swayed and held a hand against her forehead. 'If you, my girl, spent less time with those foundlings and more with your own sister, Emily would not be the *embarrassment* she is today.'

Victoria bit her tongue and knocked on the door of her father's study, well aware that this was not the moment to unburden herself to him about the tragedy she'd witnessed today in the East End.

Mr George Shelford MP, was a pleasant if ineffectual man, and in front of him lay the third draft of a very dull speech that he was due to present in the House tomorrow. When Victoria gave him her mother's message, he sighed and walked slowly upstairs to find Lady Mary lying on a chaise with a cloth soaked in cool rosewater across her forehead and a glass of sherry in her hand.

'George, something must be done about Emily! That girl made absolutely no attempt to be even remotely civil to anyone this afternoon and Lady Marchant — as well as that ill-favoured daughter of hers with a neck like a giraffe . . . '

Mr Shelford gave every appearance of listening, but he'd heard it all before. Their youngest daughter's form and features had been designed by a divine hand to illustrate feminine perfection, and now when the sixteen year old entered a room it was not uncommon for gasps to be audible.

Yet the sweet child was cursed with a pathological shyness which was as paralysing now as it had been when she was five years old. She froze with strangers. And she never had much to say to the family either.

Mr Shelford shook his head and tut-tutted several times as Lady Mary described every detail of the wretched gathering where Emily had disappeared for a whole hour and was eventually discovered sitting on the floor behind a sofa.

'Just imagine how I felt, George, when Lady Marchant — that old bag of bones — announced that she'd always considered Emily Shelford to be *simple minded* and that this had just proved it! I was outraged, but then — ' Her hand shook as she gulped the sherry. 'But then I overheard that appalling daughter of hers saying that Emily could hardly be expected to behave any better in

4

society when she came from a long line of Smithfield butchers.' She made a whimpering sound. 'After that, of course, we left the house immediately.'

Mr Shelford gave a sympathetic murmur. Lady Mary had always been a highly strung creature who liked to remind him that her disposition was governed by a faint trickle of aristocratic Woolcott blood flowing through her veins. Though their wealth and influence had evaporated more than a century earlier, the Woolcotts still clung to their titles and the faded distinction of their old rank.

Lady Mary would never have married a man she considered to be so far beneath her socially if she had not found the manners and the appearance of George Shelford to be perfectly acceptable — and his financial situation especially so.

From the time they'd met, he'd made no secret of the fact that the foundations of his family's prosperity had been laid down by generations of hard-working butchers. They'd been shrewd men who'd bought property, sent their sons off to gain a gentleman's education, and gradually inched themselves up the precarious social ladder — never moving too fast, never leaping too far in a generation.

George Shelford's marriage to Lady Mary

Woolcott had been useful in elevating his family another notch, and her connections had certainly been instrumental in helping him gain a seat in the House of Commons — by the narrowest of margins — as well as ensuring his acceptance into a couple of good clubs.

Yes, indeed, the butchers of Smithfield had come a long way in the last century, and now there were whispers in some quarters that Mr George Shelford MP might be in line for a knighthood. Bets were being laid on it in the clubs and the odds were growing shorter. He hugged the dream close. *Sir* George Shelford!

'Victoria should be giving more help to Emily!' Lady Mary's *turn* was showing little sign of abating, so he refilled her sherry glass. 'When are Caroline and Hedley coming back to town? Caroline must make a greater effort to take Emily under her wing, too.'

Mr Shelford didn't mention that their eldest daughter and her dashing husband were already home from their latest country house party. Witty, vivacious Caroline, always the life of every party she attended, had called on him this morning, asking for his help to pay off some of the debts that she and Captain Hedley Ingram had yet again incurred.

In temperament, Hedley and Caroline were

splendidly matched and Mr Shelford always considered it a great pity that his income couldn't match their lifestyle. But, as a father, he was never able to refuse a request from the delightful Caroline.

But neither could he bring himself to ask her if there was any truth in the gossip that had come to him regarding their outrageous conduct when she and Hedley were guests at a recent house party in Norfolk. He'd heard that she had been no more faithful to her husband than he'd been to her but, apparently, it had all been regarded as a great joke. The Prince of Wales had also been staying in the house at the time, and it was said that he'd laughed, too.

But if gossip was starting to spread about Caroline and Hedley's wild behaviour, how long would it take for the image of Shelford respectability to become tarnished, and for the name of George Shelford to be dropped from the list of forthcoming knighthoods? He would never, never forgive anyone in the family whose actions brought about that disaster.

* * *

When Victoria went to her sister's room, Emily had already dried her eyes and was sitting at her painting table beside the window. A folio of botanical prints lay open, ready for her to copy an exotic bloom — which would then join all the other uninspired efforts pinned around the walls.

'Emmie, what happened today? What has upset Mama this time?'

'It was awful, Vicky. The ladies were gossiping about everyone and I wanted to run to the other side of the world. I never know what to do when there's a room full of people looking at me and expecting me to say something brilliant.'

'Emmie, don't be a goose! They're only looking at you because you're so pretty, and nobody ever says anything *brilliant* in that society.'

Emily sniffed and gave a watery smile. 'They were even talking about you!'

Victoria laughed. 'Well, it must have been a very dull party indeed if they were reduced to that!'

'It started when Lady Marchant remarked that you were already twenty-one with still no prospect of marriage. That horrible Eloise started to giggle. This was too much for Mama to bear, so she said that you and Howard Royston would announce your engagement the moment he came home from Barbados. Then Mrs Royston told everyone that, yes, she and Mama had arranged the match years ago.' Emily's clear blue eyes widened. 'Vicky, what will you do?'

'Absolutely nothing. And neither will Howard. We've always known what our mothers were planning and, while I'm sure we'll remain the best of friends, there will never be an engagement. Anyhow, I think it's likely to be a very long time before he comes back from Barbados.'

She said nothing further. In his last letter, Howard had asked her not to disclose the news that he was about to marry a lady on the plantation, a lovely, honey-skinned lady who was already the mother of his son. The gossip mongers were sure to have a field day when word of *that* event reached London drawing rooms!

★   ★   ★

After spending a week in her room doing little but copying one botanical print after another and carefully inscribing the Latin name of each exotic specimen under the illustration, Emily agreed to accept Caroline and Hedley's help in overcoming her dread of facing strangers.

Generously financed by Mr Shelford, the couple threw themselves into the project with goodwill and promised that they would expose Emily to only their most respectable friends. They schooled her in the art of smiling while she recited appropriate little responses when they met acquaintances during their strolls through Hyde Park. And they took her to see lighthearted plays where they invariably met friends during an interval and often went on to supper with them afterwards.

Emily clung to Hedley's arm wherever they went, smiling prettily and saying little. At the end of the fortnight, Caroline showed a flash of irritation.

'Emmie, you've got to make an effort to be more sociable, even if you simply make a polite comment about the weather or about — about — something we've seen. Anything.'

'But I don't know what to say to people who show no interest in tropical flowers, or painting.'

'Oh, Emily Shelford!'

In an attempt to expand Emily's area of interest beyond the lacklustre watercolours lining her bedroom walls, Caroline and Hedley took her to see exhibitions of art in the great London galleries. She was elated by the experience, especially when she spied certain flowers hiding in the background of some masterpiece.

In desperation, they encouraged her to read

various items of London news that they circled in *The Times* each morning, and attempted to rehearse her in the art of inconsequential social chatter.

Within a week they felt she might be ready to accept an invitation to a grand dinner party, and she was even persuaded to attend a private ball. When they called at Hanover Square a fortnight later, they were able to report a modicum of success.

'I know that our Emmie is making a genuine effort to come out of her shell,' Hedley said, as he sprawled elegantly in the drawing room, 'but, by Jove, Vicky, I think your sister is the most boring girl I've ever met. We arranged for her to be seated beside an utterly charming fellow at a supper party last night — and she nearly had him nodding off to sleep while she went on and on again about all those wretched tropical flowers she paints.'

Caroline heaved a theatrical sigh. 'Oh, Vicky, thank goodness you're the one who's been assigned to escort her to the Egerton's garden party tomorrow.' She gave a roguish wink. 'Hedley and I are off to Ascot with the names of some sure-fire winners. We'll be rich when we arrive home!'

★ ★ ★

Lady Egerton's garden was at its magnificent best and, as Lady Mary and her daughters mingled with other guests, Emily was given opportunities to recite the pretty responses she'd been rehearsing. Victoria and her mother exchanged frequent smiles. Yes, the afternoon was going splendidly.

When guests began to drift into a pavilion set up for refreshments beside the ornamental lake, Lady Mary entered on the arm of an acquaintance and Victoria looked around for her sister. Her heart sank. Where had she gone? Surely Emily had been beside her only a moment ago when she stopped to speak to a friend over there near the arch of white roses? When had she slipped away? Why? At no time this afternoon had Emily given any indication that she was feeling overwhelmed.

Victoria hurried into the house and looked for her in the ladies' retiring room. And then, caught on a rising tide of panic, she slipped through the reception rooms, searching furtively behind sofas and curtains. It seemed ridiculous to be doing this now when Emily appeared to have been managing so well this afternoon. She stepped out into the garden with her anxiety turning into anger. Time was ticking away. If she wasn't found before their mother realized that she was missing, Lady Mary would fly into another fit of hysterics.

Emily, Emily, where have you gone?

A search of the shrubbery led Victoria along a path to a large greenhouse that held a virtual jungle of exotic plants and, through the dense foliage, a movement caught her eye. Then she heard her sister's voice.

'Oh, do come over here! See? This is another one that's been wrongly labelled!'

'By Jove, you're right again!' It was a male voice. 'Someone here clearly doesn't know the difference between an *anthurium andraeanum* from Columbia and *anthurium scherzerianum* from Costa Rica!'

Victoria moved closer to see who was speaking. He was of medium height, a plump, well-dressed young man with large ears, a fleshy nose and a terrifyingly wide mouth. But Emily was smiling up at him while his pale-blue eyes gazed down into hers. Neither seemed to be aware of Victoria's presence until she was almost beside them.

'Oh, Vicky! I'm so glad you're here.' Emily's face was pink with pleasure. 'Do let me present Mr Clifford. Mr Clifford, this is my sister, Victoria.'

The young man swept off his hat, bowed and took her hand. 'Delighted Miss Shelford, absolutely delighted.' His full-lipped mouth widened further. 'Your sister's ability to identify exotic blooms is quite remarkable.

Yes, Miss Shelford, quite remarkable.'

'Oh, but it's certainly not equal to your own, Mr Clifford,' Emily said sweetly. 'I've only learned the names of these specimens from the illustrations in my grandfather's folios, and I know nothing about the way you say you develop your hybrids from the *miltonia phalaenopsis*.' She turned to Victoria. 'That orchid grows in the jungles of Brazil and I've painted copies of it, but Mr Clifford actually *grows* it. He collects all kinds of plants and bulbs from around the world for his own greenhouse. We've been having a most fascinating conversation.'

Emily's sudden outburst of confidence stunned Victoria. 'Most interesting, Mr Clifford,' she murmured, then cleared her throat politely. 'Emmie, I'm truly sorry to interrupt, but I think Mama will be looking for us soon.'

Emily smiled into the young man's decidedly unhandsome face and held out her hand to him. 'I'm so sorry, but it seems that I must leave now. Do please call on us tomorrow morning so you can meet Mama, and then I'll be able to show you all the botanical folios in our library.'

'Nothing would give me greater pleasure, Miss Emily. Absolutely nothing.'

★ ★ ★

When Lady Mary was informed that Emily had invited a gentleman named Martin Clifford to lunch next day, she instantly asked Mrs Royston, to have enquiries made into his background. Constance Royston was an expert in this subtle art, and the report on Martin Clifford that came back couldn't have been better: old family, large estate, likely to inherit a title from an ageing uncle. And the gentleman had not yet reached the age of thirty. Lady Mary rubbed her palms together. Clever, clever little Emily!

When the gentleman himself called at the house next morning, Emily introduced him to both her parents, as well as to Caroline and Hedley who'd been summoned by Victoria. They'd lost their money again at the races and were in need of some cheerful company to lift their spirits.

After Mr Clifford had spent thirty minutes chatting sociably in the drawing room with the other members of her family, Emily got to her feet. 'Please excuse me, but I've promised to show Grandfather's botanical folios to Mr Clifford this morning. All twenty-two of them.' Emily's cheeks were rosy pink, and there was a new tone in her voice that took them all by surprise. 'Would anyone else care to join us in the conservatory?'

The family rose *en masse* and sat listening to Mr Clifford enthuse over each page he turned. 'Remarkable collection. Quite remarkable, Mr Shelford. I am torn with envy.'

As time slipped by, Victoria saw Lady Mary's eyes flicking frequently to her watch; Mr Clifford had viewed no more than a quarter of the collection by the time the butler came to the door to announce lunch.

'Ah!' Their guest let out a sigh of resignation. 'I must apologize for having taken up the whole morning with my own enjoyment.' His huge mouth widened further into a smile. 'Lady Mary, may I plead for an invitation to return when I'm next in London? I dearly wish to continue my journey through these magnificent folios.'

'Of course, Mr Clifford. Please do call again. Any time at all.'

Victoria and Caroline shared a knowing smile. They sniffed romance in the air.

During luncheon their guest entertained the family with tales about his travels to collect rare specimens for the hothouses at Cloudhill, his estate in Somerset.

'I do hope that you will all be able to visit Cloudhill sometime in the near future and see for yourselves the collection of *ephyphites* growing in my greenhouse. I promise that you won't find a better display anywhere this side of the equator.'

There were nods and smiles from all at the table, and Mr Shelford exchanged a quick congratulatory glance with his wife.

'Thank you, Mr Clifford, we would be delighted,' he said, and a mutually convenient date for a visit next month was immediately arranged.

Mr Clifford raised his brows apologetically at Emily. 'It's unfortunate, but by then I'm afraid that the *vanda coerulea* will have finished blooming. I'm so disappointed that you will miss it because it's been quite spectacular this year.'

'Oh!' There was genuine disappointment in Emily's tone as she explained to the family that this rare orchid from the Himalayas was a most unusual shade of blue.

'However I did take a photograph of the blossoms at the peak of their flowering a few weeks ago,' he hurried to say, 'and I had it faithfully tinted by a gentleman who excels at that craft.' Mr Clifford looked towards Lady Mary. 'Ma'am, do I have your permission to send this photograph to Miss Emily?'

'Oh, yes, of course, Mr Clifford. How very kind of you.'

* * *

'What a charming young gentleman,' Lady Mary sighed to her husband later as they saw Martin Clifford drive off in a hansom cab. 'Such charm and poise. Such refined manners!' She carefully refrained from commenting on his decidedly unattractive looks.

Her husband nodded. 'He's going to make Emily an offer, you know.'

Lady Mary clicked her tongue. 'Yes, but Victoria should be married before her younger sister walks down the aisle. I can't understand what is keeping Howard Royston on the plantation all this time. Poor Victoria. Even his mother says she doesn't know why he won't leave Barbados.'

★　★　★

Lady Mary was correct to speculate that when the photograph of the blue orchids reached Emily three days later, there would be an accompanying message.

Naturally, Emily replied to it promptly and that encouraged a flurry of letters back and forth between Somerset and London, until the day came for the family to set out for their visit to Cloudhill.

2

Martin Clifford had posted a lookout on the roof of his rambling redbrick house, much of which had been built in the days of Good Queen Bess. He waited by one of the tall, mullioned windows overlooking the gardens, impatiently winding and unwinding a curtain cord around his fingers, until he heard the sounds of an old hunting horn float down from the roof. It was the signal that two carriages had been sighted entering the gates.

He could barely contain his excitement as he hurried to the steps to greet the Shelford family's arrival, flanked by a line of smiling servants.

'Welcome to Cloudhill one and all.' He helped the ladies alight. 'Please come in, come in. I trust you had a comfortable journey? You are not exhausted? Refreshments are waiting in the drawing room, and then perhaps you'd like to be shown to your rooms to bathe and rest before dinner?'

As the party walked into the house, Lady Mary looked around approvingly at the paintings and tapestries hanging on the oak-panelled walls, the vast Aubusson carpets, the cabinets filled with fine porcelain pieces and an impressive array of heavy silver on display. It was also pleasing to note that there appeared to be no dust about, and that the woodwork gleamed. It was clear to her that Cloudhill was a well-run, dust-free house, with the added grace of scented flowers throughout.

'I'm coming to like Mr Clifford more and more,' Lady Mary said drily to her husband as they walked upstairs to rest before dinner. 'And becoming mistress of this great house is going to be quite a feather in our little Emily's cap. Oh! Won't that wretched Lady Marchant be apoplectic with envy when she hears the news!'

'Well, m'dear, first let's wait for the gentleman to make an offer for our daughter's hand.'

His wife gave him a smug smile. 'Twenty-four hours, my dear George. Mark my words: that young man will be coming to you within twenty-four hours.'

The sun was slowly sinking and Victoria was putting the final touches to her hair when there was a tap on the door connecting her room with Emily's.

'Vicky, please throw a shawl around your shoulders and come downstairs with me quickly.' Emily was almost dancing with excitement. 'Mr Clifford is down there and he's sending signals for me to come downstairs to see the greenhouse straight away — and — oh, Vicky, it's still daylight and everything will be perfectly proper if you're there with us!'

She went to the window and drew aside the curtain to reveal their host standing in the garden below. They waved to each other and Victoria waved too, then snatched her shawl and ran softly down the stairs behind her sister.

Mr Clifford, smiling broadly, offered an arm to each and hurried them across the parterre, then down a flight of stone steps to a long path leading through a shrubbery. Beyond this loomed a structure that appeared to be a slightly smaller version of the Crystal Palace. Inside, and lit by strategic lamps hanging throughout, was a vast, exotic world of colours and leafy shapes that made Victoria catch her breath.

Emily appeared to be transported as she looked around her; Mr Clifford's gaze didn't leave her face. Victoria sensed the delicacy of the situation and deliberately hung back while Martin and Emily wandered off along paths leading to further extravagant displays.

'Oh, Mr Clifford! This is — this is — so

much more than I ever imagined,' she heard Emily say, and when next she caught sight of the pair fifteen minutes later, they were beside a waterlily pond. Mr Clifford was down on one knee and Emily's hand was in his.

Victoria smiled to herself and hung back even further. But fifteen minutes later she did catch a glimpse of them walking arm in arm somewhere between the rows of *ixora coccinea* and *justicia brandegeana* and witnessed Emily lift her face invitingly towards Mr Clifford's. He lowered his head and touched his lips to hers in a soft kiss. And then another. Emily's arms slipped up around his neck.

Victoria's eyes widened. This was *Emily*? It was difficult to reconcile the image of her shy little sister with the eager young woman here in this greenhouse

Victoria blew a long, silent breath and stayed rooted to the spot while the couple moved on with Mr Clifford's arm now around her sister's waist.

More time passed and darkness began to fall. *Hurry up, Emily!* Victoria needed to stand under a lamp to see the hands of her watch. It was imperative for them all to be back in the house before their mother became aware of any absence.

When her patience could be stretched no longer, she went searching for the pair and found them beside the displays of *maranta leuconeura*, wrapped closely in each other's arms and clearly far away in a world of their own.

Victoria felt her cheeks heating and quickly walked to the door, wondering how to bring the pair back to earth. In desperation, she pulled a wooden stake from a garden bed and hit it loudly several times against the metal door frame.

Emily and Mr Clifford came hurrying through the potted vegetation, both looking somewhat flushed and dishevelled, and beaming with a new-found joy. 'Thank you, Vicky.' Emily seemed to have little air left in her lungs. 'I'd quite lost track of the time. Everything in here has been so *diverting*.'

No one in the house seemed to have noticed their absence and, after an excellent dinner — during which Lady Mary announced that she had never seen finer silver on any table in England — Martin drew Mr Shelford into his study and asked for Emily's hand in marriage.

With that formality quickly concluded, Martin asked her to walk out to the terrace with him, where he opened a velvet box and revealed a charmingly old-fashioned ring with a cluster of diamonds and sapphires. She caught her breath, and held out her hand. 'Oh, how lovely!'

'My darling wife-to-be,' he said, slipping it on her third finger, 'this was my mother's and, on the night she passed away, she told me that it was to be yours, Emily. Of course, she didn't know your name or who you might be, but she told me that wearing this ring had brought her great joy and happiness, and if you were the woman who had won my heart, she wanted you to wear it and know that this ring came with her blessings.'

'How lovely. Thank you, Martin, thank you — and with all my heart, I promise to make you happy.' She kissed him warmly. 'Now let's go back to the others and arrange a date for the wedding.'

★ ★ ★

Martin Clifford was no sportsman. Horses and guns held no interest for him and his stables housed only several pairs of carriage animals.

'What the devil are we going to do with ourselves all week at Cloudhill?' Caroline moaned. 'Go for walks and play billiards?'

Hedley rolled his eyes. 'We're both going to die of boredom.'

They soon discovered that it was a mistake

to underestimate Martin Clifford. On the day he'd first met Caroline and Hedley Ingram, he'd made an assessment of their characters that further acquaintance had merely confirmed. He didn't approve of their irresponsible way of life, but, as they were part of his beloved Emily's family, he'd see to it that they'd not find Cloudhill's hospitality wanting.

Lady Mary was late coming down for breakfast the next morning, but she arrived in time to hear Martin announce that he was arranging a ball at the end of the week to celebrate the engagement, and that neighbours had already sent over a couple of their best hunters for Caroline and Hedley to use during their stay.

'Yes, there's some good riding hereabouts, and my friends intend to invite you to take part in a point-to-point they've organized for Wednesday.'

'Oh, I say, Martin, that's absolutely splendid!' Hedley beamed and Caroline clapped her hands.

'And if you'd care to try some shooting, I'll have Walker, my steward, show you the guns that my late father used. I've never found any pleasure in it, but Walker knows all the best locations for wildfowl at this time of the year.' He stopped abruptly and turned to Victoria.

'Oh, forgive me, my dear sister-to-be, but should I have asked my friends to bring a horse for you also?'

She shook her head. 'Thank you, but I don't ride. I enjoy walking . . . and playing tennis. I noticed a net down there on the lower terrace.'

'Yes, indeed! Don't play myself, but I've arranged for a few young neighbours to come for a game tomorrow. And, by the way, we've all been invited to lunch at Longleat House on Thursday. I'm afraid that the marquis and most of the family are away at the moment, but Lord Bevill, the eldest son, is eager to become acquainted with you and your family, Lady Mary.'

She clattered her tea cup onto its saucer; excitement rendered her temporarily speechless. The Shelfords had been invited to dine with aristocracy! That was going to provide a superb barb for her to throw at Millicent Marchant and her wretched daughter when next they met.

'Please don't concern yourself about the distance to Longleat, ma'am. It rarely takes me more than an hour to drive there, and we'll be back well before dark.'

There seemed to be nothing that the master of Cloudhill was unable or unwilling to provide to ensure that the Shelford family enjoyed their time in Somerset. The kitchen staff provided a variety of splendid dishes each day, and neighbours were invited to dine some evenings. These meals were usually followed by dancing and cards, or games of charades and songs sung around the piano, which they discovered that Mr Clifford played quite well.

'Emmie, darling,' Victoria said as their carriage pulled away from Cloudhill at the end of the week, 'your Martin Clifford is the most thoughtful and tender-hearted gentleman I've ever encountered. You're the luckiest girl in the world to be marrying him.'

'Yes, I know I am. And I'll pray hard that some day you'll find a husband just like him.'

Victoria smiled to herself and turned to look out the window. She doubted that there could ever be another gentleman quite like Martin Clifford. He was unique.

★ ★ ★

A week later, Lady Mary — wearing an elegant new green velvet hat from Paris — drove triumphantly around Hyde Park in her open landau with Mrs Royston at her side. The engagement of Miss Emily Shelford and Mr Martin Clifford had been announced in *The Times* that morning, and Lady Mary could barely contain her elation when a steady stream of acquaintances approached the carriage to offer congratulations.

'Constance, my dear, do tell me if you catch sight of that wretched Lady Marchant and her giraffe, Eloise, here this afternoon. I want to snub the old witch for having called our sweet little Emily *simple minded!* Hah! Emily has caught herself a future viscount. I did tell you, didn't I, that dear Martin is a great nephew of Lord Fortescue, and his heir? I'd like to see Lady Marchant snare such a fortune for *her* daughter!'

Mrs Royston smiled. She'd already heard the whole story several times, and she was still amazed at how quickly a romance had developed between the unlikely pair.

'I decided that if we set the wedding a month after Emily's birthday, it will give me time to have her gown made in Paris, and — ' Lady Mary suddenly wrapped her fingers around her companion's wrist. 'Ah! Look, Constance, here come Lady Marchant and Eloise. I must make sure that neither of them miss my snub. I do hope people are watching.'

They were indeed, and Lady Mary slanted a look of glee towards Mrs Royston as Lady Marchant and Eloise were suitably cut when her ladyship ordered the carriage to increase speed just as the pair was almost beside them.

'Oooh!' Mrs Royston gasped. 'She'll *never* forgive you for having done that to them, Mary! That woman and her daughter won't stop until they've found some way to pay you back.'

'Hah! Just let them try! I'll soon have *two* daughters married well, and Millicent Marchant still can't find any poor fool willing to wed her Eloise at any price.' She brushed an imaginary speck of dust from her skirt. 'Now what was I saying about the wedding? Ah, yes. Emily is taking scant interest in the preparations, and I'm afraid to say that Victoria allows so much of her time to be taken up by charity work that I see little of her at home these days. And I do feel that she's accepting far too many invitations. She's a very popular girl, you know.'

Mrs Royston looked at Lady Mary sharply. 'Don't tell me she's formed some attachment? She must be aware that Howard is sure to be back from Barbados before long, and I know he'll be ready to make her an offer.'

*   *   *

Lady Mary felt like singing for joy when she returned home. Her little Emily was about to be the most beautiful bride ever to walk down

29

an aisle. Poor Mr Clifford could be forgiven for having inherited such an unfortunate lack of good looks when he'd been born into a wealthy family with elderly relatives who had produced no other heirs.

She was halfway up the stairs when her thoughts switched to Victoria. Yes, she'd grown into a charming, intelligent girl, though she lacked the golden beauty of her two sisters. But she'd developed something else — poise? A quick wit? Whatever it was, that spark was attracting a growing number of gentlemen to their door.

At that moment, Lady Mary heard the sound of it opening, and looked over the banister to see Victoria standing on the threshold with a man that no mother in her position could ever approve of. She blew a hiss of irritation between her teeth. No young lawyer whose father owned a small iron foundry in the Midlands would ever be considered a suitable escort for a daughter of this house. Victoria had been told repeatedly about her mother's view on associating with people who were not of their own social class, yet she still showed an infuriating streak of independence in choosing her acquaintances.

'Thank you, Oliver, it was a wonderful recital,' Lady Mary heard her saying to the slim, grey-suited man at her side.

Though she was unable to catch his reply, her blood froze when she witnessed the warm familiarity with which Victoria leaned forward and lifted her cheek to be kissed before the man ran down the steps.

'I'll see you at the Alcock's dinner on Tuesday,' she called after him, then turned to walk across the hall, smiling to herself.

Lady Mary's knuckles whitened. That little vignette sounded alarm bells in her head. When was Howard Royston going to arrive home? How far might Victoria's relationship with this son of an iron miller have progressed by then? Oh, goodness, it didn't bear thinking about!

But confronting Victoria, as her mother well knew, was never the way to persuade this young lady to change her mind. A more subtle technique was required, and, as soon as Mr Shelford returned from his day at Westminster, she bearded him in his dressing room.

'George, Victoria's association with that wretched son of a provincial iron merchant must not be allowed to go any further. We have to put a stop to it!'

It had been a bad day in the House. The debate over the proposed Slum Clearance Law was not going well, and Mr Shelford had no inclination to begin another debate over

31

the dinner table tonight with his favourite daughter.

'Victoria has always been a sensible, level-headed young woman,' he said mildly. 'I believe we can trust her to make sound decisions.'

His wife narrowed her eyes at him. 'Can we? Just think what lies at stake here, George. Your knighthood could very well hang in the balance. Having two daughters married into good families will stand for little if the third drags us all down by marrying someone so socially inferior. Someone whose family background might hold — well, er — who knows what frightful secrets that we're not yet aware of. Think about it, my dear. Consider what fodder it could supply to those who are looking for some excuse to topple your name from the list of honours.'

She saw that she'd touched the right nerve. 'But what can be done, Mary? After all, this is *Victoria* we're talking about!'

She held his dinner jacket for him while she explained the part he was required to play in her strategy. 'I have no intention of confronting her, my dear, because there are other ways to detach our daughter from this unsuitable young man. You'll see.'

Fortunately for her plan, the family was dining alone that night and, as usual on these rare evenings, the conversation was focused on Emily's wedding. The ceremony was still three months away, but the list of guests to be invited was a regular topic for discussion. And, right on cue, Mr Shelford delivered his line.

'My dear, do you think that your Aunt Honoria will be able to travel up from Devon for the ceremony?' He spoke innocently and kept his eyes fixed on his plate.

'Oh, poor Aunt Honoria! No. Sadly, I'm afraid it will be quite impossible for her to make the journey now that her health is failing.' Lady Mary looked pained. 'You know, my dear, I think she will be ninety next birthday, and she mentioned in her last letter how very frail she is becoming. I've always been uneasy about her living all alone down there.'

Across the table, Emily's great blue eyes filled with concern.

'No, Emily,' Lady Mary said smartly. 'I know that it would lift her spirits if you went down to spend a little time with her, but you can't possibly leave London when we have so many things to prepare for the wedding. And neither can we expect Victoria to put aside all her charity work and other engagements to visit such a remote part of the country.' From the corner of her eye Lady Mary saw Victoria drop her knife and fork.

'Oh, Mama, of course I can arrange time away from London. My friend Patricia will happily take my place at the hospital on Thursdays, and I'd love to stay with Aunt Honoria for a few weeks. Now I feel wretched to think that I've let myself become so caught up with things here that I haven't been down to Devon since last year. I must go down there to visit her again. Oh, please say that you'll agree to it.'

Lady Mary made a play of looking questioningly at her husband. 'What do you think, George? Can we spare Victoria?'

'Yes, yes, of course, and thank you, my dear. A most charitable offer. I'll telegraph Aunt Honoria tomorrow and say you'll be on Saturday's train.' Mr Shelford and his wife exchanged a congratulatory glance and said no more about the matter until they retired for the night.

'In all honesty, Mary,' he said, as soon as the maid had left her bedroom, 'I must confess that I'm not entirely easy about Victoria spending some time with your disgraceful old aunt.' He sat on the end of his wife's bed while she tied the strings of her nightcap. 'I've always thought that much of Caroline's wild behaviour was encouraged by the stories she heard about Honoria's scandalous past.'

Lady Mary's eyelids drooped. 'It was all so long ago, George. Yes, it's a fact that she was once married to a Prussian baron, and then to some Italian count. And of course, there were all those affairs in France.'

'Well, I think she was guilty of filling Caroline's head full of romantic stories when the girl was far too young to understand the consequences of such behaviour.'

'Oh, George, surely you're not suggesting that *Victoria* could ever be swayed by Aunt Honoria's tales?' She patted her husband's hand, settled her head on the pillow and closed her eyes. 'Our Victoria has her feet set firmly on the ground, as you well know, my dear, and when dear Howard Royston arrives home we'll announce their engagement. You'll see. Next year we'll have another wedding to prepare.'

And perhaps there would be a significant event to celebrate before then, he thought, smiling to himself as he left her room. When his knighthood was announced, his wife was sure to arrange a fitting celebration. Perhaps a grand ball?

Ah! What a night that would be for *Sir* George Shelford.

3

When Victoria's train pulled into the tiny platform at Sedleigh, old Wilf Potts, chewing on the stem of his briar pipe, was waiting for her with Aunt Honoria's trap.

'Hello, Mr Potts, how good it is to be back here again.' He gave a friendly grunt. 'How is my aunt today?'

'Fit as a heifer.'

She climbed up into the seat beside him. 'I hope you and Mrs Potts are keeping well, too?' Her great-aunt's retainers were surely both well over eighty now.

'Aye, that we are, thank 'e, miss.' This was usually the extent of any conversation with Mr Potts and Victoria attempted no more while the little grey mare clopped up and down the hilly lanes leading to Lady Honoria's house three miles away.

She slipped off her gloves, pulled the hat from her head and breathed in the sweet, earthy scents of the countryside around them. Occasional glimpses of the whitecaps dancing on the blue sea beyond the cliffs took her eye and, looking down from the bridge as they clattered over the river, she saw a vessel under repair in the little shipyard which had stood there on the bank for more than a century.

'Mr Strickland appears to be very busy in the yard.' She craned her neck to see sheets of copper being unloaded from a wagon.

Mr Potts grunted. 'Old boat down there bein' outfitted to go tradin' with the 'eathens.'

She turned on the seat and glimpsed the name *Fortitude* painted on the vessel's stern, before the trap rounded a corner and they trotted along the last mile to Aunt Honoria's pretty little cottage.

Of course, everyone in the family knew that it wasn't actually their great-aunt's own house. She had no money at all, but one of her old lovers — a peer of the realm who'd died twenty years previously — had left her a bequest of £200 a year, and the tenancy of this cottage during her lifetime.

Victoria caught the sound of Lady Honoria's laughter coming from the drawing room as soon as she walked into the kitchen where Mrs Potts was setting out a plate of plum cake along with three cups and saucers on a tray.

'Ah! What a treat it is to see you here again, Miss Vicky.' Her wrinkled face creased further and she kissed Victoria on her cheek.

'It's always a treat to be here, Mrs Potts,

but tell me quickly about my aunt. I hear that her health is failing.'

The housekeeper gave a hoot. 'M'lady is almost ninety years old, bless me! And just listen to her in there now flirtin' with her gentlemen visitors. Failing? Never!'

She placed a fourth cup on the tray, which Victoria picked up while Mrs Potts went ahead to open the door of the drawing room.

'Victoria, my darling girl! So you've crept in by the kitchen again to surprise me!' The old lady, wearing lavender silk and cream lace, was sitting like a queen in a high-backed chair with a handsome courtier on either side.

Both visitors, dressed in blue naval jackets with gleaming brass buttons, stood as Victoria walked into the room and one, a tall young man with fair hair, stepped forward to take the heavy tray from her hands and set it down on the table.

'Thank you,' she said. His face was bronzed by sun and wind, his eyes the brightest blue she'd ever seen, and, when he flashed a smile, Victoria caught her breath. She looked away quickly and saw the sparkle in Honoria's eyes.

'How delightful it is to have you here again,' the old lady said and they kissed. 'Gentlemen, let me introduce my great-niece,

Miss Victoria Shelford. My dear, here before you are two of the bravest, most handsome and gallant seamen ever to sail from Devon.' The pair stood side-by-side, smiling, and looking not in the least abashed by Lady Honoria's extravagant words.

'My dear, this is Captain Henry Latham, who has voyaged around the world a dozen times, facing hurricanes, pirates, monsters of the deep and all kinds of terrifying things.'

The older man, whose age was perhaps fifty, gave an amused smile and acknowledged the introduction. 'Delighted, Miss Shelford,' he said, and took her hand. He was of stocky build, with a bluff and hearty man-of-the-world air.

'And this gentleman, dear, is Captain Latham's nephew, Peter, who, I've just learned, is now also a captain — or master — or something very important. Did you happen to notice their vessel under repair in Strickland's shipyard on your way here?'

'Indeed I did see the *Fortitude*.' She shook hands with him. The young man's skin was tough, his grip firm, and his second smile was just as heart-jolting as the first. Her fingers seemed unwilling to lose contact with his. 'May I ask, Captain — '

He interrupted. 'Sorry, Miss Shelford, there can only be one captain on board a ship, and that's my uncle. Yes, I've just received my master's papers, but I'll be sailing alongside him as first officer.' Did she imagine it, or did his pressure on her hand increase momentarily before he released it?

'Oh, I understand.' She wriggled her fingers to restore their circulation and, with a sudden need to busy herself, lifted the teapot and began filling the cups. 'And where will you be sailing off to?'

'We're heading to the East Indies.' Peter picked up the first cup and handed it to Lady Honoria with a courtly bow. 'I've never sailed in those waters, but this old sea dog knows them well.' He and the captain exchanged a warm look. 'I've been working on Yankee clippers for the last five years, but my uncle and I always had a plan to go into partnership one day and buy a trading vessel of our own.'

'How exciting. I wish every success to you and the *Fortitude*.' Victoria took the chair he was holding for her and when her teacup rattled on its saucer she was surprised to find how unsteady her hand had become. 'How long do you expect to be away from England?'

Captain Henry answered. 'These trading voyages usually take about two years, Miss Shelford. I've sailed to the Spice Islands several times and the shipowners have always made a healthy profit when we took out a cargo from our British iron foundries and brought back a hold full of silk, tea, exotic timbers, and anything else that commands a high price here.'

'And so now you, yourselves, have become shipowners. How splendid.' Victoria was aware that the nephew hadn't taken his gaze from her face. 'And when is the *Fortitude* due to sail?'

'It will be some time yet before the shipwrights have finished and we get the masts up,' Peter answered, moving his chair closer to hers. 'After that, we need to find a crew, get the ship rigged, then make a run down the Channel to see how she handles in the Atlantic swell.'

Aunt Honoria smiled at the men. 'It all sounds most exciting. I'm sure Victoria would love to see the work going on at the shipyard, wouldn't you, dear?'

'We'd be honoured to introduce you to the *Fortitude*, Miss Shelford,' the captain said, 'though I must warn you that with ship-wrights still crawling all over her, it won't be safe to escort you on board yet.'

'Thank you, I quite understand — and I promise not to get in anyone's way. Would it be convenient if I walked down tomorrow afternoon?'

'Yes, please, do come.'

It was Peter Latham who spoke, and it was not simply his words, but the enthusiasm in his tone that sent a ball of excitement bouncing through her.

* * *

'Do you know, my dear, I don't think I've felt so well for months as I do at present.' Lady Honoria chuckled while Victoria fussed about arranging her lace-trimmed pillows at bed-time. 'Now whisper to me, m'love, have you ever before met a young man as charming and handsome as Peter Latham?'

'Yes, of course I have, Aunt. London is full of handsome — ' She blushed.

'But did any of *them* make your heart beat the way it did today when Peter Latham smiled and pulled his chair closer to yours?'

'Aunt Honoria, how can you possibly know — Oh, dear, was I so obvious?'

'I was delighted to see the glow that came into your eyes, dear girl.'

Victoria perched herself on the edge of the bed. 'A glow? No, whatever you saw in my eyes today was pure *terror*.' She gave a little self-deprecating huff. 'You know that I'm not the sort of girl who — who melts at the touch of a man, yet from the moment I met Peter

Latham this afternoon, I felt myself being drawn to him. Never before in my life have I experienced such an extraordinary sensation. And, yes, it did terrify me.'

A smile played around Honoria's mouth. 'Why should it do that?'

'Why? Because I have met him only briefly and I've absolutely no idea who he is. There's been no time to learn anything about his background, or his character, or — or — ' A flush swept into her cheeks. 'In any case, how could I permit myself to even think of getting to know him better when he'll be sailing away in a few weeks and not coming back for two years?'

Honoria raised her brows and clicked her tongue.

Victoria sniffed, then let out a long sigh. 'Oooh! Why shouldn't I be terrified of my emotions when Peter Latham and I have only just met and I know nothing about the kind of man he really is — and yet, despite all that, I can't get him out of my mind. I know I'm being ridiculous. It's all happening far too suddenly. It's totally unreasonable.'

'Oh, my poor darling, do you think that love always provides a reason?'

'Well, it should, because I'd like to know why it is that, if I close my eyes, I can see him waiting for me there on the edge of a great cliff. And, yes, he's charming and handsome and he excites me, but if I allow myself to move any closer I could very well tumble over the edge with him. And who knows what might be waiting at the bottom.'

'Hmm, I see. What a *sensible* answer that is, Victoria. You sound just like your mother.' Honoria squeezed her hand. 'My darling girl, life is all about taking chances and you must never be afraid to grasp whatever joy it offers along the way. Yes, there'll be disappointments sometimes, even sadness. But I've learned that the shadows have a way of making the rest of life seem all the more brilliant.'

Victoria lay in bed that night with images of a young, handsome mariner dancing through her brain. All common sense cried out to turn around and go home quickly to the safety of London. But she knew that it would now be impossible to resist taking just one more little step towards him on that enticing edge.

The following afternoon she almost ran to the yard where shipwrights were clambering over the vessel, hammering and sawing. Peter was working on the deck and, when he saw her coming, he scrambled over the side and down the rope ladder. They met face to face in the middle of the yard and when he smiled at her she felt a flash of fire as old as time.

'I thought — actually I couldn't believe that you'd really want to see this old ship.'

'Oh, yes, I wanted to come. Yes, I wanted to come very much.'

They searched each other's eyes and she thought she could see her thoughts reflected in his. It was a shock to realize that he appeared to be as nervous as she was.

They sat on an upturned box in the shade and he picked up a stick to draw diagrams in the dust as he explained the refitting that was being done on the vessel. She tried hard to concentrate, but his closeness made that difficult.

'By the end of next week, it should be safe enough for you to come aboard to inspect her.'

Why did she think that she could hear a deeper meaning in each word he uttered? Was her heart playing tricks with her mind? He walked home with her at twilight, stayed for supper, and submitted himself to a lengthy, light-hearted inquisition by Lady Honoria.

'Yes, I can see that you've done very well to afford to buy a partnership in the *Fortitude* — so tell me, Peter, just what age are you? Do you have family? Brothers and sisters?'

'I'm twenty six, ma'am. And no, I have no family at all — apart from Captain Latham.

My father was Thomas, his brother. He was a blacksmith but, sadly, both he and my mother were taken off by an outbreak of typhoid when I was ten years old. That's when I went to sea.'

'You did? It surprises me to hear that you were able to become a sailor at such a tender age.'

'I started as a ship's boy, m'lady, and right from the start I knew that the sea was my calling. Uncle Henry found me a place on a vessel that was captained by an officer who had a reputation for being a first-rate sailor and a fair-minded master. He worked me hard and taught me well. I have much to thank him for.'

*　*　*

'Well?' the old lady said, when Victoria came to her bedroom later to bid her goodnight. 'Are you still terrified of slipping over the edge of that cliff with a man named Peter Latham? From what he revealed this evening, I believe him to have a fine, steadfast character and a promising future. Would you not agree?'

'Oh, Aunt, I think — I think I will never again meet anyone like him.' She flung her arms wide and spun childishly. 'I've been in love several times, you know. Well, I think I have. It was always very pleasant and enjoyable, but what I felt towards Peter the moment we met, was something quite different. Utterly different! It was as if I'd been suddenly gripped by some savage, glorious madness.'

And nothing happened in the following weeks to alter her feelings. She ran to the shipyard every afternoon and learned to climb up and down the precarious rope ladder dangling from the deck.

Once aboard, Peter showed her the workings of the vessel from the pumps and the galley, to the poop deck at the stern, which was the captain's exclusive domain. The officers' cabins were below this, with a handsomely panelled navigation room built across the stern. In here, Victoria was eventually able to make herself useful by unpacking boxes of books and rolls of charts and maps, along with navigation instruments, and storing them away in their specially fitted drawers and shelves.

Peter walked home with her each afternoon and often stayed for supper with Lady Honoria. 'No, no, don't thank me, Peter, my dear,' she said, 'it's a pleasure to share your company. It makes me feel young again.'

Each evening Victoria stood with him at the

garden gate as he was leaving and, while the farewell kisses they exchanged grew increasingly heated, he resisted her unspoken invitation to explore deeper intimacy. They spoke of love, but it was she who first mentioned marriage.

'Vicky, I love you deeply and there's no other woman in the world who could ever fill my heart the way you do, but do you imagine that your parents will give their permission for you to marry a man of the sea? I've no grand connections and nothing to recommend me but what you see standing here before you.'

She put her hands on his shoulders and held him at arm's length, looking at him squarely. 'Yes, and what I see is exactly why I love you, Peter Latham. You're a fine, honest man. Anyhow, I don't need my parents' permission to marry. I'm over twenty-one and what I want is to spend the rest of my life with you, wherever you go, whatever you do.' She spoke with an odd mixture of innocence and passion. 'You've told me that wives often sail with their husbands.'

He reached for her and held her close. 'Vicky — my dearest Vicky. Dear God, what can I say? I love you with every fibre of my being, and swear that I'll look after you and make you a wealthy woman one day.'

'Oh, Peter! I don't care a jot about that. All

I want is to be with you. And I want to be *useful*. Yes, you can teach me how to navigate and I'll plot our course round and round the world so that we never have to set foot on shore again.' When she laughed he picked her up and hugged her tightly in his arms.

'Sweetheart, I really *must* write to your parents and ask for your hand. It's the proper thing to do. I want to tell them how much I've come to love you, and swear that I'll always take care of you.' He snuggled his face into her neck.

'No! Please don't write. I mean, not yet. But let's go inside and tell Aunt Honoria that we're engaged.'

★ ★ ★

Once the copper hull was in place, the carpentry below decks was completed and the masts were in position, the day came for the newly painted *Fortitude* to be slipped into the water and moored a few yards down river at the jetty where a gangplank now made boarding simple. The barque rode high until her ballast was loaded, and while that was happening, Peter and his uncle travelled to Portsmouth to sign on a crew of able seamen, as well as a cook and a sailmaker, a carpenter and a ship's boy.

They were back within a week, followed shortly by two wagonloads of men with sea chests and canvas bags — eighteen men with weathered faces, tattooed arms, ear-rings, scars, and most wearing knives and spikes on their belts. They tugged their forelocks to Victoria as they climbed aboard and carried their belongings below.

Within minutes they were back on deck and, under Peter's direction, the complicated business of rigging the three masts began. Eventually, the twenty-six new sails had been hoisted, with halyards running to the belaying pins, while the captain watched from the deck, bellowed orders about braces, buntlines and clewlines. Victoria held her breath each time Peter scrambled up a mast and worked his way along a high spar to some seaman who was securing ropes.

Supplies were brought on board, the water barrels were filled and the carpenter built chicken coops to stand beside the goat pen. While she watched the ship quickly coming to life, her heart grew heavier: tomorrow, the mooring ropes would be cast off, the wind would fill these sails and the *Fortitude* would disappear out there into the Channel.

Through their adjoining wall that night, Lady Honoria listened to Victoria pacing her bedroom floor and, long before the sun had risen, she heard a light tap on her own door.

It was Victoria, fully dressed and carrying a portmanteau. 'Aunt, I've decided to take that leap over the cliff. I'm going to beg Peter and his uncle to let me sail with them while they put the ship through her trials.' She quickly kissed the old lady's cheek. 'I'll be gone for no more than a few days — perhaps a week.'

Lady Honoria rarely found herself speechless, but this was one of those occasions.

* * *

On the other hand, Captain Latham had a great deal to say when he confronted Victoria in the dawn light, and every word conveyed his outrage at her uninvited arrival aboard his ship, as well as his fury at Peter's giddy happiness at her surprise.

'Please let me apologize, Captain, because I know that this is not at all the thing to do.' She refused let herself buckle under his tongue lashing. 'But if you give me permission to sail with you for these few days, I promise to be in nobody's way.'

They stood facing each other silently, before the lines around the captain's mouth slowly softened. 'Very well, Miss Shelford, I will give you permission to remain on board, on condition that my first officer is not distracted from his duties.'

'Captain, I promise that you won't even know that I'm here.' Without another word she bolted into Peter's cabin and threw herself gleefully onto his narrow bunk. From above her head, she heard orders for the moorings to be cast off and the sails unfurled, followed by sounds of running feet along the deck, and the soft creaks and groans of timbers as the vessel got under way.

She knelt with her face pressed against the porthole, nervous and excited as she saw the shoreline — and her old life — slipping away. Once out into the Channel, the ship began to roll gently and, when she lay her head on Peter's pillow, she dreamed of the day when she'd be his wife and part of his life at sea, on this ship or any other. A happiness greater than she'd ever known squeezed her heart.

The ship's boy brought a plate of bread and ham to her later in the morning, along with a basin. 'Mr Latham sends his compliments, ma'am, and I'm to tell you that we're makin' good headway but when we start headin' out of the Channel, there's likely to be some rough weather. Storm blowin' up on the port bow.'

With hunger gnawing at her insides, she nibbled at the food on the plate and hoped that her stomach would behave. The sky outside was growing darker and before long, she could detect an increasing pitch in the sound of the wind singing in the high rigging. The bell rang for all hands to come on deck and she soon detected a new shudder in the ship's roll as it caught a cross-swell on the building seas that were slamming against the hull. The pumps below began to thump continuously.

Hours later, Peter knocked on the door and stood grinning at her with his wet hair plastered against his head and water dripping from his oilskins. 'Are you all right, sweetheart?' he asked, looking pointedly at the empty basin.

'Can't you see that I was made for this?' She laughed and braced herself against the bulkhead as the wind howled and the ship pitched violently. 'What about you and the crew up there?'

'Fine. The men know what's expected of them, and the ship's handling splendidly.' He leaned forward and she kissed him quickly. 'I'm too wet to come in, but as soon as this weather settles I'll show you just how proud I am of you.'

The wild storm had blown itself out by sunrise the next morning, though a heavy sea still swept over the bow. Victoria woke to the sound of four bells signalling that routine had returned to shipboard life and the first watch was on its way below to catch four hours' sleep. Four hours on, four hours off around the clock — for weeks on end for everyone, except the captain and first officer who were never truly off duty.

She was still in her nightdress when Peter at last arrived in the cabin, hollow-eyed with fatigue, but grinning. 'Well, we wanted the old ship to show us what she was capable of doing in all weathers, and she came through last night's blow like a true lady.' He sagged against the bulkhead and eyed her longingly.

She swung her feet onto the pitching floor and staggered to his side. 'And standing here before you, sir, is another lady who is anxious for your approval — just as soon as we get you out of these wet clothes.' She reached up and, with fumbling fingers, began to unbutton his jacket and shirt, while the heaving ocean threw her off balance and tossed her against him again and again.

They laughed and kissed as she towelled him dry. He tasted of salt and sea and man, and she wondered if any woman before had ever sampled such potent flavours all at once. She was so happy, she thought that her heart might stop, but it didn't seem to matter. Nothing mattered in this private and wonderful world but the taste of his mouth and the touch of his skin.

When he whipped the nightdress over her head, they tumbled into his narrow bunk and lay tightly jammed together while their kisses deepened and passion soared. Finding a mutually comfortable position in the confined space created initial difficulties, but their eager bodies soon guided them to the solution.

'Now show me, Peter. Show me how to make love.' When she raised his hand to her lips and innocently ran her tongue across their tips, his aching fatigue became an avalanche of desire.

'Sweetheart, I think you'll find that old Mother Nature is a splendid teacher.'

A quiver rippled through her and she pressed herself even closer against him as he kissed her face and the curve of her neck. Her heart thundered when he shifted his weight and began languidly and knowing to lead her along paths of hot, dark, irresistible discovery until her body sang the glorious womansong that nature teaches her daughters. She rose to him and powerful sensations swamped her, lapping each secret corner of her body, sweeping her into worlds of rapture.

Replete, she lay quietly in his arms, knowing that she'd been treasured and cherished, and that nothing in her world would ever be the same again. 'Oh, Peter, my Peter. It was — oh, sublime!'

'Heaven has made us for each other, sweetheart, and when I come back with a shipload of treasures from the East' — weariness was slurring his words — 'your parents will give us their blessing and then, when I watch you walking towards me down the aisle — '

'Shhhh.' She stroked his neck, his shoulder. 'It's time to sleep now, my love. Sleep.'

He was a truly beautiful man through and through, a good man, a noble man, and she loved him utterly. But she knew that no matter how many treasure ships he brought back from the East, a mariner named Peter Latham, the son of a blacksmith, would never be accepted by her parents. They'd never give their blessing to a marriage, so there was little point in asking for it. While he lay sleeping with his head on her shoulder, she began to make plans.

When at last she was able to ease herself out of his bunk, she dressed quietly, threw a shawl around her shoulders and stepped out onto the heaving deck. There, buffeted by the salt-laden wind, she grasped a halyard to steady herself and gazed at the waves and spray breaking over the pitching bowsprit. There was nothing in view but the daunting expanse of angry grey water stretching in all directions.

It was very easy to imagine that they had sailed a thousand miles from the shores of England. There was nothing out here but the *Fortitude*. They were utterly alone in this watery world.

She stepped back into the shelter of the officers' quarters and, making no sound to wake the sleeping captain and his first officer as she slipped past their doors, she went into the great cabin in the stern. Here on the bookshelves that she'd arranged, she found the leather-bound Book of Common Prayer, and opened it at the page headed: *The Form of Solemnization of Matrimony*.

Clearly, she and Peter must be married before he sailed off to the other side of the world. It would be a simple matter to arrange: Captain Latham would perform the wedding service at sea with eighteen sailors standing there on deck to witness it.

Such a marriage would be perfectly legal. Who could deny it?

4

It took a few moments for Captain Latham to recover from his astonishment when he heard Victoria's request. Then he threw back his head and roared with laughter. 'Absolutely not! No, no, no!'

Victoria lifted her chin and looked at him squarely. 'Oh, yes, indeed I think you must, Captain! Surely you're aware that my reputation has been utterly lost aboard your ship, so now I demand that your nephew does what is right and honourable and marries me immediately.' She frowned and pursed her lips to prevent any smile from ruining her performance. 'I'm over twenty-one, you know, so I have no need to ask my parents for permission.'

The captain clicked his tongue, took the prayer book she was holding open, and scanned the pages. 'Well . . . ' He stroked his chin, frowning. 'I've never been asked to do anything like this before, but — er, why not?' He let out a hoot of laughter. 'Yes, very well, of course I'll oblige you, m'dear. Would the start of the dog watch at four o'clock tomorrow be suitable?'

* ★ ★

The next afternoon Peter and Victoria stood on the windy poop deck and exchanged their wedding vows in a ceremony that was witnessed by eighteen seamen who had all washed, shaved and dressed in clean clothes for the occasion. She felt deeply touched by that, and shook each man's hand warmly as he came up to put his signature — or his mark — on the marriage certificate that the captain had drawn up.

She felt giddy with happiness. When her parents were presented with this document, they could have no doubt that she and Peter Latham were indeed legally married. That was what she told herself as she played with the plain gold wedding band that he'd placed on her finger during the ceremony. It was much too large and had a tendency to slide off but, once she was ashore, any jeweller would be able to adjust it to fit.

Peter had been amusingly evasive about how he'd been able to produce a gold ring at the appropriate moment in the ceremony. She suspected that he must have bought it last night from one of the sailors who'd probably won it at a gaming table. Or had stolen it. But that was of no concern because joy filled her and nothing mattered now but the few

59

remaining days and nights to be shared on board with her new husband.

Dressed in oilskins, she walked the deck beside him and quickly learned to adjust her stride to the long, easy pitch and roll of the ship. He taught her how to take readings from the sun and to chart their position on the maps in the navigation room below; when they studied the night sky he pointed out the constellations that had guided generations of mariners towards the southern hemisphere.

Every day brought her new knowledge, each night fresh, sweet discovery. All the good things piled up, so that every moment, every hour, every day she spent beside Peter was better than the moment and the hour and the day before.

She felt proud to stand beside him at the helm, watching the bow slicing its way through the dark waves and listening to the loud moaning hum of the wind in the rigging, the wind that was driving them steadily back towards the coast of England.

'I don't want to leave you,' she whispered, as they lay together on her last night aboard. 'Oh, what I'd give to stay here and simply sail on and on with you. But I know I can't do that. It would be too cruel to my family to go off to the other side of the world without telling them.'

He nuzzled her neck. 'Yes, I know, Mrs Latham, but when I come back after this, you and I will spend the rest of our lives together on board. And before you spend one more night on board, I promise to have the carpenter widen this bunk.'

When the *Fortitude* tied up at Strickland's jetty to take on board the chickens and a milking goat, and gear for the bosun's locker, along with more provisions for the long voyage ahead, Peter and Victoria hurried back to Lady Honoria's house. They arrived just in time to see the village doctor leaving.

'Ah, good afternoon, Miss Shelford.' He lifted his hat to her. 'Her ladyship will be glad to see you. She suffered a slight seizure a few days ago and I'm afraid it has left her with a degree of weakness in her right side. But she is quite comfortable. I'll call again tomorrow.'

Victoria ran into the house and found her aunt propped up in bed with flowers massed on her dressing table and window sills. Her eyes opened at the sound of Victoria's voice and she gave a twisted smile. 'Tell me . . . '

Victoria sat on the bed and held out her left hand. 'Look at this, Aunt. Peter and I took that step over the cliff, but instead of falling, we were carried upwards — and we soared like eagles with a great wind under our wings. Oh, I have so much to tell you:

Captain Henry married us at sea, and when the *Fortitude* comes back, Peter and I will have another wedding — in a church with the whole family attending.'

The old lady chuckled. 'My blessings on you both, my dears, and may you enjoy many happy years together.' Her words were slurred, but her delight was clear.

'Thank you for that, Lady Honoria.' Peter lifted her hand to his lips. 'I feel relieved to know that at least one member of Victoria's family gives her blessing to our marriage.'

With the *Fortitude* ready to sail, his visit to Lady Honoria was necessarily brief. 'You have my promise that I'll be back as swiftly as I can, ma'am, with silks and treasures from the Orient for my two favourite ladies.'

He kissed her lightly on the forehead and the old lady smiled.

And the kiss that he and Victoria exchanged at the gate was almost as brief.

'I love you beyond everything, Peter. Write to me often, and I'll keep myself busy to make sure that the next two years pass quickly. I'll be waiting.' Her voice was artificially bright.

He reached into his pocket and handed her an envelope. 'This is for your parents, sweetheart. I'd give anything to be with you when you tell them about us, but in this I've tried to explain who I am, and how deeply I love you. And that I intend to be a rich man one day.'

They clung together again for a few moments before he straightened. She needed to hold the gatepost tightly and keep her chin high as he walked out into the lane. They blew a kiss to each other before he turned the corner and disappeared from view.

She'd taken a few unsteady steps back towards the house before her sobs began — and she realized that the wedding ring had slipped off her finger again. In panic she dropped to her knees and eventually discovered it lying in long grass. Once back in the house, she found a length of satin ribbon and hung the gold band safely around her neck. Next to her heart.

The following morning a letter arrived from her mother with a reminder that Emily's wedding was less than a month away. 'The other bridesmaids have all had final fittings for their gowns, so you must come home immediately.' Lady Mary added a postscript hoping that Victoria had not over-indulged herself on cream cake and gained weight during her time in Devon.

She wrote back to say that it was impossible for her to leave Devon yet as it was clear to everyone that Lady Honoria

Woolcott's life was gently slipping away. Each day she slept for longer and longer periods, and in her waking moments she sometimes smiled and whispered to people whom only she could see standing in the room.

'I need you here with me, Mama. Please come now because Aunt Honoria is sinking and soon it will be too late.'

It was her father who replied, and he was uncharacteristically curt. 'Certain worrying family matters here are giving your mother more than enough to deal with at the moment. I'm sorry, my dear, but you must attend to whatever has to be done for Aunt Honoria, and return to London as speedily as you can.'

Victoria had never felt so utterly alone. She sent an express to Caroline and Hedley. 'My dears, I beg you to come down to Devon. I'm sure that our aunt is thinking of you, Caroline, because she often calls me by your name.'

Her sister's reply didn't arrive until the morning that Honoria died. With Victoria holding her hand, the old lady smiled, gave a little sigh and slipped peacefully from the world.

Victoria had no opportunity to open Caroline's letter until she'd attempted to comfort the distraught servants, spoken with the doctor, and arranged the details of a funeral service with the vicar. The news of Lady Honoria Woolcott's death flew through the district, and a stream of tearful neighbours and friends came to offer their condolences and to reminisce. Everyone had fond stories to tell about Lady Honoria.

It was well into the afternoon before Victoria found the opportunity to read Caroline's letter.

Dearest Vicky

Hedley and I are most dreadfully sorry, my sweet, but it's quite impossible for us to get away from London at the moment. Such a to-do! We have appointments with various important legal people — all because of a wretched woman who has been looking for years to find an excuse to divorce her husband and is now about to name ME in court for having stolen his affections! Nothing could be more ridiculous, of course, but her servants have produced the most scurrilous statements about me which are absolute lies. I'm glad to say that none of this appears to have reached the ears of the London gossips yet, but Mama and Papa are both in a perfect tizz that some whisper of it will wreck his chances of receiving that precious knighthood. Can't you just imagine what glee it would give Lady Marchant and Eloise to know of our disgrace! Do give our love to dear Aunt Honoria. I'm sure she will laugh at our predicament!

Caroline's letter ended with a message that the bridesmaids' dresses were *quite divine*. And she also wondered if Victoria had heard the news that a general election had been called, which meant that their father was required to leave London immediately after the wedding and pay one of his rare visits to his constituency to start campaigning.

Victoria threw the letter to the floor and blinked back the tears of frustration. Then she washed her face and met her aunt's fussy little solicitor who had arrived to read the will.

Lady Honoria Woolcott had owned nothing of great value, but she had bequeathed little pieces of porcelain and jewellery as mementos to the wives and daughters of various neighbours and local tradesmen, as well as necklaces to the three Shelford sisters. Would Miss Shelford be able to identify all these items and see that they reached the people named as beneficiaries? the man pleaded.

When he drove away, Victoria began to cry — angry tears now as she paced up and down the drawing room. She was angry that other matters were keeping her family from being here with her during this unhappy, lonely time. Angry that —

Her thoughts were suddenly diverted by the sound of a coach pulling up at the gate and, when she peered through the curtains, she was astounded to see Martin Clifford heaving himself down the step.

'I'll get the door, Mrs Potts,' she called, and ran through the house. 'This is the gentleman who is to marry Emily in — oh, very soon now.' She flung open the door and threw her arms around Martin's portly frame.

'Martin! I can't tell you how delighted I am to see you. Thank you, thank you for coming.'

'It's little enough at a time like this, my dear sister-to-be,' he said, kissing her cheek. 'Emily — my sweetest angel — wrote to me of her concerns about you having been left all alone here with Lady Honoria in failing health, so I came immediately.'

Emily! Little Emily had been the only one in the family to understand how desperately she was in need of their help. Victoria hugged Martin tighter, then ushered him into the drawing room while she gave him the details of Lady Honoria's last weeks, as well as listing all the matters that the attorney had asked her to deal with before she'd be able to leave for London.

'And on top of that, Martin, I'm alarmed about what Caroline has told me about some divorce scandal she's become involved in. Do you know about it? Is it really as bad as it sounds?'

He nodded and cleared his throat. 'It's a nasty business, make no mistake, but your sister and her husband have accepted my suggestion that they should leave for an extended holiday in America before the matter gets to court. Passage has been booked for them on a ship due to leave Tilbury after the wedding.'

She regarded him with a frown. 'But everyone knows that Caroline and Hedley have no money and — ' Her jaw sagged. 'Oh, Martin, I doubt that Papa would ever agree to finance this escape. Surely you're not the one who is paying for it?'

'The whole business regarding Caroline is upsetting my little angel, and I will not have it!' He spoke tartly. 'Caroline and Hedley will leave quietly for Tilbury straight after the wedding and board this ship to New York. I have a friend there who is to take them across the country to visit his estate — he refers to it as a *ranch* — in some place called Wyoming. Hopefully they'll stay on that side of the

Atlantic for a year or two until the dust settles here.'

Victoria regarded him with awe. A more unlikely-looking white knight would be hard to imagine, but surely there was none whose heart was filled with more generosity.

'Martin, my dear brother-to-be, you must be the kindest man on earth to do so much for our family.' She fingered the gold wedding ring hanging under her blouse and longed to share the news of her marriage with him. But she hesitated. It didn't seem to be the right thing to do before she'd told her parents.

* * *

The days following Lady Honoria's funeral passed in a blur of activity, with Martin helping Victoria to disperse her aunt's bequests around the countryside. And he endorsed her decision that the £485 she'd found hidden in a dressing-table drawer should be given to Mr and Mrs Potts. By the time the last tearful farewells had been said to Honoria's friends and neighbours and they were on their way back to London, Emily's wedding was only two days away.

* * *

'Well, here you are at last!' Lady Mary gave Victoria's cheek a fleeting kiss. 'Tell me later about Aunt Honoria. I need to see you in your bridesmaid's gown immediately. Goodness, my girl, you seem to have *lost* weight in Devon.'

Tension in the house was almost palpable, with George Shelford distracted by the prospect of the impending election and the agony of having to travel north to his electorate and deliver campaign speeches.

He called Victoria into his study. 'Your mother has agreed to accompany me and I'd like you to come with us, too, m'dear. The Radicals are standing a very popular candidate against me and, somehow, I need to rally more support.' There was desperation in his voice. 'You and your mother must move about and talk to people up there. We'll hold dinners to woo the voters, maybe even have a ball.'

She knew how much his seat in Westminster meant to him. 'Yes, of course, I'll go with you, Papa. I'll do anything I can to help, though you know I'm a rank amateur when it comes to politics.' Caroline, of course, would have performed this role superbly, but her name was no longer allowed to be mentioned within Lady Mary's hearing.

Clearly this was not the appropriate time to

produce Peter's letter to her parents, nor to reveal the ring hanging from the ribbon around her neck. Desperate to tell someone in the family about Peter, she went to see Caroline and Hedley the next morning and found both them and their house in a state of chaos.

'Oh, Vicky, lovely to see you!' Hedley called breezily from the top of the stairs while two men carried a chair past him and put it beside others already piled in the hall. 'All this stuff is being repossessed and we're going abroad tomorrow. Have you heard?'

She ran up the stairs and found Caroline still in bed, drinking chocolate and surrounded by travelling boxes. 'Vicky, you poor lamb,' she said, pulling a long face. 'What a dreadful time you must have had all on your own down there with poor old Honoria. Sorry I couldn't lift a finger to help, but have you heard that we're sailing to America straight after the wedding?' She put down the cup and doubled over in a fit of giggles. 'Good old Martin has arranged it all with a millionaire friend over there who — who is probably going to exhibit us in some Wild West Show as a *pair of tame British aristocrats*!'

Hedley walked into the room. 'And we'll give 'em a damn good show, won't we, Caro?

Might even get an offer to join Buffalo Bill's troupe.' He gave a snort of mirth and Victoria felt a wave of irritation at their flippancy. And especially at their lack of gratitude to Martin for his generosity.

She held her tongue about Peter and found an excuse to leave their house as soon as she could. If Caroline and her husband had always been so appallingly shallow, why had she never recognized it before? Had Peter Latham changed her life so much that she now viewed everything in the world with different eyes? *Oh, my darling Peter, when will I be able to tell my parents about us?*

On her way home, Victoria visited a jeweller where the Shelfords were unknown, and had her wedding ring altered to sit snugly on her finger.

Nobody in the house noticed that she was wearing it.

★ ★ ★

Lady Marchant and Miss Eloise Marchant had been invited to Emily's wedding and were there to witness that, with Lady Mary's meticulous planning, every detail of the grand day flowed flawlessly. As the notes of the organ swelled and Victoria walked sedately down the aisle with three other bridesmaids,

72

she doubted that anyone else in the great old church could sense the pain hiding behind the carefully arranged smiles on her parents' faces.

Last night her father had received the woeful tidings that his knighthood was most unlikely to eventuate, and her mother had just heard of vague whispers starting to circulate in society regarding Caroline's indiscretions. But throughout today's ceremony, Mr George Shelford and Lady Mary held their heads high and danced gracefully, like a pair of elegant, well-oiled automatons through each step of the elaborate social ritual required to be played out.

With Martin constantly at her side throughout the reception, Emily's shyness became invisible. Victoria knew that it was still lurking there, but Martin's self-assurance became a shield that protected her.

'Our little Emmie is a very fortunate young lady to have won your heart, Martin Clifford,' Victoria murmured, as the couple was preparing to leave on their honeymoon. 'You understand my sister perfectly.'

'Indeed I do understand her ways.' He spoke earnestly. 'The years I've spent growing exotic plants has taught me that some species burst into flower quickly, while others take longer to reveal their blooms. I see my darling

Emily as a truly unique specimen, one which — with tender nurturing — will eventually display blossoms to astound us all.'

'Yes, Martin, I believe you.'

★ ★ ★

Once Emily and Martin had been waved off to their honeymoon in the gardens of Italy, and Caroline and Hedley had quietly slipped away to America, Lady Mary kept to her bedroom in a state of nervous exhaustion.

Mr Shelford spent most of his time in his study, struggling to draft his campaign speeches. His gloom deepened daily and, on their train journey north to his constituency, Victoria saw that both her parents were far too distracted by the pending contest for her to introduce the topic of her marriage.

While the train rattled northwards, she sat in the carriage trying to calculate how far south the *Fortitude* might have sailed by this date. Peter had said that he'd post letters from Cape Town, and suggested that her mail to him should be addressed care of the British Consul in Singapore. It was all so many miles away. So many miles.

Time and again Victoria tried to find some opportunity to talk to her parents, but they remained tight-lipped and distracted throughout the journey. When they finally arrived in his constituency she came to understand their apprehension about this campaign once she'd witnessed the booing and heckling that met her father each time he stepped up on a platform to speak.

Even Lady Mary's grand dinners at the hotel for some of the Woolcott family's old Whig connections failed to rally the support George Shelford needed to hold his seat.

After the votes were counted and the Radical candidate had been declared the winner, the defeated Shelfords swiftly retreated to Hanover Square. Victoria went back to work at the Foundling Hospital, while George Shelford spent much his time heaving deep sighs and staring at the fire in his study.

Lady Mary argued that they should get away from London for a time and take a house in Paris, or Rome, or Corfu. And she complained endlessly about Howard Royston's continuing absence from London.

Eventually, Victoria came to feel that she would never find the *perfect* moment to break her happy news about Peter while both parents seemed so determined to remain miserable.

She waited until they were alone one night in the drawing room after dinner. Her father's concentration was fixed on the fire burning in the grate and Lady Mary had her nose in a ladies' magazine. Neither looked up when Victoria entered.

For a moment she stood in the middle of the room clutching Peter's letter, along with the marriage certificate produced by the captain. The sound of distant thunder rumbling over the rooftops added to her unease and when wind-driven rain began to beat against the windows like angry fists, the tension inside her became unbearable.

'Excuse me, Mama, but I have something I'd like to tell both you and Papa.' Her mouth seemed to be lined with sandpaper.

For weeks, she'd been rehearsing this delicate scene and now, with a galloping heart, she started to describe her meeting with Captain Latham and his nephew in Aunt Honoria's drawing room. 'They are both charming gentlemen. Peter Latham is very handsome and he has the qualifications to captain his own ship one day. He and — '

Lady Mary sat forward in her chair, grasping its arms. 'Oh, God! Victoria, what have you done? What? I can tell by your face that you've been up to some kind of mischief!'

'No, Mama, I want to tell you and Papa that I've fallen in love and I want you to be happy for me. It happened while I was in

Devon. His name is Peter Latham and we fell truly and deeply in love the moment we met. He's twenty-six and at present he's sailing to the East Indies — '

The horror in her mother's expression told her that this wasn't going at all as she'd planned. Her hand shook as she held it out. 'See, Mama? This is my wedding ring. Aunt Honoria gave us her blessing and we were married at sea by the ship's captain. And when Peter comes back, I'm going to join him on the ship and — '

Lady Mary gave a wounded howl and scrambled to her feet. 'What? What? Oh dear God, Victoria, are you mad?' Her cheeks were drained of colour. 'Surely you're not telling me that you eloped with a sailor?' She shrieked. '*You did! A daughter of mine ran off to sea with a common sailor!*'

'This is all the doing of your wicked old Aunt Honoria!' Mr Shelford's face purpled and he suddenly scrambled to his feet, shouting at his wife. 'You wouldn't listen when I warned you to keep Victoria out of her clutches. I warned you that she would ruin Victoria just as she did Caroline. And now look at what that wretched old harridan has done to us!' His voice broke and he shook his fist.

'No! Don't say that, Papa! Please listen to

me, please *listen*! You have always understood me, so I beg you to hear me now when I tell you about Peter and what a truly fine man he is. Then you'll understand how I fell in love with him. Here, Mama, please open his letter and read what he has to say. He is strong and handsome and clever and brave. Here, please take it.'

Her mother's lips curled. She took the envelope between her thumb and finger, then holding it at arm's length as if it was filled with something contagious, she swept across the room and flung it into the fire.

'Now, this is never to be mentioned again, do you hear me?' She turned and pointed a finger accusingly. 'Think of the scandal; think what delight it would give Lady Marchant and her ilk to hear that you had eloped with such a low-class creature! Do you hear me, Victoria? I will not have another word about it! This marriage never took place!'

'Papa!' Victoria looked pleadingly towards her father for understanding. But when she saw none, her dismay flamed into anger. 'You have always been the one person I thought would never abandon me. Papa, I thought you loved me!'

She unfolded the marriage certificate and held it towards him. 'Well, look at this. Look, look! No matter what Mama might say, here is the proof that my marriage certainly did take place! This document shows that I am the lawfully wedded wife of Peter Latham, Master Mariner, and here are the signatures of eighteen witnesses who will testify to having seen us make our vows. It's a perfectly legal certificate and any court will agree, as you know.'

'No!' Her mother's eyes filled with venom. 'No, no, no!' She rushed forward, snatched the paper, tore it, screwed the pieces into a ball and threw it, too, into the fire. 'Now where is the proof that you're married, you shameful creature?' Her voice developed a harsh, metallic ring. 'No, no, no, I will *not* have it. It — did — not — happen!'

'It's no use, Mama.' Victoria glared at her defiantly. 'You can burn all the papers you like, but the captain has recorded our marriage in the ship's log. I am, and always will be, the legal wife of Peter Latham. He's coming back for me one day, and I'm going to spend the rest of my life at sea with him, sailing the world, seeing the wonders — '

'Noooooo!' Lady Mary's screams reached a pitch that brought the butler and a footman bursting into the room in time to see their mistress swing her hand and strike Miss Victoria hard across her face.

'Get out of my sight, you wanton! Get out!'

The heavy blow threw Victoria off-balance and sent her stumbling backwards. She was forced to grasp the edge of a table to stop herself from falling when her father stepped aside and turned his back to her. His rejection hurt even more than her mother's blow had done.

'Papa, please, *please* don't do this to me! Hear what I have to tell you. You've always listened to me!' But he remained slumped in his chair with his chin on his chest and his shoulders shaking.

The startled servants rushed forward in time to support Lady Mary as her legs began to buckle.

Victoria stiffened her spine and clutched the remnants of her dignity as she walked silently from the room, trying to ignore the stinging pain in her cheek, as well as the pain in her heart.

Her night was filled with a sense of unreality. How could her life have been turned so completely upside down within the space of half an hour? When she closed her eyes, the appalling scene with her parents in the drawing room triggered old images of the day that she and her sisters had been travelling with their governess in a carriage which broke a wheel and overturned on a country lane. She recalled the terrifying feeling of helplessness as the vehicle tipped further and further, throwing them all around the interior, together with baskets, boxes, rugs and books.

They'd been frightened and bruised, but they'd scrambled from the upturned vehicle and, after sitting by the roadside for a few hours, the wheel had been replaced and they were on their way again.

She saw a moral in there somewhere. Life as she'd know it had just be turned upside down, but before the next day dawned, she'd reached a decision about how to set it back on course while she waited for the *Fortitude's* return.

She packed a portmanteau, left a forwarding address with the footman and caught the first train to Somerset. Emily and Martin were away on their honeymoon, but Victoria knew that they'd offer her refuge at Cloudhill while she waited for Peter to come back.

5

When the door of Cloudhill was opened to Victoria's knock, the butler's long face broke into a smile. 'Why, Miss Shelford, how good of you to come so soon! Mrs Frost is airing your room at this very moment.' His glance quickly slid away from the bruise left by her mother's blow on her cheek last night.

The man's greeting puzzled her. She'd sent no message to inform Martin's household of her uninvited arrival, but at the sound of voices in the hall, Mrs Frost, the house-keeper, came hurrying down the stairs with a welcoming smile.

'Ah, Miss Shelford. I'm sure the mistress will be delighted to find her sister already here when she arrives.' She too, seemed careful not to stare at the bruise.

Victoria strained to make sense of whatever was happening. 'I understood that Mr and Mrs Clifford were not due back from Italy for another month or so.'

Mrs Frost nodded. 'Yes, of course, but the honeymoon has had to be cut short because travelling becomes such a misery at a time like this, doesn't it? My own poor daughter suffered the same sickness — morning, noon and night — when her first baby was on the way. Mr Clifford and the mistress are expected back any day now, and the master informed us that he was about to write and ask if you'd be able to come to be with Mrs Clifford. It's extremely kind of you to arrive early.'

Emily! Victoria's heart melted at the thought of little Emmie becoming a mother.

'Perhaps, Miss Shelford, you would like to be shown to your room and — '

Victoria interrupted. 'Mrs Frost, I must tell you that I'm no longer Miss Shelford. I was married a month before my sister and Mr Clifford, though ours was a very small wedding.' She pulled off her glove to show the ring. 'I am now Mrs Peter Latham, and my husband is abroad on business — maritime business.'

The housekeeper expressed her delight at the news, and so did Emily and Martin when they arrived home three days later and heard the full story of her time in Devon. 'I knew that neither Mama nor Papa would be delighted to hear that I'd lost my heart to Peter Latham, but — ' She heaved a heavy sigh. 'Well, Mama has destroyed my marriage certificate, but I absolutely refuse to let her destroy my marriage.'

'Oh, Vicky, dearest,' Emily said weakly, as she settled back on her pillow following another bout of nausea, 'your Peter sounds perfectly wonderful, and how romantic to think that you'll be sailing away beside him one day. Yes, I know you're going to be so happy. As happy as I am.'

'Yes, I will — some day.' But for the time being, Victoria was glad to settle into a routine that revolved around Emily's care and comfort. The doctor confirmed that the baby was progressing well, but no matter what was tried, nothing seemed to relieve her bouts of sickness. Whenever her strength permitted it, Emily asked to be taken to the greenhouse to be with Martin while he tended his plants, and Victoria soon found herself making most of the day to day domestic decisions at Cloudhill.

'I hope I'm not seen to be interfering in your excellent management, Mrs Frost,' she said, after she'd signed the monthly household accounts and checked the kitchen orders. Tomorrow morning she was to interview a local girl for the position of parlour maid. 'I'm sure it won't be long before my sister is well enough to take on her duties of mistress of this house.'

Sporadic correspondence arrived at Cloud-hill from Caroline and Hedley in America, amusing letters describing how the couple were unashamedly playing their *British aristocrat* roles to the hilt and being entertained in high style everywhere they went.

Hedley and I have concocted various little English scenes which are very popular when we perform them at house parties. It's hilarious to give the impression that we attend court regularly, and then to observe the enthusiasm of our republican hosts as they watch us demonstrate the correct protocol to be followed when meeting the Queen.

My dears, you would die laughing if you could see them practising how to bow and curtsy without wobbling.

Christmas arrived, and with Emily still unwell, it was Victoria who took on the role of hostess when the usual collection of Clifford aunts, uncles and cousins of all ages descended on the great house for the family's traditional Yuletide celebrations.

It was a busy time for the household, but as long as the kitchen staff kept up a supply of splendid food, the relatives were perfectly able to organize their own entertainment. Victoria found them a pleasant, easygoing group who were happy to play charades, billiards and cards, or sing popular songs around the piano. They went for long walks and danced in the evening, and sat for hours drinking tea by the fire while they exchanged an endless supply of family gossip.

Emily came downstairs to join the company whenever she felt sufficiently well, and she was fussed over by them all.

As Victoria stood on the steps and said farewell to the Clifford relatives, she thought that this had probably been the jolliest Christmas she'd ever spent. No commotions, no formality.

'Emmie, have you heard from Mama and Papa?'

Emily shot a glance towards Martin. He frowned. 'Victoria, I invited your parents to join us here, but they declined. They've leased the house in Hanover Square to some family from York, and are taking a villa in the south of France. Permanently.'

★ ★ ★

Victoria's happiness soared when mail from Peter began to arrive — first, a bundle of letters that he'd posted from Cape Town. He reported that he and his uncle were in the best of health, the *Fortitude* was sailing splendidly, and later he was able to describe the splendid trading opportunities they were discovering in Burma, Siam and Java. Perhaps her happiest moment came when he confirmed that he had collected all her letters that were waiting for him at the British Consulate in Singapore.

My dearest, when I held them in my hands, I could almost imagine that it was you I was holding. And, yes, of course I took them to bed with me — not that they could ever truly replace the joy we shared. By the way, you'll be delighted to hear that the carpenter has already widened the bunk and it's waiting for you — for us, my darling Vicky.

In May, Victoria wrote to him with the news that Emily had produced a healthy baby boy and named him Tobias: *Emily and Martin are happy for me to make my home here with them until that wonderful day when you come back and take me on board the Fortitude. That's where I truly belong.*

It wasn't long before Emily began to feel unwell again and the doctor confirmed that there was another baby on the way. 'Vicky,

I'm so glad to have you here with me still. What would I do without you?' she said, placing Toby in her arms. At six months he was a happy, alert little fellow who sat gurgling contentedly on her lap and tugging at her necklace.

'Well now, Master Toby,' Victoria said, trying to distract him for a moment while she released his grasp, 'you and I have much to talk about because Christmas is fast approaching and the puddings are hanging in the pantry. Your dear mama has asked me to arrange the festivities here again, so we'll decorate the house with holly, have the piano tuned, and ask cook how many geese we need to prepare. Oh, little one, I wonder where your Uncle Peter and the captain will spend their Christmas this year?' She hugged him tightly and spun in a circle. 'Soon they'll be sailing back to England! Soon, soon, very soon you'll meet your Uncle Peter.'

She sat down at the kitchen table with Mrs Dobson, the cook, to discuss menus for the guests. *Where will I spend Christmas next year?* she asked herself and went upstairs to check the visitors' bedrooms, and then down again to talk to the staff who were rearranging chairs in the drawing room and setting out extra card tables. *Will I be aboard the Fortitude next year, sailing across some great blue ocean? Will we be eating bananas and coconuts on a white beach beside a coral lagoon?*

With Emily's wretched sickness sometimes confining her upstairs for days, it was Victoria who again took on the role of mistress of the house, greeting the relatives, allocating bedrooms, arranging the seating at dinner.

Martin never failed to kiss her cheek and thank her at the end of each day. 'I don't know how we'd have managed without you, my dear sister.'

It wasn't a burdensome job; in fact, she enjoyed it. But nevertheless, she was bone weary by the time the last party had been waved off and the staff began the task of restoring order in the old house. She was on her way upstairs to gossip with Emily when a footman hurried after her. 'A letter just come by special delivery for you, ma'am.'

She frowned at the handwriting on the envelope and continued to walk slowly upstairs as she ripped it open. At first it was impossible to comprehend the words on the paper, written by a shaking hand and signed *Henry Latham*. Her eyes skimmed the pages again in disbelief. No! This had to be some mistake; it could *not* be true. It couldn't be! Peter could not have become so ill that he died out there in the Indies. So suddenly! So far away.

The pain inside her was beyond tears and she was suddenly swamped by a huge, cold and angry emptiness. Her heart thudded and she gasped for breath. Why was the captain telling her that Peter had been stricken with a tropical fever in the Celebes, just when she had begun to count the weeks till they'd be reunited? Peter had said that he'd soon be on his way back to her. Of course he was sailing back for her. She was waiting for him, wasn't she? He'd *promised* that he would come back.

Her whole body began to tremble and she seemed to have forgotten how to breathe as she burst into Emily's room to stand panting at the foot of the bed, ashen-faced.

'Oh, Vicky, what is it?' Emily threw off her covers and held out her arms.

Victoria rushed into her sister's embrace while a silent scream of agony caught in her throat. She felt her heart shatter as her world was tipped off its axis. Oh, Peter! My Peter! No, no, no! Don't leave me. You *promised* to come back for me and I promised to wait for you. I am waiting, see? I will always be waiting. Peter, come back, please come back.

★ ★ ★

'Poor Victoria — Ah! To be widowed so young.'

'Poor Victoria, such a tragedy. But just look how bravely she's holding up,' the neighbours and relatives whispered to each other when they called at Cloudhill to offer their condolences.

Each morning she woke with the feeling that she'd been hollowed out in one vicious scoop by some malevolent force. While in company she resolutely hid behind a mask of calm civility to cover the rage of grief tearing at her insides night and day. She endured the platitudes delivered by well-meaning people who called in a seemingly never-ending stream and referred to her constantly as *poor Victoria*. She cringed inwardly, but sent the good people away with the impression that *poor Victoria* was bearing up to her loss remarkably well.

No one was aware of the nightly dreams in which Peter called to her with an urgency that left her in tears when she woke. Neither did they notice how her breath caught and she tensed with anticipation whenever footsteps were heard approaching the house, or a shadow appeared on a wall. Twice she'd called for the carriage to stop when she thought she'd glimpsed him amongst the crowd of shoppers at the markets in Wells. Her head told her that it could never be Peter returning, but her heart refused to abandon hope.

'I doubt that poor Victoria will remain a widow for long once she comes out of mourning,' the ladies said over their teacups, whenever they tallied the names of eligible gentlemen who began calling at Cloudhill.

But Emily and Martin sensed the depth of her grief when they saw her setting out for long, solitary walks into the countryside, or spending her days in a whirlwind of unimportant domestic activities. Toby occupied hours of Victoria's time, too, as she played with him on the nursery floor or took him out into the garden on a sunny day.

She maintained a correspondence with Captain Latham, but he spoke of no plans to sail back to England yet as he'd found a lucrative market in San Francisco. His first letter only hinted at the grief torturing him when he described Peter's sudden illness and his burial three days later on a remote island in the Java Sea.

I am devastated that when the fever struck I was helpless to save him, even though he was dosed with every drop of quinine we had on the ship. When he knew that he was dying he instructed me to write his Will, and asked for all your letters to be placed with him in his grave. The last words he spoke were of you.

When she was alone, Victoria sobbed her loneliness and heartbreak until she could cry no more. In company she continued with the pretence that her pain was easing.

Emily's confinement came on the September day that was expected, and another baby boy, Harry, was delivered safely into the Clifford family. Amidst the joy and congratulations, Victoria put aside the letter from London which had come that morning, and it wasn't until Emily had been comfortably settled for the night and baby Harry was feeding, that she went to her room to open it.

The contents left her puzzled. It came from Mr Horace Bartley-Symes, a solicitor of Oxford Street, stating that he had been given the honour of handling the Last Will and Testament of her late husband, Captain Peter Latham, and that she, Victoria Latham née Shelford, had been named as sole beneficiary of her husband's estate. This comprised a half-ownership of the barque *Fortitude*, as well as the late Peter Latham's share of the profits accrued in recent business enterprises, namely £9367. Would

Mrs Latham, at her earliest convenience, be so good as to notify the lawyer how she wished to receive her bequest?

'Oh, Martin! I can't possibly claim half the ship. The *Fortitude* belongs to Uncle Henry and I don't feel I have the right.'

'Vicky, m'dear, Captain Latham is quite aware of your husband's bequest. He was the one to write the will for Peter, remember?' He lay a comforting arm around her shoulders. 'Your husband has made you a wealthy lady, and in leaving you his share of the ship, he's made sure that your fortune is going to increase. My recommendation would be to invest your inheritance in the *Fortitude*'s future ventures.'

But Peter's money could never fill the emptiness in her heart. For that to happen she needed to find some purpose in life. But where should she turn when she left Cloud-hill? Even though Emily and Martin had made it abundantly clear that they considered her to be part of their family and urged her to stay, Victoria felt a growing restlessness. She needed to find a path of her own. But where did it lie?

★　★　★

Caroline and Hedley remained in America and their letters invariably raised laughter around the family table.

Darlings, you'll never guess what Hedley and I are doing now! We have become actors — professional thespians, no less. A gentleman who saw us putting on one of our funny little scenes at a party in Philadelphia, has written a wonderfully romantic play for us, and we are now performing it in a theatre here in San Francisco. We even sing and dance on the stage. The newspapers are saying the most flattering things about us and money is simply rolling into our pockets! Now we've been booked for a season in Boston, and perhaps New York after that.

Vicky, darling, why don't you come over and spend some time with us?

She thought about it for weeks. Was Caroline's invitation the lifeline that she was looking for? Was sailing across the Atlantic to a new country the direction she should consider taking?

★ ★ ★

When Emily was well again, it was clear that being mistress of a great house carried responsibilities that she was ill prepared to take on. She was perfectly at home in Martin's greenhouse, but even *he* came to

95

hint that his wife might like to learn a little about the management of Cloudhill and its staff.

'Vicky, please, please stay a little longer and show me what I'm expected to do.'

'Yes, of course I will, Emmie.' Victoria knew that staying on to help her sister was providing a very convenient excuse to postpone the effort of looking for a new direction in her own life.

She threw herself cheerfully into the task and discovered that Emily proved to be an enthusiastic pupil of household management. Above all, she wanted to please Martin, and quickly filled the notebook she kept close beside her to record all Victoria's practical advice and schedules. Emily's task was made easier by the fact that the servants loved their young mistress and went out of their way to oblige her.

By the time that Christmas came again, Emily was at last ready to step into her role as mistress of the house, and Martin radiated pride when she stood beside him greeting their guests and was able to take her place at the head of the table.

In addition to the usual number of family members spending the festive season at Cloudhill this year, was Nigel Pelham, a quiet, long-legged cousin of middle years who was here on home leave from his administrative post in India.

'We must look after poor Nigel during his visit,' Martin murmured as they watched him arriving. 'His wife met with an accident on the voyage home to England. No matter how bad the weather, Maud always insisted on taking her daily constitutional out on deck, but this time when she walked out in a storm, she was thrown off her feet and struck her head on a railing.' He clicked his tongue. 'Had to be buried at sea.'

Nigel seemed like a lost soul amongst the gathering. He had little to say, but the expression in his gentle brown eyes and the grey-streaked curls falling across his forehead, reminded Victoria of a very sad spaniel.

'Poor Cousin Nigel,' said a stout aunt, drawing her aside. 'He's been staying at our house for the last month and — well, he's just so dreary. Always has been. Maud did all the talking.' Her voice dropped to a whisper. 'I can't tell you how glad I am that he's going to spend the remainder of his leave here at Cloudhill.'

A small, bird-like great-aunt fluttered up to them. 'Poor Nigel. He insists that he must go back to Kashmir, but how he will survive out there without Maud beside him, heaven alone knows. She was forever telling him what jacket to wear, what time to go to bed, what invitations to accept.' The ladies frowned at each other and shook their heads.

As Victoria listened to the cousins gossiping, she learned that for the last twenty years Cousin Nigel had held the position of Deputy Controller of Revenue in the State of Kashmir. Every five years, he and his redoubtable wife, Maud, had come back to England on leave and set out on a circuit of visits around the family — following the schedule drawn up by Maud.

'I don't know how he'll ever manage without Maud at his elbow,' said a grey-haired uncle. 'I swear I've never met a more useless fellow, though they say he's perfectly efficient when it come to his ledgers in Kashmir.'

'Don't worry, I'm sure there will be any number of ladies waiting to become the wife of Nigel Pelham when he gets back there,' a bright-faced young niece added. 'He's always been an uninteresting creature, but he's quite presentable, don't you agree? Besides, he earns a big salary and lives in a house filled with Indian servants. Oh, yes, I can see a long line of husband-hunters over there rushing to fill Aunt Maud's shoes.'

After Nigel had spent two days at Cloudhill, Victoria came to understand the family's comments. Bleak January weather had delivered sleet and mud to the district, marooning them all in the great house, and though Martin tried to entice his cousin to visit the greenhouse, Nigel made it clear that horticulture failed to rouse his interest. Nothing else appealed to him, either.

Victoria offered suggestions: 'A game of billiards? Chess?' But Nigel seemed to want nothing more than to settle himself quietly with a book beside the fire in the library. Poor, sad Nigel, she thought, of course he wants to be left alone in his grief.

While other guests were gathered around the piano in the music room, she walked upstairs to the nursery and found Emily's boisterous little boys romping in high spirits while their nursemaid was coughing and sneezing with a feverish cold.

'Polly, you should be in bed!' Victoria touched the girl's forehead. 'Quickly, off with you. I'll take care of these young gentlemen and they can play with me in the drawing room today. Yes, I insist!'

Baby Harry was now on his feet and toddling everywhere in the wake of three-year-old Toby, so she filled a basket with an assortment of toys and herded her noisy little nephews downstairs.

Before long, the hullabaloo made by their

games in the drawing room drew Nigel from the library next door. 'Oh, I'm so sorry we disturbed you,' Victoria said, as she looked out from behind the curtain where she'd just caught Toby hiding.

'No, no, not at all, I enjoy the sound of children's laughter.' He sat on his haunches to watch little Harry attempting to fit a wooden peg into its slot. 'My wife and I were never blessed with a family, y'know.' He ran a hand over the child's head.

Toby skipped to him and demanded attention, too. 'Read me some of my book. Please. Look, there's a tiger on this page.'

Nigel smiled and settled cross-legged on the floor with the picture book. Harry deserted his pegs to move closer. Nigel soon had them squealing and giggling at his attempts to produce the growls and howls, yelps, roars and hisses of each wild creature pictured. It wasn't long before he was on all-fours, trumpeting like an elephant and crawling around the room with Toby and Harry swaying on his back.

'Believe me, Martin, your cousin was a changed man when he was with the children today,' Victoria said that night, after Nigel had gone up to his room. 'He sang little songs and made up all sorts of games for us to play. He even tipped over the drawing room chairs and built a marvellous fort for the boys.'

Martin shook his head in amazement. 'Good heavens! I've never in my life seen him enthusiastic about anything, apart from collecting revenue in Kashmir.'

Emily looked up from her embroidery. 'Poor Nigel. However is he going to manage without Maud to run his life when he goes back?'

'Don't worry, m'love, I'm sure he'll soon find some energetic lady to do that,' Martin muttered from behind his newspaper.

Victoria frowned. 'Yes, Martin, but I've gained an impression from the relatives that Maud was utterly unselfish, and whatever she did for Nigel was entirely for *his* benefit. Aren't you concerned that when he sets foot back in Kashmir he could be snapped up by some lady who'll put all her own interests first and make his life miserable?'

'Hmm. I recall my cousin being raised by two older sisters who doted on him and *taught* him to be helpless. I think they promoted his marriage to Maud because they saw her as a lady who *needed* to be kept busy — so the marriage was a perfectly balanced one.' He nodded thoughtfully. 'The only thing missing, of course, were half-a-dozen children to keep Maud fully occupied. She had no one but Nigel to pour her prodigious energy into caring for.'

Emily set her embroidery aside and sat forward. 'Vicky, I want you to do something to help Nigel. Now, now, please don't look so alarmed.' She checked to make sure that Martin was listening, too. 'When Nigel sails for India at the end of January, I think it would be an excellent plan for you to go with him and spend a lovely holiday over there.'

'Ah!' Martin's mouth widened and he raised an eyebrow. 'Emily, my sweet angel, I can read your mind. Yes, splendid. Victoria can stay in Srinagar and be in an ideal position to survey the field of candidates for Nigel's affections. Yes, Vicky, you'll be there to select a sensible lady — an unselfish lady — to fill Maud's shoes. Then you can quietly steer his choice towards her.'

Emily clapped her palms together. 'Yes, please, Vicky. Please stay over there for a little while and help poor Nigel avoid falling under the spell of someone who might treat him abominably.'

Victoria looked aghast. 'No! Absolutely not! You're asking me to behave just as our own mother did with my friends — to be intrusive, controlling, judgmental. No, Emmie, I will never agree to anything like that, so please don't ever mention it again. Ever! Good night!'

She swept from the room and closed the door behind her with a resounding bang.

6

Victoria stood alone at the ship's rail as it headed into the wind, pitching and rolling on its way to India through a buffeting sea. The modern steam engine alone was unable to produce sufficient power to drive the vessel through the heavy weather, and she watched tensely as seamen were ordered up the two wildly swaying masts to unfurl the sails.

The scene reminded her of the times she had seen Peter performing some such feat on board the *Fortitude*. She felt him very close to her out here on the ocean. It was well over four years since their first meeting at Aunt Honoria's house, but nothing had dimmed her memories of every single moment they'd shared. And now, feeling the ship's pitch and toss, hearing orders shouted to the seamen, listening to the bells ringing for each change of watch, sniffing the salty tang of the sea —

Peter was standing right beside her. She could feel his closeness. If she looked around she'd be able to see his smile, and if she reached out —

She swallowed hard, closed her eyes and gripped the rail, lifting her face into the whipping, salt-laden sea spray. This was just another fantasy. Peter could *never* come back. She spun away from the grey water, and heaved open the door into the saloon.

Sea-sickness had prevented all but a few passengers from venturing beyond their cabins since leaving Aden, but two very determined, pale-faced ladies were presently sitting one on either side of Nigel. He, like Victoria, hadn't missed a meal.

At first, the relationship between Mr Pelham and Mrs Latham had aroused a deal of speculation amongst the other passengers, but once Victoria had made it clear that she was simply travelling to spend a holiday in Kashmir with her cousin, she had a foretaste of what was lying ahead for the widower. Though Nigel spent most of his time with his nose in a book, it appeared to her that every female on the ship between the ages of eighteen and eighty was drawn to him. Some fussed about and tried to lift his spirits with bright chatter, a few openly flirted, and one woman regularly attempted to divert him with topics of deep philosophical content.

Nigel obliged them all with his gentle smile, and said little.

Without doing it consciously, Victoria began to evaluate the ladies on the ship and soon saw that the task of finding the right wife for Nigel was not going to be straightforward. So many variables were being presented. By the time they reached Bombay, Victoria had decided that her only reliable measure of the *right* wife would have to begin with the level of Nigel's own interest in a lady.

And on the voyage, not one candidate had shone in that aspect. Hopefully, Kashmir would prove a better hunting ground.

★   ★   ★

The Frontier Express they boarded at Bombay was a badly misnamed train, she discovered, as they rattled slowly northwards towards the Himalayas. But through the dusty window of their compartment, she watched the passing scenes with awed fascination. The country was so vast and so ancient, with all its colour and splendour and squalor sitting side by side. She saw oxen in the fields turning water wheels, and stately processions of brightly dressed women walking away from wells with gleaming brass pots balanced on their heads. Beyond the fields of crops, she caught glimpses of camel convoys and painted elephants, great hill-top forts, distant palaces and areas of jungle where little brown monkeys sat in the trees.

At the end of the first day on the dusty train, it occurred to her that Peter had not crept into her thoughts more than once or twice. It gave her an odd, almost guilty, feeling.

After three days with very little sleep, she was struggling to keep her eyes open when she became aware of Nigel observing her closely. He swallowed and moistened his lips.

'My dear Cousin Victoria,' he began awkwardly, 'I admit to being a dull man, but I'm not a stupid one — though clumsy I may be — but I have far too much respect — indeed, affection for you, er — to permit any degree of misapprehension to exist between us.'

She blinked at him, struggling to follow his gist.

'Victoria, I am quite aware that the subject of matrimony was in the air at Cloudhill when my cousin and your sister proposed that you should accompany me to Kashmir. But I must tell you, my dear, that as fond of you as I am, I have never been a passionate man and I fear that I am not one who could ever bring you — er — contentment.' He nodded to emphasize his statement. 'Maud and I suited each other's temperaments, you see. She was not — oh, as I say, we suited each other well and I shall miss the good lady, but it would be a grave mistake for me to make you an offer, my dear.'

Her jaw sagged. 'Truly, I had — I assure you that there are no expectations of any kind. You're quite mistaken, Nigel.'

'Well, m'dear, I'm certain that Emily and Martin — who have nothing but your best interests at heart — are hoping that if you and I are not to form a union, I will at least introduce you to some acceptable gentleman in Kashmir — someone who will win your heart and take care of you. You shouldn't remain a widow.'

She made a throaty sound of dismay.

'Oh, yes, there are a great number of single men in India who live in hope of meeting a lovely young lady, just like you. Actually, I know some very sound fellows belonging to the regiment in Srinagar whom I'm sure — '

'No, Nigel, no! *Please* don't give any of your friends the impression that I'm out here to catch a husband! I want you to make it quite clear to everyone from the outset that I've come simply to spend a short summer holiday in Kashmir. Perhaps a very short one!'

'Really? Very well, m'dear, we'll say no more about any marriage business.' He scrubbed his fingers across his chin. 'I must warn you, however, that I'm expecting a

107

mountain of work to be waiting for me when I arrive back in my office, and, for a time, you're likely to find me a very poor host.'

'Nigel, please don't be concerned. I'm not expecting you to entertain me. Actually, I look forward to seeing new sights and exploring the countryside.'

'Oh, you won't be short of company, m'dear. The ladies of our community will make sure that you enjoy your holiday. They have tea parties and all kinds of social events, and some are very keen sportswomen. You might even like to join the Amateur Dramatic Society. Yes, I'm sure your time will be happily filled once you've met Maud's friends.'

* * *

Nothing that Nigel had told her about the drive up to Kashmir prepared Victoria for what lay ahead when they left the train and climbed into a small canvas-topped vehicle pulled by a relay of sturdy, thick-coated mountain horses. This trail into Kashmir led upwards through the wrinkled foothills of the Himalayas and entered the almost perpendicular gorge of the snow-fed Jhelum River. They climbed a winding pass that seemed to be little more than a shelf cut into the rockface, and while the journey was spectacular and thrilling, she expected that at any moment their wheels would slip off the edge and plunge them into the torrent below. Or that she'd hear the rumble of an avalanche sweeping rocks down from the side of the mountain towering above.

But the relays of horses plodded on steadily up the trail. The temperature continued to drop and she pulled a rug higher. Her head drooped.

She didn't know how long she'd been asleep, but her eyes flew open when the pony-cart stopped for another change of horses. They were on level ground now and she gasped at the beauty of the huge white-crested mountains encircling them. It was a scene like no other, with snow still lying thick between the trees in the surrounding forest of tall pines, and acres of pale mauve alpine primulas growing by the hundred thousand on the short cropped winter grass of the *marg* — the meadow stretching before them.

Straight ahead on the far side of the valley, a drift of cloud moved to unveil a blue-white wall of ice where rays of sunlight sparkled on a majestic peak towering above all the other mountains in the unbroken range. The sight of it touched something profound and deep inside her. It brought a lump to her throat.

'Welcome to Barramula, gateway to the Vale of Kashmir,' Nigel said and followed her gaze to the mountain. 'That's Nanga Parbat — you can see it for miles in all directions.' He helped her to climb down stiffly from the pony cart. 'Come along now, we've time for hot tea and toast in the rest-house while they bring up the fresh horses. We should be home in Srinagar tonight.'

She remained standing where she was, spellbound by the magnificence of the lofty mountain looming above them. The sunlight struck diamonds of light off the ice, and, as the minutes ticked by, she became increasingly infused with a strange feeling of having reached — what? A turning point? Or was it simply exhaustion addling her brain? She gulped deep lungfuls of the sweet, cold air, and stood gazing up at the dazzling, untrodden snows of the great Nanga Parbat. The peak was so clear, so magnificent. So unreachable.

The massive mountain seemed to be standing there before her as a reflection of her marriage to Peter. So far away. So unreachable. She shook with a silent sob as she sensed for the first time since she'd received the news of his death, that Peter had gone beyond her reach. It was a shock to find herself quite alone up here amongst the towering mountains. It was final. Peter had truly gone.

Her chin trembled as she gazed up at the sparkling summit where a long plume of snow was whipping away across the heavens in a gale which, here in the valley, was no more than a light breeze on her face.

The mighty Nanga Parbat was demonstrating that it could no more hold the snow on its heights than she could continue to hold Peter in her life. He was lying on the other side of the world with all the love that she had poured into her letters placed next to his heart. She was here alone. Memories would remain with her, but the man who'd created them had gone to his rest. The moment had come for her to take the final step and call a silent goodbye.

With her eyes closed, she lifted her face to the heavens and whispered his name.

* * *

Exhaustion blurred Victoria's impressions of their arrival at Nigel's house late that night, but she remembered a line of tearful servants speaking to Pelham-Sahib in the local tongue, Urdu. Duleep, the head house servant, was the only one amongst them

111

who understood English.

But the gentle woman who led her upstairs needed no instructions. Clearly, she had been well trained by the late Pelham-memsahib to serve a good pot of tea and toast to a newly arrived guest while a warm bath was prepared and a feather bed made up with lavender-scented sheets.

Victoria fell into it gratefully, and the sun was up when she woke to lie staring up at the plastered ceiling, trying to recall where she was. The hands on the clock showed that it was nine o'clock. What day was it? Did it matter?

Unfamiliar scents and sounds drifted in through the shuttered windows and when she flung them open, the Vale of Kashmir lay before her like a green bowl cupped in the palm of the mighty Himalayas. Her bleary gaze swept the long, meandering lake and the unique little craft on it, the willow trees and poplars lining the banks, the tall, close-packed houses that she could see in the distance with brown-cloaked people going to and fro about their business.

And here came a man in a blue jacket cantering briskly past their gate on a gleaming chestnut mare with a white blaze and four white socks. Her eyes followed the beautiful horse until it was out of sight, and

112

she envied the man who was riding out on such a perfect morning.

She rang the bell and Duleep answered, carrying a breakfast tray. He set it down on a table beside the window and held a chair for her.

'Thank you. Is Pelham-sahib still at home?'

'No, memsahib, he left very early for his office.' He gave a nervous little cough. 'Will memsahib be wishing to discuss menus for the week?' He lifted the pot and began to pour her tea.

'No, Duleep, I am here as a guest.' She saw the relief in his eyes. 'I won't require any changes in your household routine.'

Nigel had already prepared her for the protocol observed amongst the British residents of Srinagar. 'Your first caller is sure to be Lady Phillips, a most charming woman. As the wife of the Resident, she's the senior lady in Kashmir.'

'And so I should wait in the house for her to call?'

He'd nodded apologetically. 'And the second call will be made soon after by the regiment's senior lady, the wife of Colonel Moncrief. And then all the others will start arriving. As soon as they've introduced themselves you'll be flooded with invitations to luncheons and musical afternoons, dances

— and goodness knows what else. Maud was always kept busy.'

His prediction was right. The Resident's wife called that afternoon and Victoria liked her immediately. Lady Phillips, was a dainty woman in her middle years who seemed genuinely distressed by Maud Pelham's tragic shipboard accident.

'What a tower of strength that dear lady was in our little community, especially when we had the annual flood of visitors arriving to escape the heat on the plains. Mrs Pelham could always be relied on to arrange a splendid array of entertainments for them — concerts and croquet and debates on all kinds of subjects. We will miss her sorely.'

Next morning, Colonel Moncrief's wife, the senior lady in the military establishment, made her call. Mrs Moncrief was a sharp-faced woman who rarely smiled, but she did so several times while she was giving Victoria examples of the sound moral guidance that the late Maud Pelham was quick to pass on to young officers in the regiment.

'Englishmen serving in India are always starved of suitable female companionship, you understand, Mrs Latham, and when the so-called *fishing fleet* arrives each year with eager young women who have failed to make a match at home, it can stir bad feelings amongst the officers. Some become despondent, rivalries quickly erupt, and occasionally hearts are broken. It can quite undermine morale in the whole regiment.'

Victoria nodded. 'Yes, I imagine so.'

'Fortunately, Maud Pelham was a remarkable judge of character and she had no hesitation about stepping in to save many a young man from rushing into a disastrous alliance with a silly girl who was determined to go home with an engagement ring on her finger.'

'Really?' Victoria appreciated that insight into Maud's line of thought. It made her feel slightly less guilty about any attempt she might make to manipulate Nigel's choice of a new wife.

Once Lady Phillips and Mrs Moncrief had made their calls, the other British ladies came in twos and threes throughout the next week. Victoria was required to do no more than chat, and Duleep was delighted to be kept busy serving tea and cake to the visitors.

Victoria's new acquaintances were eager for her to join their card parties, luncheons, croquet games, china-painting groups and book readings. Did Mrs Latham enjoy shooting?

'You'll find some very good game up there

in the mountains at this time of the year. We're setting up a hunting camp next week. Would you like to join us?'

'Thank you, but no — I don't ride and I know nothing about guns.'

She heard the news that rehearsals for the Amateur Dramatic Society's new production of *The Scarlet Cloak* were going well, and that the new ballroom being built onto the clubhouse at the polo field would soon be completed. A committee had plans well in hand for its inaugural ball on the Queen's birthday.

'How we all miss dear Maud at a time like this!' Victoria often heard that remark. 'Now there was a lady who knew how to organize a splendid function!'

Victoria's diary was soon filled with invitations, and though she told Duleep that she could easily walk the short distances to any of these houses in the cantonment, he clearly disapproved of the notion and insisted on rousing Maud's little old syce to harness the pony trap for each visit.

'Pelham-memsahib never walked!'

As Victoria watched how her new acquaintances occupied their days, they reminded her of a tribe marooned on an island, snuggled tightly together, hugging their Englishness close, and doing their best to ignore the great tide of Kashmiri humanity swirling around them.

They lived their lives in neat rows of well-tended gardens planted with English flowers, comfortable in bungalows filled with English furnishings, and servants for every domestic task. There was no reason why a mem-sahib would do a stroke of any kind of work, apart from organizing entertainment and trying to keep in step with everybody else.

Most sons, and some daughters, were sent off to schools in England at the age of seven or eight. 'Yes, it's heartbreaking to part with them, Mrs Latham,' said the regimental doctor's wife seated beside her at lunch one day, 'but children are inclined to become far too attached to the Indians if they remain here. Yes, they must — '

'Shh!' The magistrate's wife frowned at the speaker and nodded towards a thin woman who was sitting nearby and staring expect-antly out the window. 'M'dear, please take care not to talk about children within Mrs Buckley's hearing.'

While the topic of conversation at the table quickly turned to the latest catalogue that had just arrived from England, the doctor's wife whispered to Victoria that poor Mrs Buckley's little daughter had been kidnapped several years previously. 'Not surprisingly, Rose

Buckley quite lost her mind with grief, and it's only lately that she's even been able to leave her house.'

'That's dreadful. How did it happen?'

The doctor's wife shook her head. 'Child stealing is a very old and well-organized business in this part of the world. The kidnappers work swiftly and probably sell the child to one of the beggar masters in some big city. Or worse. Thank heavens, it doesn't happen often now, but we must remain vigilant.'

*　*　*

Victoria began to play tennis once a week; and three officers she'd met at a garden party called on her regularly as a trio. They flirted with her lightly, invited her to watch them play polo, and escorted her to the regimental band concert. She found their company pleasant enough, but when she gave them no encouragement, they went off to find other more lively targets.

The people she met in the cantonment and the invitations she accepted were all perfectly pleasant and agreeable, and Victoria came to feel a prickle of guilt at her own desperation to escape from this tight little circle and explore further afield. Kashmir must offer much more than this corner of England, she thought. Where were the three marvellous old Mogul gardens that Martin had told her about?

'Oh nobody visits them now, Mrs Latham,' said Mrs Simpson, the rector's wife. 'My husband took me to the Shalimar Gardens once, but we found them to be in a very poor, overgrown state. I'm sure I saw a snake.'

Victoria continued to wake early each morning, lying in the half-light and waiting for the now familiar hoofbeats to come pounding past the house. It was easy to recognize the sound of the splendid chestnut as it galloped off into the dawn, and by the time the man in the blue jacket came riding steadily back to town — always close to nine o'clock — she was up and dressed and standing at the window to watch him pass.

No, she corrected herself. It was the beautiful horse that held her attention. Just who its stern-faced rider was, or where he went, was neither here nor there. There were often days when the sight of that animal tempted her to go out and buy a horse of her own, then have someone teach her to ride it. She needed to broaden her horizons and discover for herself what lay around the bend in the road. But the idea came to nothing.

The more time Victoria spent in Srinagar,

the more futile she saw her mission to steer a new Mrs Pelham into Nigel's arms. He gave no signs of a particular interest in any of the pleasant ladies they met at the evening card parties and dinners they attended. After all, hadn't Nigel told her plainly on the train that he was not a passionate man? And with Duleep to oversee everything in the house — even reminding Pelham-sahib of his appointments and laying out the appropriate clothes for each occasion — a new Pelham-memsahib in Nigel's life seemed to be rather superfluous.

Victoria wasn't sure how long her visit to Kashmir would be, but she made a determined effort to step warily through the tangle of military and civil cliques which she saw constantly forming and reforming amongst the wives in the cantonment. It was a delicate business, but for Nigel's sake she was careful to remain on good terms with them all.

A feeling of impatience hit her again this morning as she stood at the window and watched the man on the chestnut horse riding past at nine o'clock. To date, she'd seen nothing of the city beyond the cantonment and the residency compound. On impulse, she sat down and wrote a note of apology to her tennis group, saying that she'd be unable to play today.

'Duleep, I'm going for a walk into the market, so please have this note delivered to Mrs Chambers. I'll be back for lunch.'

She didn't stop to hear his protest, but she suspected that he sent one of the young servants to shadow her into the old town — a jumble of lanes and tall, narrow brick buildings with timber balconies overhanging the street. It lay a mile away, sprawling around one arm of the lake and well out of view of the British community.

As soon as she entered the lanes, she was struck by the intangible and rich odours of the place — the smell of humanity, sweet and sour, of dust and refuse and boiling ghee. Surprised stares were thrown her way, but they were not unfriendly, and she made her way slowly through the throng of men and veiled women, overloaded donkeys and handcarts bringing cherries, peaches and mulberries to the market.

She was intrigued by everything she saw around her. Shops on either side of the street opened directly onto it, with men sitting cross-legged on the floor while they worked at their crafts. She was aware of being watched by families living above and when she smiled up at the women and children standing on their balconies, they called down a greeting. At least, it sounded to her like a greeting.

She admired the rolls of fabrics in the silk merchant's shop, as well as a display of the finest of woollen shawls woven with paisley motifs in the next one.

A dentist, flanked by an audience, performed his work on a patient sitting on a chair in his doorway, while a few yards away, a barber was shaving a customer out on the street. A pile of jewel-coloured carpets caught her eye, and she paused to marvel at the speed of the grain merchant's fingers as they flew to and fro, clicking the beads of his abacus as he sat crosslegged on the floor of his shop.

A herd of goats trotting down the narrow road forced her to step aside quickly, and around the next corner she stopped at the sight of the familiar chestnut horse standing outside a woodcarver's workshop on the opposite side of the lane. A lad held its reins while the rider was talking with the craftsman inside.

From this position, Victoria had her first clear view of the tall Englishman's features. Whenever she'd seen him riding past the house, she'd always considered his expression to be somewhat forbidding, but now his sun-tanned face appeared to be — if not handsome — at least good-looking, despite the thin white scar running down one cheek.

He looked younger, as well. And that was especially so as he flashed a wide smile when the toymaker brought out a brightly decorated wooden elephant standing well over eighteen inches high. She found herself smiling, too, when she saw the craftsman position a gold-painted *howdah* on the back of the toy. The Englishman picked up two small wooden figures to sit in it, and then a *mahout* to place astride the elephant's neck.

When the Englishman pulled the toy across the floor, she noted how cleverly the trunk had been made to sway from side to side as the wheels turned. What child wouldn't be delighted with such a toy? She could just imagine how excited Emily's little boys would be if she arrived home with a gift like that for them.

The man gave a boyish laugh, ran the toy several times again up and down the small floor of the workshop, and then shook the toymaker's hand.

Victoria stood where she was until the painted elephant had been wrapped in calico and the man had ridden off with it. Then she approached the woodcarver and attempted — with every pantomime gesture she could produce — to tell the craftsman that she wished to buy a toy just like the one he had sold to his last customer.

When the man shook his head repeatedly, she wasn't sure whether it was because he was unable to comprehend her request, or whether he was refusing to oblige her. Finally, she gave up and retreated in frustration. If only she could speak a few words of Urdu — just a few.

7

'Nigel, I'm afraid that I upset Duleep this morning.'

He smiled when she told him during dinner that night about her unescorted visit to the markets and the impressions she brought away. 'Strange smells, yes, but I found it all quite fascinating — and the people seemed to be friendly.' She didn't mention the Englishman she'd seen at the toymaker's.

He smiled and clicked his tongue at her. 'Vicky, English ladies don't go down there to shop. If you want to buy something, simply tell Duleep and he'll have the merchant bring his entire stock up to display on the veranda for you. That's the way it's done here.'

'Yes, but before I leave for home, I'd like to see more of the real Kashmir. Martin told me about the old Mogul pleasure gardens on the other side of the lake but the rector's wife said that the one she visited some time ago was completely overgrown. What do you know about them?'

'Haven't seen them for years, Vicky. Not quite Maud's cup of tea, you understand.'

When Victoria tactfully suggested to her art group that a painting excursion to the Shalimar Gardens next week would be a novelty, only quiet little Mrs Simpson, the rector's wife, was willing to forego their usual Tuesday morning still-life exercise.

Thinking that the outing might be beneficial for poor Mrs Buckley whose daughter had disappeared three years ago, Victoria asked her if she'd like to join them, too. But the suggestion only increased the woman's distress. 'Oh, no, I mustn't leave the cantonment. What will my little Margaret do if she comes home and finds that I'm not here?'

Duleep was clearly not happy when he heard that the memsahibs intended taking no servants on their outing in a *shikara*, the little canopied punt rowed by a *manji* standing at stern with his oar. But Victoria had made up her mind, and once he'd organized the loading of their picnic basket, rugs, umbrellas, Mrs Simpson's easel and two satchels of art materials, he was forced to watch anxiously as the little craft pushed off from the *ghat* and skimmed silently out onto Dal Lake.

Sunlight danced on the water and Victoria experienced a bubble of delight bouncing inside her as she lounged under the scalloped canopy while they drifted through a blaze of floating lotus blossoms with the flashing blue and gold and green of kingfishers and bee-eaters diving amongst them.

She shared a smile with Mrs Simpson. On a day like this, it was such a relief *not* to have a companion who chattered constantly. With a frieze of snow-capped peaks circling the valley, the shallow labyrinth of waterways that made up Dal Lake meandered for miles, sometimes spreading widely, sometimes narrowing in places where arms of land reached from opposite banks and causeways were built across with little arched bridges for water traffic to pass under.

She watched merchants in their *shikaras* rowing to and fro around the lake with baskets of fruit and vegetables, sacks of grain and flowers and doing business with farms and hamlets sitting on the banks. A melon-seller pulled close and held one out to them, but they shook their heads and he skimmed off towards a small farm on an island.

At one point they passed a long wooden houseboat being poled along slowly by four men. Every inch of visible wood was carved with delicate patterns of trees and blossoms.

'How lovely,' Victoria said as they drifted past. 'Are all the houseboats on the lake decorated in a similar way?'

Mrs Simpson nodded. 'Some are very splendid indeed, and there's a truly magnificent one that's sometimes moored near the Shalimar Gardens, so I hear. It belongs to the wealthy widow of a khan and she spends each summer up here. Not that we've ever been invited aboard. I mean, it just wouldn't do, would it?'

'It wouldn't? Why?'

'Why? Well, because we're English, and while the begum might be considered a very grand lady, she's of mixed blood.' The rector's wife dropped her voice to a whisper. 'They say that her mother was Persian and her father a Frenchman! So you see that a clergyman and his wife could not — would never — '

Victoria made an effort not to smile. 'And does this lady visit anyone ashore?'

Mrs Simpson tipped her head towards the Hari Parbat Fort looming on the hill across the lake. 'Well, I've heard that she sometimes visits the maharaja and the ladies of his *zenana*.' She leaned closer to Victoria. 'Actually, when we first arrived here nearly twenty years ago there was a great deal of gossip concerning the begum and a certain senior officer in the regiment who, um . . . ' She raised her eyebrows suggestively.

'You mean that the begum and a British officer had an affair?'

Mrs Simpson coloured. 'You must understand that the begum's background is obscure, so that kind of thing is just not done, my dear. It does no good for the races to mix.'

Victoria bit her tongue.

However, a pleasant surprise was waiting for them at the Shalimar Gardens when their *shikara* nudged in beside a grand one already moored at the *ghat*.

'Oh, splendid! The grass has all been cut since I was here last,' Mrs Simpson said, looking around her. 'How pleasant it looks now with the trees and roses pruned.'

The glory of the Mogul garden might have faded a little in the 300 years since it had been built by the son of the great Akbar, but the sound of running water and splashing fountains met the ladies as they stepped ashore. Like all Persian gardens, these were divided into quarters by spring-fed water channels and planted with lines of poplars and fruit trees. In the distance, a marble pleasure-pavilion stood at the end of a long, straight path, with terraces climbing the high hill behind it, and all linked by tumbling cascades.

Victoria and Mrs Simpson spread their

rugs in the shade of a gnarled pear tree and the rector's wife immediately began to set up her easel and stool. 'Look at the light on the hill over there! I must catch that before it goes.'

Victoria looked about. 'This place is absolutely enchanting. Would you mind very much if I leave you to go off and do a little exploring? I won't be long.'

How much she would have to tell Martin and Emily about this delightful setting, she thought, as she wandered along well-tended paths that ran past rose gardens and beside long water channels with their lines of bubbling jets. There was no sound but a distant call of birds and the splash of fountains.

Far ahead lay the entrance to a white marble pleasure-pavilion. When she reached it, Victoria found the interior dim after coming in from the glare of the garden. She'd taken only two steps over the threshold before she collided hard with a small girl who was running to the doorway, dragging a wooden elephant on wheels.

The child slipped and the toy tipped onto its side, spilling little figures from the *howdah*. Victoria quickly scooped them up and held them out to the child. 'Don't cry, little one. Look, they're not hurt.'

'Annabelle!' a deep female voice called from the other side of the pavilion, and a statuesque, grey-haired woman wearing a blue and gold sari swept across the black marble floor. 'Oh, madame, I do apologize for the child's carelessness. Annabelle, you must tell this lady that you are very sorry for not looking where you were going.'

The words were duly whispered in a strong French accent, and Victoria smiled into the child's big amber eyes. 'Thank you, your apology is accepted.' She leaned closer. 'I think that if I had a beautiful elephant like yours, I'd find it hard to keep my eyes off him, too.'

The little honey-skinned girl tugged at the strand of brown hair curling over her shoulder and studied Victoria shyly for a moment. 'He's my special friend.'

The serenely beautiful woman gave Victoria a warm look and took the child's hand. 'Thank you for your forbearance, madame. I bid you good morning.' She signalled an *ayah* to pick up the toy and to follow her and the little girl from the pavilion.

A Sikh servant who'd been hovering in the background, needed no instruction. He was a giant of a man, middle-aged, and sporting a moustache of monumental proportions, along with a large black pistol tucked into his belt.

131

Victoria was intrigued as she watched the group moving in formation down the path to their *shikara* waiting at the *ghat*.

How interesting to find that little girl playing with a painted elephant. Had it come from the man on the chestnut horse? Or perhaps there were dozens of children in Kashmir who owned painted elephants. But was it possible that the regal lady she'd just encountered had been the legendary begum? Mrs Simpson had said that her houseboat was sometimes moored in this area.

Urged on by curiosity, Victoria walked to the rear entrance of the pavilion and began to climb the long flight of steps leading up to the four terraces built into the hill behind it. She was puffing hard by the time she reached the top, and grateful to find a stone seat at the head of the cascade. Looking out from this height, she had a splendid view over the lake and she could see the grand *shikara* being rowed towards a huge houseboat moored off the far bank. The melon-seller they'd encountered earlier was paddling his way towards it, too, but as soon as the party was aboard, four men with long poles began to move it. Within fifteen minutes, it was out of view, with the melon-seller drifting in its wake.

'Ah, there you are at last, Mrs Latham,'

Mrs Simpson said, when Victoria eventually rejoined her. 'Did you discover anything interesting on your walk?' She dabbed another green leaf onto her almost-completed painting.

'I'm sorry to have been away for so long, but I find everything interesting in Kashmir.' She decided not to discuss her brief meeting with the woman and little girl.

★   ★   ★

In her next letter to Emily and Martin, Victoria said that she would soon be making plans to leave Kashmir because there was little more she could do for Nigel.

> *Everyone here shows great fondness towards him, but he seems quite content to continue his bachelor life. I have enjoyed a very pleasant holiday, and now I feel the time has come for me to leave. I don't belong here.*

She put down her pen and looked at those words. No, of course she didn't belong here, but where did she belong? Her parents' house in Hanover Square had been leased to a family from York; Cloudhill had been a haven when she'd most needed it, but it was Emily's home — not hers. The latest statement to come from the London solicitor showed that her wealth was growing fast each year. She could afford to travel anywhere in the world. Or should she buy a house in the country? Buy a farm? Find a useful life!

★ ★ ★

All week, Nigel had been losing sleep over the prospect of having to play in the annual cricket match between a team from the regiment and the 'Resident's Eleven' — a group of civil servants who were rallied annually for this match.

'It's the same every year, Vicky!' he said miserably when he came downstairs in his spotless whites. 'Damn it! Unless I'm lucky enough to trip and break an ankle on the way there, I can't avoid playing.' A note of woe crept into his voice. 'I've told Sir Ian that I can never see a ball coming, let alone hit one with the bat. I'm an embarrassment.'

The one bright note in his sorry cricketing saga was the news that this year the Resident had turned a blind eye to the rule book and had recruited his military attaché to play on the civil servants' team. 'Perhaps Captain Wyndham might save us from our usual utter and complete disgrace.'

Inside the white picket fence surrounding the cricket ground, Victoria took a seat in the marquee where the memsahibs, dressed in their starched muslins and lace, sat sipping cool lemonade served by barefooted servants. The ladies chatted as the regimental band played jolly tunes to entertain them while they waited for the start of the match.

Victoria noticed a brown-haired, freckle-faced girl wearing a shabby patchwork skirt hovering outside the picket fence. She'd observed this lass sometimes wandering alone past Nigel's house, and now when the child tried to sidle past the attendant at the gate, the man quickly sent her packing.

'Who is that girl? Why isn't she allowed in?'

'Oh, that's Molly Collins, and this enclosure is reserved for officers' families,' said the woman sitting next to her. Victoria gave a puzzled frown.

'Molly is living with some family in the ranks until the chaplain can find a relative in Ireland who'll take her.' Victoria looked even more puzzled. 'She's an orphan. Her father was killed in a skirmish up in the hills, and her mother died three months ago.'

'The poor child! Is there no other family?'

'Yes, two younger brothers, but of course the Regimental Benevolent Fund pays for orphaned boys to be sent down to boarding school in Lucknow.'

'And what about Molly? Who does she live with?'

'Can't say I know exactly, but she's sure to have been taken in by some trooper's family. At least for the time being.'

'Poor child. Does she attend school here?'

The woman shrugged. 'Probably not.'

'So what does the Regimental Benevolent Fund do for an uneducated girl like that if some relative doesn't claim her and provide her with a home?'

'Oh, she won't be abandoned. She'll be given her passage back to England, along with a purse of twenty pounds so she can buy clean clothes and find work.'

'But Molly Collins is still a child! And if she has no family to offer shelter or protection, do you realize what kind of work she'll find on the streets of any city?' Dark memories of death in an East End tenement shot into her mind. 'Believe me, it would be kinder to smother Molly in her bed tonight than send her to that fate!'

'Really, Mrs Latham, how you do dramatize the situation! Besides I think that she's at least twelve. Quite old enough to become a scullery maid.'

Victoria felt herself heating. She was

preparing to continue the argument with the well-dressed, well-spoken woman, but at that moment the teams came out onto the field and everyone in the pavilion began to clap.

As well, there were audible titters of excitement amongst the young ladies who'd just arrived in the fishing fleet. Those who knew the social scene in Srinagar were quick to point out to the visitors which man was married and who was unattached, what rank was held by each, who was next for promotion. And which men to be wary of.

Victoria caught the look of strain on Nigel's face when the officers won the toss and went in first to bat. He took up his position on the field and began by missing two easy catches. But when the next ball hit him squarely in the chest, he instinctively clapped both hands over it and seemed stunned when the umpire called 'Out!' A burst of applause came from the spectators in the marquee.

A frisson of surprise ran amongst the ladies when the new bowler came across for the second over. Victoria recognized him as the man on the chestnut horse whom she'd seen in the toymaker's shop. He tossed the ball in the air twice before running up and sending a sizzling delivery down the pitch.

'Who is that fellow bowling now?' she

asked the woman seated next to her, wondering if she might find an opportunity later to approach him and ask how she could make the toymaker understand that she wanted to buy a painted elephant like the one that he'd bought.

'That man? Oh, that's the military attaché, Captain Wyndham — and surely the most unsociable creature in India. Refuses every invitation, unless it's for some official function where he's duty-bound to put in an appearance.'

The lady sitting behind them leaned forward to add her opinion. 'Yes, but even then he just stands about, or goes off to find a billiard table or card game. Never asks a lady to dance. Such a pity that he's inherited none of his father's charm. Did you know, Mrs Latham, that he's the son of General Gordon Wyndham? Now there's a truly sociable gentleman!'

'And he's not nearly as handsome as his father, either,' Victoria's neighbour added with a sniff.

She held her tongue and asked no more about General Wyndham's unpopular son. Actually, she rather liked his dark, brooding looks, and she certainly enjoyed watching the way his long limbs moved as he ran up to the pitch to deliver each fast ball. Eventually he toppled two army batsmen in quick succession and earned a lukewarm ripple of applause at the end of the innings. But, as he walked off, Victoria clapped until her palms were stinging.

After the break for lunch, Captain Wyndham was sent in as first bat for the civils, with Nigel as his opening partner. Poor Nigel, it will be his turn next at the crease, she thought, knowing how much he was dreading it. But when Captain Wyndham sent the first fast ball sailing past the fieldsmen, they safely scored two runs with Nigel racing up and down the pitch as if his life depended on it. When the captain was back in his place at the crease for the next ball, he hit another easy two runs and their score continued to mount by twos, with an occasional six, before he was eventually caught out.

A few moments later, Nigel was standing awkwardly in front of the stumps, fumbling with the bat while he pulled out a handkerchief to wipe his forehead. But his agony proved to be short lived when he was bowled out for a duck and left the pitch looking relieved. When Victoria saw him heading off towards the players' pavilion, she excused herself and went to find him to offer whatever kind words were needed at a time like this.

139

She'd almost reached the pavilion when she heard the sound of crashing glass coming from the rear of the building — followed by angry shouting, children's squeals, and Nigel calling for someone to stop. She also heard a female voice raised in fury: 'Kitty Cameron! Now look what they've done! I told you to leave those wicked imps at home with the *ayah*!'

Victoria rounded the corner of the building and almost collided with the wife of the forestry officer. The woman was far too tight-lipped with anger to do more than roll her eyes heavenwards as she swept past.

At the rear of the building, a slim young woman with curls the colour of corn silk, stood below a broken window of the club-house kitchen with her shoulders slumped and a handkerchief held to her eyes. Several brown-skinned faces were looking indignantly through the shattered pane, then someone inside threw a cricket ball down onto the grass where it rolled to a stop at the young woman's feet.

During all this, Victoria caught sight of Nigel galloping after two small boys who had reached a fence surrounding the croquet green and were now trying to scramble over it.

'Oh, dear, oh dear!' the young woman said

and, when she took the handkerchief from her eyes, Victoria saw that the moisture in them was coming from uncontrollable laughter.

'Oh, dear, oh dear!' she said again and her smile was enhanced by a delightful pair of dimples. 'I never could throw a straight ball. Should I confess that I was the one who smashed their window? It was meant to go straight down there, but — ' She gave another peal of infections laughter. 'And now that nice gentleman is rescuing my naughty twins. Do you know him? I must thank him for his kindness. My name is Kitty Cameron.'

'How do you do, Mrs Cameron. I'm Victoria Latham, and yes, I know Mr Nigel Pelham very well indeed. I'll be happy to introduce you.'

Nigel was coming towards them now, not only holding each boy by one hand, but also holding their attention by whatever he was saying to them. 'My cousin Nigel is very fond of children.'

'How extraordinary! I've never before met a man who could tolerate small, noisy boys and their endless tricks. Their own father certainly couldn't!'

Victoria looked at the pretty woman quickly, wondering what was behind her matter-of-fact tone. And her use of the past tense.

'Yes, I'm a widow, Mrs Latham. My husband drowned in the Jumna last year.'

'Oh, Mrs Cameron, I'm so *very* sorry.'

'Thank you.' Clearly she wished to say no more, and turned to face Nigel who was now only a few paces away. She spread her arms towards the boys and when Nigel released their hands, they ran to her. She rewarded their rescuer with a beatific smile.

'Mrs Cameron, please allow me to present Mr Nigel Pelham, a gentleman who not only tolerates small boys, but who tames them as well.'

Nigel whipped off his cricket cap. 'Mrs Cameron, it was my pleasure. You have fine, bright lads. They're a credit to you.'

For a long moment the pair stood looking at each other, smiling, while the twins watched on with interest.

'Nigel,' Victoria said, 'if Mrs Cameron agrees, I'd very much like to invite her to dine with us one evening. Soon.'

'Thank you, Mrs Latham,' the widow said without taking her eyes from Nigel's. 'I'd be delighted to accept. Any evening at all. I'm staying with my cousin — George Harris, the forestry officer.'

'Then may I suggest two days from now? Friday?' His voice had acquired a new, deeper tone. 'I'll call for you in the gig at seven. Will that be convenient?'

'Perfectly, Mr Pelham, thank you. Perfectly.'

★ ★ ★

Before Nigel dressed and set out in the gig to collect Mrs Cameron, he had Duleep cut his hair. Shorter. Smarter. Victoria smiled to herself and made no comment about how much younger it made him look. Though there was still a light dusting of grey at the temples, he'd lost every trace of the sad spaniel look produced by the old curls falling on his forehead.

The cook excelled himself that evening and the dinner party was deemed to be a great success, with Duleep bringing out the best dinner service and overseeing every detail. Later, Nigel opened the pianoforte in the drawing room and invited their guest to play.

'Yes, Mr Pelham, I do play, but not at all well, I'm afraid,' Kitty said, when he led her to the piano stool and propped up the score of a popular song in front of her. 'I'm afraid it's been a long time since I touched a keyboard, but I'll do my best.'

Victoria sat listening as Kitty began to play and sing — hesitantly and rather poorly at first. But when Nigel surprised them both by joining in with a pleasant tenor voice, her nervousness started to fade and she fumbled over fewer wrong notes. They even began to harmonize during several sentimental songs, and after they'd sung *Drink To Me Only With Thine Eyes* once, they sang it again.

'Delightful, Mrs Cameron.' Nigel swallowed hard. 'Thank you, but I mustn't tire you.'

'Thank *you*, Mr Pelham. I'm not at all tired.' Her dimples deepened.

'Then perhaps you'd care to walk into the garden with me to see the Night Flowering Jasmine? It's doing exceptionally well this season.'

'Oh! Yes, I noticed a beautiful perfume in the air when we arrived.' She looked towards Victoria. 'Will you come, too, Mrs Latham?'

'Er — yes, of course. But please go ahead while I get a shawl.' She took care to walk upstairs very slowly, found a wrap for her shoulders, and walked downstairs even more slowly. A dish of bon-bons standing on the drawing room table distracted her as she was passing it, and choosing the right one to slip into her mouth was a process that couldn't be rushed. After that, she took her time in choosing another.

When she at last stepped out onto the garden path, the fragrance of the blossoming vine drew her towards the far end where two figures stood facing each other in the moonlight. Even at a distance, she could tell that any initial interest that either Nigel or Kitty might have had in the blossoms had vanished. They were standing apart, but reaching out to each other with fingers entwined.

For a moment, astonishment held Victoria rooted to the spot and she felt like an intruder. Perhaps she should slip back to the house?

'Oh, there you are, Vicky,' Nigel called, when he became aware of her presence. 'Do come over here and enjoy this glorious perfume.' He and Kitty stepped apart, though neither stopped smiling.

And at the end of the evening Nigel drove Kitty home and Victoria was already asleep in bed before he returned.

He was looking particularly cheerful the next morning at the breakfast table. 'Victoria, m'dear, I've invited Kitty and the boys to lunch on Saturday. Will that be convenient for you?'

Victoria smiled. 'Splendid.'

Fortunately, Kitty also brought the boys' *ayah* to lunch that day. Together, this patient lady and Victoria, along with Duleep, kept the four-year-olds occupied at the far end of the garden to ensure there was little interruption to the engrossing conversation that Nigel and Kitty appeared to be having under the willow tree.

After that day, letters began to pass between them frequently, and Nigel sometimes found a reason to call on her of an evening.

Only two weeks after their first encounter, Nigel Pelham, Deputy Controller of Revenue in the State of Kashmir, did something that he'd never done before in his whole career. He absented himself from his official duties for no reason other than to spend a whole day of diversion and pleasure in the company of Mrs Kitty Cameron, picnicking in the solitude of the Shalimar Gardens.

He returned to the house that evening engulfed by love for a lady who had clearly returned his affections. Victoria noted that the outing appeared to have left him looking ten years younger.

'Vicky, I can't describe how I feel when I'm with her. I could climb mountains. Fight a tiger! And she asks for nothing but to share my life.'

Victoria smiled to herself as she recalled Nigel having told her once that he was not a passionate man. But, clearly, that was before he and Kitty Cameron had found each other.

How dear Aunt Honoria would have applauded this delightful romance.

* * *

Barely a month after their first meeting, the engagement of Mr Nigel Pelham, widower, and Mrs Kitty Cameron, widowed mother of four-year-old twins, was announced.

The English community was agog and the ladies tut-tutted over their teacups. Surely the forestry officer's pretty cousin was far too young and *disorganized* to take Maud's place? And what havoc would those two unruly lads cause in Maud's well-ordered home?

Victoria held her tongue because it was clear from the moment they'd met that any wear and tear inflicted on the fabric of Maud's house would be well and truly compensated by the joy that Kitty and her little boys were bringing into Nigel's life.

'Can you believe it, Vicky, there's a difference of only fifteen years in our ages,' he said to her, apropos of nothing one evening, as he closed his eyes and smiled to himself, clearly lost in pleasurable thoughts.

Victoria wrote to Emily and Martin about the surprising turn of events in Nigel's life, and said that she now intended to stay on in Srinagar for the wedding.

Kitty and her boys are like a breath of fresh air that is blowing all the old cobwebs away from Nigel. Whenever the naughty twins are with him, they behave like lambs — well, most of the time. Kitty herself is a truly sweet-natured soul, and not in the least demanding, but Nigel insists that the whole house must be refurbished before she comes to live here. And he is the one who is organizing the changes and replacing all Maud's dark velvet curtains and coverings with Kitty's choice of chintz roses, roses, roses on everything.

I've grown very fond of Kitty Cameron. She might have the looks of a Dresden doll, but she has many unexpected strengths. I know that she'll make Nigel a very happy man.

Even to Emily and Martin, Victoria would never reveal the tale that Kitty had confided to her one afternoon as they sat together watching Nigel throwing a ball to the twins.

She talked about her first marriage and revealed that it had been a misery, almost from its beginning. Once they arrived in India, her new husband's heavy drinking had

148

turned him into a beast, and for ten years she'd been forced to endure his violence.

'He seemed to take pleasure in beating me and I was terrified of him. In a drunken rage one day, he threw me down the stairs and that caused me to lose my first baby. I loathed him. Deeply.

'He built bridges for the railways so we always lived in isolated places where I had no one to turn to, and he soon drank away the little money of my own that I had to start with. For years I tried to stand up to him as best I could, until the twins came into the world. But when he began to hurt them too, I prayed to see him dead.

'Then, one day as I was standing by the river, I saw him stagger down to the opposite bank and order the little punt to bring him across. There'd been heavy rain in the hills and the water was running so fast that the old ferryman didn't want to cast off, but George used his riding whip to persuade him. The punt capsized halfway over and I saw my husband thrown in to the water.

'Think what you will of me, Vicky, but I confess that I felt nothing — absolutely *nothing* — when I saw him floundering in that torrent. While I stood there on the bank and watched him being swept out of my life forever, I sent my thanks to whichever river deity had heard my prayer and smiled on me that day. I felt no grief then, or at any other time — simply enormous relief to know that I'd become a widow.'

'Thank you for trusting me with that, Kitty.' Victoria had squeezed her hand. 'All I can say is that I have nothing but the greatest admiration for the courage you showed during those years, and I think Nigel is a very lucky man to have found you.'

'Of course, I've told him everything, so now I intend to close the book on that chapter of my life and spend the rest of it being the best wife that he could ever wish for. Oh, Vicky, don't you think that Nigel is the most the wonderful man you've ever met? Every day he goes out of his way to find fresh new ways to make me happy.' She coloured. 'Do you know that he's even planning a new nursery for — well, for some time in the future.'

Victoria smiled to herself. Kitty Cameron had been talking about the man who — not long ago — had been called *dreary* by the cousins at Cloudhill.

8

Kitty's charm soon softened any apprehension that Duleep might have had about the impending arrival of a new mistress in Pelham-sahib's house. She'd been quick to reassure him that when she and the boys came to live here, there would be absolutely no changes required in his splendid domestic routine. But would it be possible sometimes to have an early dinner served under the willow tree in the garden? And could the downstairs windows be opened as soon as the sun was up each morning? And would he translate her recipe book for the cook? There was a lamb dish on page seventeen which she thought that Pelham-sahib was sure to enjoy.

Victoria smiled to herself and stepped away from the daily buzz of activity in the house. A tailor with his sewing machine now seemed to be permanently encamped on the floor of the veranda, busily stitching acres of new curtains, while painters and upholsterers moved from room to room creating chaos.

As often as possible, she escaped from it all by borrowing Maud's pony-trap and having the little *syce* drive her away from the cantonment. She'd already begun to withdraw from the tight little groups of wives and their activities.

'Sorry I won't be able to come for cards this week. With so little time left here, I need to do a little sketching in the hills before I leave Kashmir.'

This became her standard excuse to avoid being caught up in the renewed swirl of tea parties and luncheons that the ladies of the cantonment were organizing for a fresh wave of new arrivals from the hot plains.

Victoria had never had any great enthusiasm for art. And very little talent, either, she reminded herself as she perched on a boulder and looked down on the long, narrow valley running beyond the little stream rushing over rocks at the foot of the hill where she was sitting. Up on the road behind her, Maud's fat little horse stood dozing in the shafts of the trap, while the thin little *syce* lay curled up on the seat, snoring.

She sketched the outline of the hill across the valley and tried to draw its tree-covered folds running down to the long stretch of green grass below. The lake and the Shalimar Gardens probably lay not far beyond that hill, she calculated. Holding the sketch pad at arm's length to study what she'd done, she screwed up her nose at the wretched effort and threw the book onto the ground beside her.

She wrapped her arms around her knees and let her mind drift while the white clouds overhead slowly changed shape until they began to resemble a flock of woolly sheep. Perhaps she should consider buying a sheep farm. In Australia?

The sound of pounding hoofbeats suddenly brought her back to earth and she sat up straight to watch the familiar chestnut beauty sweep into view around the hill. From having seen him on the cricket field, she knew that the rider was Captain Wyndham, but who was the small girl he was holding in front of him on the saddle? Was she the child with the elephant who had collided with her in the Shalimar Gardens?

Once onto the flat, the captain urged the horse into a gallop and both the man and child were laughing as the horse flashed past her vantage point.

It wasn't long before she heard the galloping hoofs again echoing from the rocks, and the horse thundered back along the valley floor with her legs stretched and her coat shining like molten gold in the sunlight. For one moment she seemed to be almost flying over the grass, and in the next she tripped, staggered, and seemed unable to right herself. Victoria saw the captain whip his feet from the stirrups at the first stumble, then as the horse crashed, he and the child were tossed to the ground, both tumbling awkwardly and rolling.

'Oh, no!' Victoria sprang to her feet and began to slip and slide her way downhill over the loose rocks and, lifting her skirt, she dashed through the fast-flowing ankle-high stream to reach the scene. Initially, the man and the little girl were not moving, but, by the time she'd raced across the valley, Captain Wyndham had raised himself into a sitting position and was holding the unconscious child in his arms, rocking her.

Not far away, the chestnut squealed in agony, lying on her side and thrashing as she struggled to stand on a damaged foreleg. Broken bone protruded through the skin.

'Belle, Belle — oh, God! Annabelle, open your eyes, sweetheart. Look at me.' The man seemed unaware that Victoria had reached his side.

'Captain, I think the child should be kept still,' she said gently, kneeling beside him and putting a restraining hand on his arm. 'Don't move her like that — just let her lie quietly.' She picked up one of the little hands to feel the fluttering pulse, then rubbed the fingers between her own. 'Sir, I'm going to untie your scarf and wet it in the stream so we can wipe the blood from her forehead.'

His face was ashen, making the thin white scar on his cheek barely noticeable. He made no response, but the look of dread in his eyes tore at her heart when she reached across the little girl to untie the knot under his chin. She ran across to the stream to wet his scarf in the icy water and, back beside them again, she wiped the child's brow, then held it against the bleeding wound on her scalp.

'You hand is hurt, sir. Is there a handkerchief in your pocket that I could use as a bandage?'

'No.' Only then did he show surprise at finding her beside him. 'What the devil — How — ?'

'I was up there, sketching,'

His frown deepened and he jerked his head towards the pitifully thrashing, squealing horse. 'Well, for God's sake, go over there and put the poor creature out of her misery.'

Victoria looked at him dumbly. 'I — I can't. I know nothing about — I've never handled — '

'Oh, Lord! Just get my rifle from the saddle, put the muzzle between her eyes and pull the blasted trigger. It's loaded.' His jaw tightened. 'She can't be left to suffer like that.'

Like an obedient child, Victoria stood and, with her knees turning to straw, she went to the stricken animal lying there, all white of eye and foaming mouth. Terrified, she heaved great gulping breaths as she dodged the flailing legs to snatch the rifle. For a moment she looked down at it in her shaking hands, felt its weight and glanced across to the captain, hoping for some signal or direction. Or a little encouragement. But his gaze was still on the child's face.

Gathering every ounce of her resolve, she moved cautiously to the mare's head. 'Oh, you wonderful, beautiful creature, please, please forgive me. It breaks my heart, but I must, I must do this.' Perhaps it was coincidence, but the animal ceased its violent struggle at the sound of her voice and watched her as she placed the muzzle carefully between its eyes, braced herself, held her breath and squeezed the trigger.

Silence. Nothing happened. She clamped her lips to stifle a wail of panic. The captain was still looking the other way. She'd never handled a gun before. What was she to do now? Common sense whispered that there must be a safety catch somewhere on this weapon. Where? Her damp hands shook even more when she turned it and located a lever beside the breech. It moved smoothly when she lifted it, then positioning the muzzle between the mare's eyes, she tried again.

This time she forgot to brace herself and the rifle's recoil slammed the butt painfully into her shoulder and sent her staggering backwards. But the bullet had done its job and the mare lay still at her feet.

For the next few moments she could do nothing but stand and stare in horror at what she'd accomplished. She'd killed this glorious animal! Her numbness quickly passed and she began to shake. She wiped a sleeve across her eyes, swallowed hard and turned away to carry the rifle back to the captain.

The little girl in his arms was whimpering and he shot a glance up at Victoria. 'Quickly, look at this — see? Watch her eyelids.'

The dark lashes fluttered and the child's eyes opened a crack. 'Oh, Papa, it hurts. It hurts, Papa.'

The man kissed the little girl's forehead and Victoria saw the moisture in his eyes. Then, still holding the child across his arms, he climbed to his feet.

Victoria knew that the sound of the gunshot was sure to have woken the sleeping syce, and, sure enough there was the little man already scrambling down the hill towards them. 'Captain, I have a vehicle waiting on the high road. Can I take you and the child wherever you need to go?'

'Thank you, but no. I'll carry her — not far. But if you would be so good as to slip the strap of the rifle over my shoulder?' By the way he moved it, she could tell that he was in pain.

At last he looked across to the mare. His lips tightened and she saw the misery in his eyes. 'She was — I am most grateful for your assistance, ma'am.'

Victoria didn't trust her voice not to break if she tried to speak. So they simply looked quickly at each other and exchanged a nod, then turned their backs and walked away in opposite directions.

Climbing back up the steep hill to the pony trap was made more difficult by the fact that she seemed to have little control of her limbs and her vision was blurred by unstoppable tears. She'd never be able to forget the expression in the mare's eyes as she held the rifle against her forehead. She couldn't bring herself to look back on what she'd done. It was too awful. But just then, she glimpsed the begum's big Sikh servant come running from what she deduced must be the direction of the lake.

Pieces of today's puzzle kept teasing her as the pony clopped its way slowly back to the cantonment. There was obviously much more to Captain Wyndham than the gossips of Srinagar realized. A little girl named Annabelle had called him papa, and she was, without doubt, the child with the painted elephant whom Victoria had seen being taken out to the begum's houseboat near the Shalimar Gardens.

What was the captain's connection with that grand lady with whom the British people of Srinagar refused to become associated? Why was the child in the begum's care?

Where was Annabelle's mother?

★ ★ ★

Andrew Wyndham's shoulder ached, his head ached, and he was bruised from the fall. Fury at the whole episode burned inside him; the nightmare of Annabelle's brush with death today would live with him forever. And his heart ached for the beautiful mare. One false step, one unexpected depression in the surface where her hoof had struck. Damn, damn, damn! Half a yard to the left or right and there would have been no fall. It was his own blasted fault. He'd been riding like a madman.

He poured a brandy and stood at his window, staring out into the night and trying to make sense of the events. The sudden arrival of the young Englishwoman at the scene had been most fortunate, but what tale would she carry back to the gossips? Who was she, this green-eyed girl who'd shown such a cool head in the emergency? No, her eyes weren't truly green, they were hazel —

Whoever she was, he should at least try to find her and express his gratitude. But how could he do that? Knock on every door in the cantonment?

He turned from the window and pulled off his jacket. Of course, he should have left Srinagar two years ago. That had been the original plan he'd made with the begum: she would raise Annabelle for a year or so, spending winter on her estate near Amritsar and summer on the houseboat in Kashmir where Andrew was able to pay regular visits. And during those twelve months, he was to have resigned from the regiment and found himself a position somewhere in the Indian Civil Service — some place where he, himself, could raise his child.

But now Annabelle was three years old and here he was, still procrastinating. The begum had been his salvation, but how much more could he ask of her?

In reality, though, where could he and Annabelle settle down quietly as father and daughter? He'd turned down a job in the

Madras Customs Office last year when he was hit by panic at the prospect of spending his life sitting at a desk reading endless cargo lists. The position of Deputy Forestry Officer in Bangalore had sounded promising — especially as a bungalow was to have been provided. But when news came that the whole area was ablaze in a series of confused and bloody religious riots, he withdrew his application. Perhaps he could find a position in Calcutta with a merchant house? Or learn whatever skills were required to become a banker? Pity that his application for the position of manager of a tea plantation in Darjeeling had been turned down. Perhaps he should never have mentioned that he knew nothing about growing tea.

He turned away from the window and began to undress for bed. Damn it, the army had been his whole life. The regiment was the only family he'd ever known and he had no real desire to walk away from it.

But where in that masculine and often lonely world would there ever be a place for his motherless child? He had to look elsewhere to provide whatever Annabelle was going to require along her path to womanhood. Though, with his funds in such a sorry state, would he ever be able to provide enough?

He opened the safe and took a great ruby ring from its box. It was valuable and it would be Annabelle's one day. When she asked him where it had come from, he would tell her the story of her beautiful Indian mother who lived in a far-away place called Gwalinpore.

The old ache for Ishana remained buried deep in his heart. Ishana, whose love had restored life to his broken body. Did she sometimes fret for the tiny, precious gift that she'd sent to him three years ago? In that time, had any of his messages reached her in the palace *zenana*? Had the healer relayed the news that her beautiful daughter was well and thriving?

★　★　★

Andrew realized that it would only be a matter of time before information filtered through to his father that he had been applying for a variety of civilian posts, and he seemed to be the only one in Srinagar who wasn't surprised by General Wyndham's unscheduled visit to inspect the regiment. The adjutants had barely sufficient warning to ensure that everything was in order before the general's party was sighted.

Colonel Moncrief welcomed General Wyndham

with full pomp at a dinner in the officers' mess. All the grand regimental silver was put into service and the general was in fine form at the head of the table, brimming with affability, generous with his praise.

Wearing full dress uniform with rows of decorations on his chest, Gordon Wyndham sat like a victorious Roman caesar about to send in the lions to devour the one man in the room who had *not* earned his praise this evening.

Andrew was placed well down the table, far enough away to catch only snatches of his father's conversation, but perfectly able to interpret his performance by watching the admiration glowing on the faces of the men around him. General Wyndham was a hero, the victor of great battles. To the men in the ranks, he was known as Wyndham the Widow-maker.

Andrew studied his father and felt all his old resentment resurfacing. The general's handsome features were beginning to coarsen, but though his hair was almost white, it was still thick. His brown eyes — Andrew himself had inherited those eyes, and so had Annabelle. He smiled inwardly as he sipped his claret, imagining what a trump card he might play one day when his dazzling Annabelle had reached womanhood and he at last introduced the general to his grand-daughter. *You see, Father, now you can't deny that I've achieved at least one success in my life.*

At the end of the evening, during which the general had made a point of ignoring his son, he called Andrew to drive back with him to the guest bungalow where he was staying. And as Andrew had anticipated, that was when the general's affability ended.

With his hands clasped behind his back, he stood rocking on his heels, frowning down at his son lounging in a chair with his long legs crossed at the ankles. The strained silence between them grew, until the general exploded. 'My God! What a lily-livered disappointment you've proved yourself to be.'

Andrew's brows lifted in mock surprise.

The general's voice always rumbled deeper when he was furious. It made subordinates quake. 'It's to my everlasting shame that my only son should have inherited every one of his mother's character flaws, all her weakness and sentimentality.'

'But, sir, I well remember you whipping all that kind of nonsense out of me thirty years ago.' His voice was flat. 'And what a fine job you made of it.'

The general took the chair opposite Andrew's and leaned forward aggressively.

'Did I indeed? Then kindly tell me what has happened to your loyalty, pride, honour, fortitude? I'd like to know how long you think you'll be permitted to fritter away your life here in Srinagar?'

Andrew continued to regard him dispassionately. 'Well, what can I say, sir? Actually, I'm looked on here as something of a wounded hero for trying to save the little Raja of Gwalinpore from being blown to pieces by that assassin's bomb four years ago. Didn't succeed, of course, but the palace healer managed to keep me alive and, since then, I'm sure the regimental surgeon has informed you about each stage of my recovery.'

'Ah, yes, Doctor Lovell.' The general didn't disguise his sneer. 'He's a good friend, I assume? Willing to keep you on the 'Unfit for Active Duty' list for a little longer?'

'Naturally, I follow his professional advice, sir.'

'And that includes playing a great deal of polo and cricket?' A little twist in one corner of his mouth always appeared when the general became sarcastic. 'And that morning gallop around the lake is most beneficial, too, eh?' His smile became a leer. 'I understand that you come back into town each morning, positively brimming with fitness.'

Andrew saw the track that his father's

thoughts were taking. Nobody knew about his early morning visits to Annabelle on the begum's houseboat, and it gave him a perverse pleasure to play along with the general's hint that he was keeping a little *bibi* somewhere in the hills.

'Well, sir, I seem to recall that you had a similar arrangement in Benares.'

The general gave a quick, knowing grin. 'Hmm. You were obviously more observant at the age of ten than I realized, but I can assure you that whatever time I spent on *amusements*, I never lost sight of my career. I was a lieutenant-colonel by your age, a full colonel by forty and a general at fifty!' He poured himself a whisky, tossed it down and thumped the empty glass onto the table beside him.

Andrew braced himself for what he knew was coming: 'Now give me one good reason, damnit, why you're sniffing around for a job in the civil! Have you married some damned woman like your mother who refuses to knuckle down to army life? Or got yourself into a scrape with a female down on the plains?'

Andrew gave a cynical chuckle and shook his head. 'Absolutely not! I keep telling you that I'm simply a wounded hero.'

His father scowled. 'And I'll lay a bet that

you were fool enough to come away from that débâcle in Gwalinpore with empty pockets, too. Why didn't you have the wits to tell your royal hosts that a contribution from the palace treasury would be the appropriate compensation for your injuries?'

Andrew kept a straight face. 'But I've always been told that kind of thing is against regulations, sir!' God alone knew how much his father had accepted in gifts and bribes over the years.

'Lord, Andrew! Have you no ambition? No thought of what the future holds for you? It's been ten years since you were made captain, and here you are, thirty-four years of age and still a bloody captain with the job of running messages between the soft-headed British Resident here and that lying old rogue of a maharaja up there in the fort! Military attaché, be damned! You're nothing but a lackey!' Now he was shouting.

Andrew held his temper and offered no denial. The general gave a huff of exasperation, pulled a cheroot case from his pocket and offered him one. For some time they sat facing each other, smoking in silence. His father rested his head on the back of the chair, brooding as he blew perfect smoke rings and watched them wobble their way towards the ceiling.

'You're a bloody fool, Andrew,' he growled at last. 'If you burn your bridges and leave the army, I'll have done with you and you'll get not one penny when I'm dead.'

When Andrew simply lifted one shoulder and said nothing, the general again lost patience. 'Why the devil won't you spare a thought for your career? Before that Gwalinpore business you were well regarded at the highest level, and with my influence you had every chance of getting a command of your own before long.' He glared at Andrew, ground the stub of his cheroot into the ashtray and waited for an explanation. None came.

'Listen to me! The North-west Frontier is still the place to see real action and make a name for yourself. I could have arranged your transfer into the Guides, y'know, and if you'd proved your worth with them, you'd soon have been given command of one of the forts they're building along the border. Very likely, you'd have been promoted to lieutenant-colonel by forty.'

'How splendid.' Andrew gave an exaggerated yawn. 'I'll sleep on it. Now, if you'll excuse me, sir, I must say goodnight.'

His father's voice echoed in his head as he mounted his horse and rode back to his own quarters in the residency compound. Being accepted to serve in the elite Corps of Guides in Mardan was the goal of every ambitious officer, but if he should ever win a place with them, it was going to be on his own merits and not because he was Gordon Wyndham's son. His mind played with the thought. What if he did apply now to join the Guides?

Challenging images of commanding a frontier fort filled his head as he prepared for bed. He could see it clearly: bringing his junior officers and the troops to the peak of readiness, settling quarrels and negotiating peace between the warring hill tribes. God! How he wanted to be given that kind of responsibility. And those forts were built with accommodation for the commander's family.

He lay on his bed watching the moon shadows on the ceiling and wondering how the Corps of Guides on the North-west Frontier would view the arrival of an unmarried officer with a small daughter of mixed blood and her *ayah*?

It was impossible. Annabelle would never be accepted. He gave a grunt and heaved himself on to his side. The whole evening had left him with an aching weariness, and the sane part of his brain told him to forget about the Guides and go to sleep quickly. The other part kept him awake. Might there be some way to change the impossible?

After another hour of sleepless tossing he flung back the sheets and went to his writing desk. Why shouldn't he put his name forward for a transfer to the Guides? Not through official channels at this stage, just a polite enquiry in a personal letter to Major-General Roberts at Mardan.

Andrew's pen flew over the paper as he diplomatically reminded Bob Roberts of their meeting five years previously when his company had fought alongside the Guides at the Bolan Pass. Modesty prevented him from mentioning the medal he'd won in that action. In any case, he didn't think that the major-general was a man who would forget the night that Lieutenant Wyndham, as he was then, had used his initiative to move his company out under cover of darkness, circle a hill, scramble up over rocks and boulders to rout a large force of hidden Pathans. It was an action that had prevented a surprise dawn attack on the main force.

Roberts himself had recommended him for the medal. 'Just the sort of man we want for the Guides,' he'd said at the time. So why shouldn't Andrew see if that was still the case? But what would he do about Annabelle? Was there a kind-hearted woman somewhere who would be prepared to become mother to a soldier's child and go out to the frontier with him? Hah! The only candidate for such a position would have to be a woman with lunacy in her family, and he already had enough of that running through his own.

* * *

Even with a stream of craftsmen at work throughout Pelham-sahib's house, Duleep insisted on noise being kept to a minimum.

But next day, as Victoria sat reading in the last of the afternoon light in the garden at the side of the house, a great hullabaloo broke out indoors. A moment later, she was startled to see the orphaned child, Molly Collins come scrambling out of the drawing room window and dropping to the ground with something in her hand. The girl darted across the lawn and into the shrubbery, just as a young cavalry lieutenant along with two troopers pulled up in a flurry of dust at Nigel's gate and ran to the front door.

Victoria could hear the officer speaking urgently with Duleep and a moment later, they turned the corner of the house together and strode across the grass in her direction. From the corner of her eye, she caught a glimpse of Molly's patchwork skirt moving amongst the bushes.

Until she learned what trouble Molly had

got herself into this time, she was reluctant to give away the child's hiding place.

'Why, Lieutenant Woodley, this is indeed a pleasant surprise. Whatever has brought you here in such a lather?' She stood quickly and walked towards the spotty-faced young man, wearing her brightest smile and hoping that this might divert his attention from the bushes beyond.

He pulled off his white helmet. 'My apologies for disturbing you, Mrs Latham, but I'm searching for a child named Molly Collins. I have orders to take her back to the regimental chaplain.'

'Oh! Does that mean he's been able to locate her relatives in Ireland?'

'No, ma'am. But she can't stay any longer with Mrs Williams because the 24th Rifles have been ordered to Jaipur, and all the wives and families are packing up to follow them.'

'Oh! But is there no other family here prepared to look after the poor girl?'

The young man blew a long breath between his lips. 'Not Molly Collins, ma'am. She's known to be too much of a handful.'

Those words send Victoria's heart plummeting. 'So what does the chaplain plan to do with her? *Please* don't tell me that he's going to put her on a boat and send her back to England on her own!'

'No, I assure you that won't happen, Mrs Latham. He's made arrangements for her to be sent to a mission station outside Poona. The good Christians down there might be able to teach her to change the error of her ways.' He lifted his high-bridged nose. 'Are you aware that child has just stolen certain property from this house?'

That child. 'The girl has a name, Lieutenant! It is Molly Collins and in the last twelve months she has lost her father and her mother, and even her two little brothers have been sent away to school. And, as you know, when they finish there, those boys are likely to serve the rest of their lives in the army, so when will she ever see them again?' Victoria's throat tightened and her voice became thin. 'Don't you agree that Molly must feel that the world has been very unfair to her? Perhaps she wonders how she is to survive if she doesn't take matters into her own hands.'

The young officer's face turned scarlet and Victoria took pity on him. After all, he was simply the messenger. She drew in a deep breath and changed her tone. 'Well, thank you for telling me about the chaplain's plans, Lieutenant. I'll know what to do now if I should happen to see Molly.'

'Oh, oh — thank you, Mrs Latham. Yes, if you do see her, please send a message to the chaplain's office and he'll — well, he'll — ' He replaced his helmet quickly and adjusted the chin strap. 'Good evening, ma'am.'

'Duleep,' she said, watching his dark eyes scan the shrubbery. 'Not one word of that conversation is to leave this house. I will speak with Pelham-sahib as soon as he comes home, and then we will decide how best to handle the matter concerning the young person who is at this moment hiding in those bushes.'

She raised her voice a little and spoke clearly so that her words carried. 'Tell me, Duleep, what did Miss Molly Collins take from this house?'

'Pink velvet ribbon, memsahib. About two yards that the upholsterer had cut for — '

'Oh, it was something pretty. I see. Thank you, Duleep, I'll not keep you from your duties any longer.' She sat on the chair again, opened her book and pretended to read until he'd walked back into the house.

'Well, Molly, I'm not cross with you, but I'd like you to come out of the bushes now and let me know what you think about the chaplain's arrangement to send you to Poona.' She heard the rustle of leaves, but the child didn't appear.

'Has any one ever asked Molly Collins where she'd like to go?' Victoria kept her head down, but from the corner of her eye she saw a movement and a peep of colour. 'I'd like to talk to Molly about this. Perhaps she'll come over here and tell me about it, and what she'd like to do when she grows up.'

'Mil-ner.'

Victoria strained to catch the soft voice coming from her left. 'Did you say that you'd like to become a *miller*? A *flour* miller?'

'Nah! A *mil-ner* that makes 'ats for ladies.'

'Of course! A *milliner*. And I'm sure a milliner always needs pink velvet ribbon, doesn't she?'

The girl slowly emerged and sat cross-legged on the grass several yards away from Victoria's chair. 'Major Fairweather's wife always wears the best 'ats. Flowers and feathers and veils. And she's even got one with a pearl brooch on the front.'

'That sounds very smart. Perhaps I'll be able to come and buy a hat from your shop one day.'

When Molly looked up at last, her eyes were awash with tears. 'I'm sorry I took your ribbon, missus. But I don't want to be sent away to a mission. *Please*.' She moved closer and put the now grimy length of velvet onto Victoria's lap. 'And if you tell me that I've got to go back to school, I will.'

'Thank you for the ribbon, Molly, and yes, I think that school is very important for someone who wants to become a milliner. There'll always be letters to write to customers and money to add up at the end of the day.' The girls tears began to overflow onto her freckled cheeks.

'Now, Molly, my name is Mrs Latham, and this house belongs to a very kind man called Mr Pelham. As soon as he comes home I'll talk to him about the plans that the chaplain has been making for you.' Molly sniffed loudly and wiped her sleeve across her eyes. 'But first, I think that a warm bath in my room would be the best idea.'

That bath was a novel experience for the girl, and it was followed by a big supper arriving on a tray. Though Duleep couldn't hide his disapproval, a bed was made up for Molly beside Victoria's, and her clothes were taken away to be washed.

'Duleep, until I discuss this situation with Pelham-sahib, I don't want one word about the child to leave this house. Is that understood?'

The sun had barely set when Molly's head settled on the pillow and she was asleep well before Nigel arrived home.

'Oh, no, Victoria! She can't possibly remain here,' he said, when she presented him with Molly's predicament. 'You mustn't meddle. It's a matter for the regiment to handle. This child is *not* your responsibility!'

'Oh yes, she is, Nigel. An unprotected girl is the responsibility of all decent people.' She looked at him squarely. 'From what I've learned about your Maud, I'm certain that she would have had no hesitation in doing all she could to help Molly Collins. It's just a matter of deciding *what* will be best for her.'

When Kitty arrived for dinner and heard the story, Victoria immediately gained an ally. 'Nigel, my darling, we need to consider this carefully, so you must write to the chaplain right away to say that Molly Collins is here, but a little unwell and not fit to be moved until Mrs Latham deems it advisable.'

While Nigel went into his study and put pen to paper as she'd directed, Kitty and Victoria began searching for a possible solution.

'If only we could find another woman to take her in — a capable, tolerant woman — kind, but firm,' Kitty said.

'And if the Regimental Benevolent Fund isn't prepared to pay for Molly's board and lodging for a few years, I'll do it myself,' Victoria added.

They drew up a list of names. It was a very short list that was quickly whittled down to one: Mrs Pettigrew, wife of the deputy health officer.

'Oh, it's hopeless!' Kitty threw down her pencil. 'Mrs Pettigrew is leaving here in two weeks. She's taking Oliver home to start school.'

'Well, my dears,' Nigel said when he rejoined them, 'I've sent a message to the chaplain, though you must realize that keeping Molly here for a few more days is merely delaying the inevitable. This can't become her haven.'

Victoria frowned as she scribbled mindless circles on the pad. Nigel was right: Molly needed to find a *haven*. Just as she, herself, had needed a haven following that dreadful night in Hanover Square when her parents cast her out of their lives.

But she'd found her haven at Cloudhill with Emily and Martin. If only she could talk to Martin about Molly Collins.

She voiced those thoughts to Nigel. 'Can't you just imagine Molly being cared for at Cloudhill and going off to the village school each morning? Perhaps Mrs Frost could train her to become a parlour maid, or she might be given work with Mrs Dobson in the kitchen and even learn to cook if she showed some aptitude.'

Nigel agreed. 'Any girl with a good reference from Cloudhill would have no difficulty finding employment in any great house.'

Victoria chewed her bottom lip. 'But even if Mrs Pettigrew said that she was willing to take Molly back to England with her in a fortnight, I can hardly pack the poor girl up and send her over there without first writing to Martin and Emily and asking if they'd be prepared to find a place her at Cloudhill. Even if they said yes, it would take — oh, I don't know how long to hear back from them.'

'Then why not send Martin a cable?'

'Is that possible?'

'Of course. There's not a corner of the Empire that can't be reached by undersea cable these days. We could telegraph your message to Bombay and it would be relayed from there to England. It's possible for an answer to arrive back here within a week.'

Actually, it took five days to receive Martin's reply. 'Happy to oblige. Send arrival details.'

When Victoria and Kitty put the proposal

to Mrs Pettigrew she was less than enthusiastic, but her attitude softened and she almost smiled when Victoria proposed a purse of £50 to cover Molly's travel expenses. 'I think that this should cover any out-of-pocket charges that you might meet along the way, Mrs Pettigrew.'

'I won't pretend that I'm delighted to take on the responsibility of delivering Molly safely to your relatives in England, Mrs Latham, so please tell her that she must do everything I say. And remind her that I will tolerate no bad manners.'

Once the arrangements for Molly had been settled, Nigel presented them to the regimental chaplain. 'Yes, the child has recovered her health — and my cousin in Somerset has offered to provide a place for her in his household. He'll see that she's given training in some useful area.'

The chaplain shook Nigel's hand warmly. 'Thank you, m'dear chap! You've taken a great weight from my shoulders. And I only hope that your cousin in Somerset has a strong constitution!'

Even though Victoria went to great pains to explain these plans in a positive light, Molly, who had grown up in a tumbledown house behind the barracks, was overwhelmed by the size of the changes that were about to come into her life.

'The first thing, Molly, is to learn good manners and always remember to use them. We'll start right now.'

Molly seemed eager to follow Victoria's demonstrations on how a twelve-year-old girl should behave in adult company, how to handle her knives and forks at the table, how to chew her food quietly, how to keep her hands and face clean at all times.

'You see, Molly, learning good manners is really like learning the rules of a game, or finding the answer to a secret code that everyone else knows. Once you know the rules and always follow them, the walls that keep people apart begin to disappear. Mrs Frost and Mrs Dobson at Cloudhill will teach you all kinds of useful things and help you grow up into a capable young lady.'

Molly's anxiety eventually started to disappear when Kitty arrived at the house with six dresses — all donated by families whose own daughters had outgrown them.

With her tawny hair washed and brushed and tied back with ribbon, Molly tried on each one, and gazed in disbelief at the reflection she saw in Victoria's looking glass. 'You mean I can keep every one? Oooh!'

Nigel permitted her to dine with them several times before she left for England.

'You're a bright girl, Molly m'dear, and a credit to your mother and father,' he said, and slipped a gold sovereign into her hand as she was saying farewell to them all.

'Remember to always eat slowly with your mouth closed, blow your nose quietly, don't forget to say 'please' and 'thank you' — and you'll do very well, m'dear.'

9

Nigel Pelham was beaming with pride as he entered the new ballroom at the clubhouse with Mrs Kitty Cameron on one arm and Mrs Victoria Latham on the other. They were almost the last to arrive because when Nigel and Victoria had called to collect Kitty from her cousin's house, one of her blue satin dancing shoes couldn't be found.

The whole place was in turmoil, and it wasn't until Nigel had taken the boys aside for a few minutes that the shoe revealed itself.

'Oh, Nigel, doesn't the room look absolutely splendid with all the flags and greenery and flowers,' Kitty said, giving his arm a squeeze as they entered. 'I don't mind if you dance once or twice with Victoria, but you simply must claim me for all the others.'

He smiled at her adoringly. He'd never been a dancer, but he had every confidence that his dearest Kitty would tonight teach him the steps of each dance, just as surely as she was teaching him the steps of lovemaking. For the first time in all his forty-six years, Nigel Pelham was feeling like a young man.

Colonel and Mrs Moncrief received the trio of latecomers and had just introduced them to the great General Gordon Wyndham who was standing with them, when the Resident's party entered the building to officially open the ball.

Sir Ian and Lady Phillips acknowledged acquaintances to the left and right as they passed along the line, and their youthful daughter, Lucy, bubbled with excitement as she entered on the arm of her escort for the evening, Captain Wyndham.

'Lackey!' Victoria heard a deep voice mutter, and looked up to see the general beside her, scowling at his son.

This was the first time she'd seen Captain Wyndham wearing his uniform, and here in his red jacket with heavy gold braid and a row of decorations on his chest, she thought he looked very distinguished. She watched his glance sweep along the line of guests until he caught sight of her standing there. A flash of recognition lit his eyes and he looked away instantly.

'Ah, good evening, Andrew,' the general said loudly as his son and youthful partner were about to pass. Without warning, he grasped Victoria's arm and pulled her forward a step, blocking the couple's way. 'Mrs Latham, I'm sure you know Miss Lucy

Phillips, but have you met my son, Captain Wyndham?'

Whatever reason lay behind the general's sudden move, Victoria had a sense of being clutched like a trophy in the man's fist.

'Good evening, Lucy,' she said, then turned her eyes to the captain and shook her head. 'No, we've not been introduced, have we, Captain Wyndham?' With a calm smile, she held out her hand. 'How do you do?'

'Delighted, Mrs Latham.' His expression remained tight, but instinct told her that he would ask her to dance before the night was through. She hoped he would.

The orchestra, seated on the stage, had been brought up from Lahore for this gala occasion, and the ball was opened by the Resident and the colonel's lady completing a circle of the dance floor, to the applause of the guests. They were then joined by Colonel Moncrief waltzing sedately with Lady Phillips. The applause continued, and all the time Victoria could feel the uncomfortable presence of General Wyndham so close behind her that she could hear his breathing becoming heavier.

Then, to her mortification, he whipped a hand around her waist and, without a word, swept her out onto the dance floor to join the two official couples. She stiffened with embarrassment at being dragged into the opening ceremony. It was an arrogant intrusion, but the general held her close against him, flaunting his strength and crushing her gown. Resentment flushed her cheeks and she found herself disliking him even more when she looked up and caught his triumphant expression. Self-important, swaggering, rude, overbearing —

Andrew was perfectly aware that his father's crass behaviour towards Mrs Latham was a display put on exclusively for his son's benefit. *Watch me, lackey, while I demonstrate how a man can always get exactly what he wants if he steps straight in and takes it.*

When all the other couples were invited onto the floor, the general still refused to slacken his tight grip around Victoria's waist. Over his shoulder, she could glimpse Captain Wyndham waltzing with little Lucy Phillips and, when the music stopped, she remained tight-lipped as the general escorted her to a chair. She sat down and turned her head away with no intention of thanking him for the dance.

From his position with the Resident's party, Andrew observed her from across the room. So, now he knew that her name was *Mrs Latham*. Time and again each day since the accident, he'd thought about the capable young woman who'd come to his aid when Annabelle was hurt and the horse was injured.

He cringed inwardly each time the memory of that dreadful afternoon came back to haunt him. Asking this unknown young lady to put the mare out of her misery had been outrageous. He should, at least, have expressed his gratitude to her right there and then, instead of simply walking away as he had done.

Since then, he'd kept his ears open for any faint whisper of gossip buzzing around the cantonment regarding a British captain with a child — and a horse so badly hurt that she had to be put down. But, clearly, he need have felt no concern about Mrs Latham's discretion.

The mare's injury was easy to explain in the regiment. 'I was riding too hard and she broke a leg when she fell. There was nothing for it but a quick bullet.' The grey gelding he'd bought next day wasn't a patch on the mare, but it was the best he could afford.

Andrew continued to stand where he was, watching the elegant Mrs Latham across the ballroom floor as she danced with one gentleman after another. There was something about her that was most appealing — the lively beauty in her face, the ready smile, her smooth high forehead. Not to mention the quick thinking she'd exhibited in front of his father when they'd come face to face this evening. *No, we've not been introduced.* A clever answer.

He signalled across the ballroom floor to a shy young officer to come and dance with Lucy, while he moved towards Mrs Latham as soon as she returned to her chair and thanked her partner.

'May I have the honour of the next?'

She stood quickly, smiling. 'Thank you, Captain. Yes.'

He was a full head taller than she and, for a man whom the gossips had said rarely danced, Andrew Wyndham held her confidently and moved lightly around the floor.

'The little girl?' she whispered. 'I hope she has recovered?'

'Completely, thank God.'

'And your shoulder?'

Her query seemed to surprise him. 'Better, thank you.' He bent his head closer. 'I'm afraid the whole incident was entirely my own fault, and I don't know how I can ever apologize sufficiently for behaving as I did that day. Asking you to — well, asking you to do what had to be done was reprehensible. I'm profoundly sorry that you were thrown into the situation, though, I must say, that your aid was my salvation.'

'It was an accident, Captain, and it was sheer good fortune that I happened to be there at that moment. I simply did what needed to be done — though I still don't know *how* I was able to do it — but we won't mention it again.' She looked up directly into his eyes and smiled.

'Just let me repeat, Mrs Latham, that drawing you into my predicament was an unforgivable imposition and I remain deeply in your debt.'

She raised a brow at him, and a sparkle lit her eyes. 'Actually, Captain, if you would care to repay that debt, I'll tell you exactly how you can do it. Er — look, they're serving punch on the veranda, so perhaps we might go out there and have a glass while we speak?'

They left the dance floor and she waited by the veranda rail while he fetched the punch. He squared his shoulders and looked down at her, frowning. 'Now, ma'am, please go ahead and ask of me what you will. Anything at all.'

'Please don't look so anxious, sir. I simply want to request your help in buying a toy elephant for my little nephews in England.'

'Elephant?'

There was a little mischief in her chuckle. 'Yes, I was in the market one day and I happened to be passing a woodcarver when

189

I saw you buying a most beautiful elephant with a trunk that waved. After you'd left the shop, I went in and tried to tell the man that I'd like him to make one just like it for me. But he seemed to have no idea what I was talking about, so now I'd be most grateful if you would write a note in the local language for me to take to him: *This lady wishes to buy an elephant*. Or something like that? Seven little words in Urdu would repay any outstanding debt between us, I assure you.'

His stern face softened, then broke into a wide, white smile. 'Ah! But nothing in India is ever as simple as you've suggested, Mrs Latham. The only solution is for us to visit the woodcarver together and talk to him about the matter. Say, tomorrow afternoon at three? May I call for you so we can ride down together?'

'Thank you, but I don't ride. I walk.' The music had stopped and she saw her next partner coming from the ballroom to claim her.

'Walk? Then I'll walk with you.' He spoke with some urgency.

'Actually, I think it best if we just happen to meet at the woodcarver's workshop at three. You know how tongues here are likely to wag if we're seen on the road together.'

Victoria arrived at the shop early but the captain, wearing his uniform, was already talking with the craftsman while a boy stood outside holding the reins of the grey horse.

'Good afternoon, ma'am.' He turned to greet her and the corners of his eyes crinkled when he smiled. 'Allow me to present Thakur, the finest toymaker in Kashmir.'

She acknowledged the little old man who was watching her shyly.

'Thakur has been telling me that he remembers you well, and he certainly did understand what you were asking on the day you came in here. However, he wasn't able to explain to you that he couldn't produce a copy of the elephant you saw because it had been made specially for me and, as a matter of honour, he'd vowed never to produce another.' He spread his hands apologetically. 'It wasn't my request, I assure you, and I know that's not the way English craftsmen do business. But this isn't England, is it?'

'No, it's certainly not!' There was laughter in her voice and she inclined her head towards the toymaker. 'Captain, please tell Thakur that I apologize for my impatience last time I was here.'

Andrew spoke a few words and the

toymaker gave a solemn bow in her direction. 'Anyhow, Mrs Latham, I've already given him permission to make another elephant like it for you, along with a howdah and, as it's for your nephews, why not ask him to make a couple of little princes to sit on the elephant's back? But now you'll have to decide how you'd like your elephant to be decorated.'

She pulled off her hat and sat beside him on a bench while the woodcarver produced a box of parchments and explained — with Andrew translating — the significance of the intricate swirling, colourful pattern illustrated on each sheet.

'As you see, Mrs Latham, every great occasion has its traditional design for the elephants taking part in it. Weddings, funerals, coronations, festivals, holy days.'

'Oh, how can I possibly choose? They're all so wonderful. Look at this one — and this!'

'Annabelle's toy is decorated for the wedding of a princess.' There was a hint of pride in his tone. 'Why not give your nephews something that's used only by very great maharajas at festival time?' He showed her a design with intricate swirls of red and gold, blue, green and white. 'You won't see anything more impressive than that!'

'Yes, it's certainly magnificent, but will it be ready by the end of the month? I'm leaving here after my cousin's wedding.'

'Thakur won't disappoint you, I can promise.'

'Splendid. Now, how do I say 'thank you' in Urdu?' She held out her hand to the craftsman.

'It's *shukria*.'

She said it, and the man smiled as their hands touched.

'Well, at last I've learned one word of the local language,' she said lightly as they left the shop and the boy holding the horse moved towards them. 'Thank you very much for your help, Captain. *Shukria*, as we say in Kashmir.' They shared a smile. 'See, I'm learning! But I mustn't delay you any longer this afternoon.'

'You're not walking back to the cantonment now? Is there something else here that you'd like to see?'

'Yes, actually. I want to see anything and everything — I enjoy watching people going about their business.' She shrugged. 'I still have so few impressions of the real Kashmir to take away with me.'

'Then, with your permission, Mrs Latham, I'd be delighted to stroll with you.' He told the boy holding his grey horse to lead it back to the Residency stables while he and Victoria set off through the twisting lanes with their odours of apple blossom, donkey dung, enticing spices and smells from the tanning vats.

Andrew surprised himself with this singular readiness to postpone his duty this afternoon and escort the delightful Mrs Latham through the streets of Srinagar.

Anyhow, it would be of no great consequence if the Resident was kept waiting for an hour or two to receive his report on the wily old maharaja's latest move in the diplomatic cat and mouse game he regularly played during his weekly audience with the British Military Attaché.

His Highness delighted in dropping very unsubtle hints that he might be about to break the treaty he'd signed with the British and switch his loyalty to the Russians who'd always been eager to win a foothold in India. All through today's audience, the maharaja had flaunted a new gift from the tsar — a heavy gold ring emblazoned with the Russian eagle.

'By the way, Captain' — Mrs Latham's voice cut across his thoughts — 'I've had no opportunity before this to mention an encounter that I had not long ago with your daughter and a most elegant lady at the Shalimar Gardens when I went there on the pretext of painting.'

'Aha! So you were the nice lady who wasn't cross with Annabelle when she ran into you? She's told me about you.'

'I've mentioned the incident to nobody, I assure you.'

'Thank you.' They shared a smile. 'As you must have guessed, it's not known here that I have a daughter, or that the Begum Raziid Khan is caring for her at the moment — summers on the houseboat, winters on her estate near Amritsar.' He paused for a moment. 'The begum was extremely kind to me when I was a boy and when Annabelle arrived in my life, she was the only one I could turn to for help.'

Victoria was intrigued, but ingrained tact prevented her from asking any of the myriad questions flying around in her mind. There was much more to this tall, dark man than he seemed willing to reveal.

'And, by the way,' he added with a knowing grin, 'the begum is on very good terms with the old maharaja up there on the hill, and it was she who persuaded him to have the Shalimar Gardens put back into order. She's finding it increasingly difficult to keep a growing child confined to the deck of a houseboat.'

Victoria chuckled. 'I can well imagine — ' Before she could say more, they came to a display of shawls hanging outside a cave-like shop. She halted and, in an instant, the sharp-eyed merchant appeared in his doorway, draping more shawls over his arms.

'Oh, they're beautiful.' She fingered the ones held out to her. 'How fine they are. Actually, I'd love to buy a couple of these for my sisters. Captain, would you be kind enough to come in and show me the way business is done in this town?'

The merchant's sons rushed to bring chairs for them while the shelves were emptied and, one by one, every shawl was unfolded and displayed. With so many to choose from, the selection was a pleasant, time-consuming exercise and, in the end, she thought that the price negotiated by the captain and the merchant seemed ridiculously low. Five English shillings for two? However, as they walked from the premises with her purchases wrapped in brown paper, all parties were wearing satisfied smiles.

They stopped to watch a goldsmith working at his craft, and then a potter throwing clay on his wheel and forming it into a long-necked urn within a few minutes. A little further along the lane, their way became blocked by a cluster of people around a frail-looking old man in a brown cloak who was seated on a stool with a shallow dish of hot oil standing before him on a brazier. The crowd parted as they approached.

'Well, look at this! Here we have an augury at work.' Andrew raised his eyebrows at her. 'Would you like him to look for omens, or tell you what he can see in your future? He can read them all on the surface of his oil.'

'No, certainly not, thank you. I don't believe in any nonsense of that kind.' She laughed as if it was a joke and was about to turn away when the old man lifted his rheumy gaze. It locked with hers, and suddenly she found herself rooted to the spot while swirling, iridescent patterns on the surface of the hot oil began to move. The man's toothless mouth worked soundlessly, until at last he gave a nod and looked down to study whatever messages he could read in the shifting, changing patterns and colours of the oil. All at once she found herself breathing fast, as if she'd been running.

Andrew stood close beside her and offered his elbow. She slipped her hand into it and stood mesmerized as the soothsayer frowned and muttered, lost in his own mysterious world. When he began to speak, his voice was cracked.

'The black water that stole what you most treasured is now calm.' Andrew translated the old man's words and whispered them into her ear. 'Children are waiting to come into your life, many daughters, and you must not allow yourself to be hindered by doubt or trepidation. Look in the right direction and you will discover your destiny is waiting all around you. Close your eyes and see it with your mind. Search for it in your heart.'

When the old man looked up, the light seemed to leave his eyes and he held out his hand to collect the coins that Andrew offered.

'Oh!' Victoria felt a shiver shoot down her spine and she tightened her grip on Andrew's arm as they walked away. 'Whatever was he talking about? How ridiculous he was. How could he possibly see my destiny in that oil?'

She scoffed, but out of nowhere, an image flew into her mind of the nameless young woman lying dead in an East End tenement. And of Molly Collins, the motherless daughter of a dead trooper. Why should these totally unconnected girls both tumble into her thoughts at that moment?

A few paces around the corner they came to a small teahouse. 'I'm sorry if the old fellow's ramblings have upset you, Mrs Latham. Perhaps a cup of tea will help.' He led her inside to a table.

'No, I'm not perturbed, Captain. Just puzzled.' Deep in thought, she took several sips from the cup brought to her and then looked up at him. 'It's strange, but I think I can understand what was behind that message regarding the *black water being calm now*. My husband died in the East Indies nearly four years ago, and when I first received that news, I was thrown into a raging black ocean of grief. I was drowning in it and for a long time I could barely keep myself afloat. Such a long time.' She bit down on her lower lip.

'It was only when I came up here into the mountains that I was able to face the fact that Peter had gone to his rest and that I was quite alone. And once I could acknowledge that truth, I felt my wild black ocean grow calm.' She tilted her head and smiled softly. 'You see, I can even talk about him now, and that's how it should be, because Peter Latham was a fine man who shouldn't be forgotten.'

As Andrew listened, he longed for the ability that some men possessed to find the sensitive, appropriate words that moments like this required. He wanted to tell her that no man could ever hope for more than to have his wife express these heartfelt sentiments in his memory. But he was too clumsy and ill-practised to attempt to express tender feelings, and could do no more than give a slight nod of understanding. She looked at him with a tentative smile, and he returned it.

'It might seem incredible, Captain, but

when Peter and I first met, we fell in love between one heartbeat and the next. It was extraordinary to feel so sure, so quickly, about something like that.' She stopped abruptly. 'Oh, do you mind me talking to you like this?'

'No, not at all. Please — '

'Well, you see, I went to stay with an elderly aunt in Devon, and she lived near a little shipyard where Peter and his uncle had their vessel under repair . . . '

He rested his elbows on the table and listened to the tale of her meeting with Peter and his uncle, and the adventure of sailing with them on the *Fortitude*.

'Captain Latham married us at sea, but Peter died of a fever over there on the other side of the world, so he never did come back for me.'

He heard the faint tremor in her voice, but she drew in a deep breath to steady it and went on to tell him about Aunt Honoria and her worldly advice. 'She always said the dark moments that come into our lives make the rest of it seem all the more brilliant. And I'm sure she was right.'

He leaned closer. Her voice was musical, and she had a way of subtly colouring her words to reveal shades of feeling. He was captured by her ability to speak openly about her emotions and permit him to look into her heart.

'Peter and I had planned for me to sail with him on his next voyage and, after that, I was going to spend my life at sea. I wanted to learn how to navigate and make myself useful on board.' For a moment she gazed thoughtfully into the distance. 'I've always felt the need to be *useful*, y'know, but it's so difficult for a woman like me to find something worthwhile to fill her life.'

Again, he longed to produce some kind of appropriate response, but the right words evaded him.

She swung her gaze to meet his and frowned. 'Oh, Captain! What did the augury say about children?'

'*Children are waiting. Many daughters.*'

'Many children are waiting for me? How extraordinary. I once worked with the volunteers at a hospital for foundlings — helping to bathe and feed them, or looking after them when they were ill.' She gave a sceptical frown. 'But that's all years ago now. Besides there was rarely a shortage of volunteers, so they can't possibly be waiting for *me* to come back.'

'But perhaps you *will* work there again when you go home to London.'

She shrugged. 'Captain, I'm not sure where

I'll go when I leave Kashmir. I have no home — either in London nor anywhere else. The house I grew up in is now leased to strangers and my parents have gone to live in the South of France.'

'Will you be joining them there?'

'Hah!' She shook her head. 'They've declared me *persona non grata*. They've never forgiven me for eloping with a sailor and creating a scandal that provided all the ammunition needed by Mama's longtime foe to win their endless, point-scoring battle.' She spread her hands in a gesture of helplessness.

'Mama and this lady were bitter rivals in their youth, and the situation between them grew increasingly spiteful as the years passed. They both went out of their way to make sure that their paths crossed at every opportunity, and each time they did, they'd both unsheath their claws and try to draw blood.

'I can't tell you how many times I saw that happening. And it's the main reason why my mother flew into such a rage when she heard that I'd lowered the social standing of the Shelford family by marrying Peter, and therefore providing her enemy with a perfect weapon to deliver the *coup de grâce*.'

For a moment she sat with her own thoughts. 'I grew up believing that, no matter how unforgiving my mother might be, I'd always be able to rely on my father to listen to whatever I needed to talk to him about. I was sure that he'd stand by me. But — no, I think that this was the very first time in my whole life that I'd ever disappointed him, yet he instantly turned his back on me. Literally. I can't tell you how much that still hurts.'

He recognized her genuine distress and felt deeply for her. 'Hard to believe,' he muttered inanely.

'Oh, it's true enough. That's why my parents and I are no longer on the best of terms.'

Tentatively, his hand slid three inches across the table towards hers. Then thinking better of it, he pulled it back and reached for his cup. 'You have my sympathy, Mrs Latham. I'm not on the best of terms with my parents, either, but then, I can't recall a time when we were ever on good terms.'

'Hmm.' She straightened on her chair. 'Yes, I certainly saw no sign of affection between you and the general at the ball last night.'

'It's always been like that. When I was three, my mother found the courage to run away with her lover, and I haven't heard a word from her since. My father packed me off to a well-known 'flogging school' in England at the age of six — one of the places designed to put backbone into miserable little boys and set them on the road to becoming brave

British soldiers. He told me that I'd thank him for it, but I'm still waiting for that day to arrive.'

She passed her cup for more tea. 'It's supposed to be against all the rules of nature, Captain, but I'm afraid that parents do sometimes let their children down badly.' She looked up and gave him a slow, warm smile. 'But I know for certain that, no matter what twists and turns Annabelle's path through life might take, you would never turn away from her. You'd listen and you'd at least *try* to understand. She's a fortunate little girl indeed to have you as her papa.'

'Annabelle is all I have. And I'm all that she has, Mrs Latham.'

'Oh please do call me Victoria. We're friends now, aren't we — Andrew?'

He found it disconcerting to realize how swiftly their conversation had slipped into these sensitive, personal areas. He'd never before spoken of his private life to anyone. In fact, he'd been taught to conceal feelings and to regard emotion as a weakness. Emotion made a man vulnerable. But until now he'd never encountered a woman quite like the one who was sitting on the other side of this table.

'Friends, indeed, Victoria. I thank you.'

'I can't tell you how much I've enjoyed our

time this afternoon.'

He was hit by a strong reluctance to part from her. 'Perhaps I could show you a little more of Kashmir before you leave? Different civilizations have come and gone in this valley for a thousand years and more, and I can take you to visit some splendid sights up in the hills around Srinagar — glorious views, the ruins of an old royal observatory, a Hindu temple. We could a picnic and — '

'Thank you, yes, I'd enjoy that very much, if you're sure you can spare the time. So far, even after being here for weeks, I still understand very little about this country because nothing ever seems to be clear or straightforward.'

He laughed. 'Yes, if you don't view life the way an Indian does it's hard to make sense of the things you see going on around the place. I hope I might be able to throw a little light on a few aspects when we get away from the cantonment. Sorry I can't suggest a day until I've checked my duty list for the next week, but may I send you a message?' He became aware that he was suddenly grinning like a schoolboy.

'My time is my own, Andrew. Any day that's convenient for you will suit me perfectly.'

As dusk had begun to settle over the town by now, there was no question of Victoria walking home unescorted. When they left the teahouse, she slipped her arm through his again and, with her hat swinging by its ribbons in her hand, they strolled back to Nigel's house, still talking and unconcerned about whether or not they might be observed together.

10

Andrew's hopes of finding the time to ride out one day soon with Victoria Latham rapidly faded when he saw the list of duties waiting for him in the next week.

Colonel Moncrief required him to attend a briefing on the intelligence that had just come in concerning a Russian scouting party having been intercepted while they were surveying mountain trails through the Hindu Kush. The rumblings of unrest were growing louder along the North-west Frontier — broken alliances, tribal skirmishes and *jehads* which seemed to have been deliberately ignited by an outside interest: Russia.

Which way would the maharaja jump if the tsar's force reached the borders of Kashmir? Captain Wyndham was instructed to gain this information from His Highness on the hill — by threats, by wheedling, by offering inducements.

And if this wasn't enough to keep Andrew busy, the Resident wanted him to be available to act as an escort for a lady and her daughter who were coming to spend a holiday at the residency.

The ladies were acquaintances of Lady Phillips's sister in London, but if it had been the Queen herself arriving, poor Lady Phillips could not have been in a greater flurry of anxiety about the visit.

'No, not those dishes — I said I wanted to use the Minton service! And please put the new quilts on the beds. Oh, do make haste to change those carpets!'

Andrew groaned when he was given his list of escort duties in the week ahead. Lord, if he didn't soon move out of this job, he really *would* turn into the lackey that his father had accused him of becoming. At least it was a relief to know that the general had gone up to the mountains to hunt bears and leopards, and wouldn't be here to witness the kind of work that his son was being required to perform.

At the conclusion of his official inspection of the regiment, Gordon Wyndham had surprised everyone by going off into the mountains with a hunting party which also included Mr and Mrs Cooke, visitors from Bombay.

There'd been winks and nudges in the officers' mess when the general had announced a change of plans and delayed his return to Delhi after meeting the enticing Beatrice Cooke at dinner one evening. Wyndham was a master of any sport which involved guns or women, but Andrew didn't pause to wonder what success his father might be having in this current game of hunting another man's wife. Even if he captured the lady, it wouldn't last. These affairs of his never did.

Andrew sent a note of apology to Victoria, expressing regrets that his free time this week had been eroded, and hoping that there would be an opportunity for their picnic next week. In quiet moments, he often thought about her. She was quick witted and perceptive; a woman with no artifice, affable without being effusive, a woman with whom a man would find it possible to form a true friendship.

And one night before he dropped off to sleep, he came to the conclusion that her hair wasn't truly brown at all: in the sunlight, it became the colour of newly-sawn mahogany — auburn, chestnut, copper, bronze.

One afternoon, as he rode down at sunset from the fort, following one more long, inconclusive audience with the maharaja, he felt far too weary to spend another evening in the company of Lady Phillips's visitors from London.

Both mother and daughter were painfully self-important and patronizing, and his own meagre supply of social chit-chat had been exhausted during the first fifteen minutes in their company. Sir Ian's new young aide, he decided, would have to perform the expected niceties that night at the dinner table.

So, instead of reining in at the residency compound, Andrew rode on to Nigel Pelham's house. It was over a week since he'd parted ways with Victoria and the impulse to see her again had been growing stronger in him all day. How much time remained before she packed her bags and left Srinagar? After he'd knocked on the door and asked to see Mrs Latham, he stood slapping his riding crop impatiently against his riding boot. Once she was on her way back to England, their paths were unlikely to ever cross again.

'Andrew!' The taffeta skirt of her cream dinner gown rustled as she hurried down the stairs, smiling. 'How good it is of you to call. Do come into the drawing room; we actually have some chairs ready to use again.'

He caught a pleasant scent about her like fruit and flowers. 'Thank you, but no, I can't stay. Sorry. I just wanted to give you my apologies for having failed to honour my promise to — '

'I won't hear another word,' she scolded gently. 'I know you have a busy schedule, and *you* know that I'll be glad to see you at any time.'

The warmth in her voice made his weariness fade, and he was hit by an uncharacteristic and utterly irresistible impulse. 'Victoria, I know it's short notice, but I'd like to take you for that picnic in the hills tomorrow, if you have no other engagement. There's a lot to see up there, interesting places to visit.'

She gave a laugh of surprise. 'Oh, yes, but you do remember, don't you, that I've never ridden a horse? We'll have to go very slowly. Shall I come down to the stables? What time would you like me there?'

He felt like a schoolboy thumbing his nose at the detention given by a bad-tempered headmaster. Young Wyndham was going to climb from the schoolroom window tomorrow morning and escape for the day. Damn the old maharaja playing spiteful games in his hill-top fort, damn the Russians marching towards the border, and damn Lady Phillips's painful visitors! Let them all stew for a day, he thought wildly. Sir Ian's poor young aide could have the wretched duty of escorting the London ladies to a regimental band concert tomorrow afternoon because Captain Wyndham would be in the mountains, enjoying the company of the delightful Victoria Latham.

'Is nine o'clock too early for you to be at the stables?'

'Not at all! And thank you again, Andrew. I look forward to it.'

★ ★ ★

Andrew grinned to himself as he rode back to his house in the Residency compound. He claimed pressure of work when he sent his apologies to Lady Phillips and called for dinner to be brought to his study.

Ah, yes, tomorrow. He was about to share a whole day with a woman who was like no other he'd ever known. In the short time he'd spent in her company, he'd found her to be warm and open, with no whiff of coquetry in her manner. It was ridiculous to be feeling like a schoolboy at his age, yet each time she came into his mind, she roused a dangerous longing within him — and one that was not *entirely* carnal.

He drew in a deep breath and steadied his breathing. Then, with his shirt sleeves rolled up, he rallied his concentration and settled down at the desk to write the day's reports and open his correspondence. Most of what lay before him were routine matters, and he found his mind drifting back to Victoria. There was a well-behaved black horse in the stables which would suit her perfectly — tall, but with easy gait, mouth as soft as butter and —

He opened the next envelope. It was from the Intelligence Office in Simla and contained the annual report on the political and military activity in various independent states throughout the country. As these provinces were beyond the reach of British law, the princely states frequently became involved in tangled dynastic power struggles, complicated by long-running, bloody wars with their neighbours.

Inevitably, all this confusion made it a fiendishly difficult task for the officers who were assigned to collate the information, and their reports were usually well out of date by the time they were distributed.

Andrew turned the pages quickly. His interest lay in one state only — the little kingdom of Gwalinpore far away on the edge of the Rajasthan desert. He skimmed the page for any mention of —

His heart lurched. That name. It couldn't be — yet, there it was! He sat staring at the blunt words disbelievingly and read the report again. The breath left his lungs and, for a split second, the pain of the news was like a red-hot steel whip slashing across his soul. He closed his eyes and tried to picture the scene in his mind. Dear God! It hurt almost more than he could bear. No, no, no!

He swept the papers from his desk, folded his arms on it, and gave way to emotion.

★ ★ ★

The other occupants of the residency were still at breakfast when Victoria arrived at the

213

stables next morning. Andrew's greeting was a little distant, she thought, and he looked as though he'd had very little sleep.

A *syce* led two saddled horses from their stalls and, without another word, Andrew cupped his hands to boost her onto a tall black mount. His expression softened when he saw her look of alarm.

'It's all right, Victoria. I know he's big, but Rex is a perfect gentleman who'll give you no trouble, I promise.'

She took a deep, nervous breath as he swung her up onto the lady's saddle. She settled her leg over the knee rest and arranged her skirt while he adjusted the length of the stirrup, then handed her the reins. She wriggled to test her balance on the high seat. 'Will you stay close and tell me what I should do?'

'Of course.' He sprang onto his grey. 'Now, just loosen your reins and nudge your heel gently into his flank. He'll understand.'

Her heart thumped wildly, but Andrew was right. The tall, well-mannered animal responded to her signals and they moved off at a fast walk along the road that wound its way out of the city.

'That's it. Keep your back straight, elbows in and your hands low. Excellent.'

She concentrated fiercely until she grew

familiar with the horse's gait. Only then did she allow herself to relax a little and look around at the scattered farms they passed, the fields of flowering saffron and mustard, the orchards of quince and almond trees.

Andrew was not an easy man to read, and today he seemed to be lost in his own deep thoughts. For some time neither spoke. 'I'm sorry to be so dull this morning,' he said suddenly, turning to look at her, 'but I had — ' He frowned and broke off.

'You don't have to keep me *entertained*, Andrew. I'm enjoying this tremendously — and what a splendid view of everything you get from up here on the back of a horse. I should have taken up riding years ago. And look what's coming down the road towards us now! How wonderful — a family setting off for somewhere on their elephant. What a sight to write about in my next letter to Emily and Martin.'

He gave a murmur of agreement, and they rode on in silence again for some time. His dark mood puzzled her, but it was easy to ignore that when all her concentration was needed on this new experience of horse riding. She tried to relax further and leaned forward to pat the horse's neck.

'Are you all right?' he asked suddenly, and she nodded. 'Then let's pick up the pace a little now and try a slow canter along this stretch. Just keep the ball of your foot in the stirrup.'

Her heartbeat rose as Rex surged forward at the touch of her heel and the road seemed to fly beneath his hoofs. But within minutes she had settled herself to the steady rhythm of his stride and gradually began to enjoy the excitement.

The long road wound its way upwards, until at last the deserted stone buildings of the Pari Mahal, the old royal observatory, came into view, standing out high on a distant spur. It took them another hour's riding to reach it and, when they did, Andrew dismounted and stood beside her while she eased her leg over the knee rest and slipped her foot from the stirrup.

'Slide down now.' He raised his arms to help her to the ground, and continued to hold her by the waist until she'd regained her balance. 'You've done very well this morning,' he said, as she gave a groan and stretched to ease her muscles. 'We've a lot more to see this afternoon, so I hope I haven't tired you too much.'

'Thanks, I'm perfectly fine. At least I think I am — but I'm sure to feel even better after I've rested a little.'

He tethered the horses and took a canvas

square from his saddle-bag to spread on the edge of the spur at a point from where Victoria had a vista of mountains, trees and sky that seemed to stretch to the end of the world.

'How wonderful!' she sighed, settling herself on the ground. 'Thank you, Andrew, it's absolutely perfect.'

There was no wind to stir the trees, no sound to be heard from the waterfall and the racing torrent in the gorge far below. Nothing moved. It was as if the whole world was standing still and holding its breath.

She glanced across at Andrew. He'd taken off his jacket and rolled up his shirt sleeves, revealing brown arms knotted with lean muscle. She was momentarily discomposed by an impulse to run her hand up his forearm as she would have touched some piece of bronze sculpture, just for the pleasure of feeling its shape.

She looked away quickly, drew up her knees and wrapped her arms around them.

Andrew was stretched out on the grass a few yards away, propped on one elbow, and gazing out into the distance with his mind clearly miles away. His mouth was tightly set and there were dark hollows of weariness under his eyes.

She shifted position and let her own thoughts drift to the fast-approaching end of

217

her holiday. How much more she'd now have to tell Martin and Emily about her time in Srinagar. What would she say about the enigmatic Captain Andrew Wyndham? Who was the real man living behind that wall of reserve? The devoted father of Annabelle? The bitter son of a British general? Certainly a man she would like to have known better, if time had allowed it.

She threw another glance at him. He was still leaning on his elbow, but now he was watching her. For a long moment their glances held before he ran his tongue over his lower lip.

'Victoria, I'm sorry to be such a deadly bore today, but — you see, I discovered only last night that Annabelle's mother had died.' His jaw tightened. 'Actually, it happened almost two years ago, but I had no idea until I read about it in an official report.' He sat up quickly.

She sucked in a sharp breath. 'Oh, Andrew, I'm so terribly sorry. Of course, I know how you must be feeling, and — '

'No, you don't know, Victoria! You can't possibly know!' His harsh tone jolted her; a little nerve began to pull at one corner of his mouth. 'I'm sorry — but she didn't just *die* — Ishana committed *suttee* on her husband's funeral pyre.'

For a few moments Victoria could only stare at him and shake her head. 'But I — I thought that kind of thing didn't happen any longer.'

'Yes? Well, the British have tried to ban it in areas that are under our control, but very few of the old ways have changed in the princely states — like Gwalinpore.' He clenched his jaw and turned his head.

She sat motionless. Her heart ached for him and, when he turned back to her, she saw the misery in his eyes.

'They say, of course, that the act of committing *suttee* brings great honour to a woman — to her memory. Of course, they claim that no coercion is used on the lady, that she is given no drug, that she feels nothing but elation when she — But how could they — ?'

He bowed his head and held it between his hands. 'Victoria, what in God's name will I tell my daughter when she's old enough to ask about her mother? How can I ever explain that the beautiful lady who created her, the woman I adored, was Ishana — the raja's favourite wife — and that she had thrown herself on to his funeral pyre to die in the flames? How can I tell her?'

Victoria felt her head spin. She stared at him wordlessly while her imagination tried to picture that scene of unspeakable horror; it forced her to take a number of deep breaths.

'Let me ask *you* a question, Andrew,' she said at last, quietly. 'Why should Annabelle ever need to know the truth about the way her mother died?'

He swung to her sharply. 'Because she's going to ask me about her mother one day, so what must I do? Lie?'

'Well, please look at it this way for a moment. You've taken your daughter away from her mother's world where you say that such an unthinkable act is viewed with honour. Now Annabelle is growing up to look at the world through the eyes of a little English girl — a girl with a father who loves her dearly, a father who's prepared to protect her by slaying every dragon that might come wandering across her path through life.'

'Of course.'

'In this instance, though, I think that knowing the truth about her mother's death is likely to become a dragon of such monstrous proportions that not even the strongest and most loving father would be able to kill it. That monster could stalk a little English girl for the rest of her life. And perhaps devour her one day.'

His forehead creased and he scrubbed a hand across his chin. 'So?'

'So, perhaps, when she asks about her mother, you need to tell Annabelle only a few simple facts — construct a fairy-tale about how you and Ishana met and fell in love. Let your daughter know how dearly her mother treasured her beautiful baby, and how sad you were when Ishana became ill and died. That's all Annabelle needs to know, Andrew. Just simplify the truth.'

He dropped back on to his elbow and broke off a long stalk of grass to twirl in his fingers before he looked up at her and shook his head slowly. 'The truth, Victoria? Where do I begin? I don't know how the truth could ever be simplified because this is a tale of India, remember?'

'Very well. Tell me, and I'll put aside my English ears.'

He gave her a half-smile. 'In the first place, what was I doing in Gwalinpore? Well, our government might consider that princely state to be an unimportant, insignificant place, but it's vital for us to keep on good terms with whoever is ruling there because it sits directly on the army's swiftest route into Afghanistan.

'There was another dynastic upheaval in Gwalinpore four years ago, and a lot of blood was spilt before a new raja — just a boy — was chosen to sit on the throne. I was given the wretched duty of transporting the

British Government's gift to the new Highness — a hideously ornate black marble clock decorated with gilded cherubs and draped in the Union Jack. It was to have been presented during the coronation ceremony.

'Well, the palace officials were most impressed when they saw me arrive with it. They assumed that I must be the personal emissary of Queen Victoria and that she, herself, had placed the royal clock in my hands. That fable seemed to add a little more significance to my presence in the palace, so I didn't disabuse them.' He turned his gaze to the tips of his riding boots.

'There was a huge crowd gathered in the great durbah hall for the coronation ceremony, but halfway through, an assassin threw a bomb. It killed the little raja, along with a lot of others, demolished Queen Victoria's marble clock, and left me, her emissary, with wounds that took months to heal.'

'Oh, Andrew! What about Ishana? Was she hurt?'

He looked at her in surprise. 'Good lord, Victoria, she wasn't there. The ladies of the palace never show themselves in public. They live totally secluded lives in the *zenana* — the women's quarters — though there are passageways built in the walls for them to move about in certain areas and watch what's going on from behind marble screens.' His expression softened. 'And sometimes there are doors concealed in the walls. That's the way that Ishana came to my chamber to offer me comfort when I was hurt. And, dear God, how I needed it.'

Questions flew around in Victoria's mind like bats in a cage, but she kept her lips tightly closed and continued to listen.

'My legs were burned and useless, I'd lost my sight. Never in my life have I so longed for a quick death to release me from the pain, not to mention the fear that I'd be crippled and blind for life. Every day the healer came to my bed to treat my burns with his potions, and to pour his oil into my eyes.

'And each morning he brought a fresh apology from the new raja, who happened to be an uncle of the dead boy, and was probably the one who'd orchestrated the assassination. It seemed, however, that the man who'd been given the job of throwing the bomb had mistimed it badly and, therefore, had brought great dishonour to their princely house by insulting Her Britannic Majesty. Not only had Gwalinpore destroyed Queen Victoria's royal gift, but it had also nearly killed her personal emissary.

'The new raja asked his auguries and

soothsayers what offering could be made to restore the honour of Gwalinpore. And can you guess what the answer was?' He flung the question at her as a challenge.

Her eyes looked straight into his. 'Yes. I think he offered you the services of Ishana.'

Her frank answer surprised him. His tone changed. 'She came to my room each day and provided me with the kind of comfort that makes a man want to live. I fell in love with her — desperately, and I knew that she truly loved me in return. What my arrogant English manhood couldn't comprehend was that Ishana, the favourite wife of the new raja, wasn't required to stop loving her husband in order to give me her love as passionately as she did.

'It was a long time before my sight returned and I could walk unaided. By then I was utterly, madly in love with Ishana and I even dreamed of finding some miracle that would keep us together. Could she escape from the *zenana*? Would she ever be accepted into my English world?' He looked at Victoria and slowly shook his head.

'What I'm about to tell you, remember, could happen only in India: When Ishana informed her husband that she was carrying my child, he consulted his auguries, and their readings gave him the news that he most wanted to hear. The birth of this baby, they promised, would provide the means to remove the veil of dishonour from the face of Gwalinpore.'

Victoria frowned. 'I think I'm becoming a little lost.'

'Ishana's husband came to me and confirmed that the baby was undoubtedly mine as he had not lain with her since he'd sent her to comfort me after I'd been wounded. An unusual situation, yes?'

'Indeed!'

'Now he hoped that I would accept Ishana's child as a gift, and that this offering would serve to expunge the great dishonour earned by Gwalinpore when Her Britannic Majesty's magnificent clock was destroyed. And her emissary almost killed. The baby was due to be born in five months' time. Where did I wish it to be sent — along with its wet nurse and servants?'

Victoria's jaw sagged. 'The begum?'

He blew a long breath between his lips. 'I'd had no contact with that lady for fifteen years — ever since my father's affair with her had ended. But, amazingly, she remembered me, and I think she's taken some pleasure in helping me keep my secret from him during the last three years. The initial arrangement we made was for her to take care of Annabelle for twelve months, or until I'd left the army and found a situation where I could raise a child. And here I am three years later, still floundering.' He picked up a pebble and threw it into the gorge below.

'I can't impose on the begum for much longer, so perhaps I should present Annabelle to the ladies of the cantonment as a stray child that I found along the way — '

'Hah!' She could tell that he wasn't being serious. 'No, Andrew, nobody seeing you two together could doubt that Annabelle is yours. She definitely has your eyes.' She raised one brow a fraction. 'But how fortunate for her that she hasn't inherited your nose.'

He gave a guffaw and rolled onto his back while the horses dozed and their riders gave no further thought to visiting any further sights this day. They stayed where they were on the edge of the ravine, growing increasingly easy in each other's company, allowing their conversation to drift from one topic to another.

'Time to eat?' he asked at last and went to his saddle-bag for the egg sandwiches, the apricots and nuts, and flasks of lime juice that had been packed by the kitchen staff.

'Here, you must be hungry,' he said and settled beside her again.

She nodded and neither spoke while they

ate. After she'd brushed the crumbs from her skirt, she gave a little sigh and stretched full length on the grass with her hands locked behind her head and her eyes closed. 'Thank you, Andrew, that was perfect.'

He watched her and, with each passing moment, he could feel his emotional barricades crumbling. As a man who'd always lived much within himself, he couldn't put a name to the sensation, but he knew that it was to do with her closeness. Again, it wasn't purely the physical closeness.

'Tell me about yourself, Andrew,' she said, without moving or opening her eyes. 'Tell me about India.'

With no particular starting point, he began to talk about the places he'd been stationed, some of the actions he'd taken part in, a few ironic incidents that made her chuckle, as well as his forlorn hope of transferring to the Guides. He spoke of friendships that had been forged amidst warm blood and cold steel, as well as the times of monumental boredom when friction between men was quick to erupt.

'Tell me about the scar on your cheek. How did you get it?'

'Can't you guess?'

'I think — ' She sat up and looked at him narrowly, making a play of puzzling over the answer. 'Yes, either you were grazed by an enemy bullet during some heroic campaign up in the hills, or perhaps that wound was inflicted by the point of a duelling sword. Did a jealous husband catch you dallying with his wife and call you out?'

He gave a hoot of laughter. 'Well, let there be no secrets between us, ma'am. There's nothing heroic or noble about it, I can assure you. I got the scar brawling in a native bazaar when I was more than a little drunk and a pickpocket tried to make off with my money. I caught up with him and, while we were scuffling in the dust, he pulled a knife. But I got my purse back and probably left him with a few broken ribs. So what do you think of that?'

Her hazel-green eyes looked straight into his. 'I think you're a man who protects what is his, and in this instance you acted with appropriate boldness and determination. I'm sure the end justified the means. Isn't that what your friends in the regiment would have said at the time?'

He felt physically winded by the feelings she was stirring in him. 'Ah, yes, the regiment. It's certainly a family that takes care of its own — at least it looks after its men. Wives are another matter, of course, and there are many ladies who can't survive the constant loneliness of living on the periphery of the regiment.' For a few moments he lapsed into a thoughtful silence.

'That makes it easier to understand why the ladies out here have to keep themselves busy by arranging their tea parties and card parties — and occasionally having affairs with other men to put a little spice into life. After all, they have servants to do all the work, they've sent their children back to be educated in England, so, of course, they need their social activities to fill in the days until a husband's home leave comes around every five years. Then they can escape from India for a few months — though some marriages can't survive that long.

'My own mother had enough after four years out here, and I can still remember watching her walking — no, *running* away from the house and driving off with some man. My father gave me a sound whipping when he found me crying for her to come back, so, as early as he could, he sent me off to a school that had a name for putting backbone into soft little boys. I think that the masters there did a first-rate job because I came back to India as a young man with lots of backbone and very little else inside him.'

She rolled onto her side and lifted herself onto her elbow. 'You're utterly wrong,

Andrew. I've known you only a short time, but I can see so much to admire in your character. I know you to be a strong and honest man with a tender side that you try very hard not to reveal. Actually, I feel quite envious towards Annabelle for having a father like you. Did you never wish to marry some nice lady and — '

'Marry? Frankly, no, Victoria.' He grinned. 'Perhaps that was due to the fact that, in the course of my life, I've known so very few *nice* ladies.'

She laughed aloud. 'It's not too late for you to change your ways, Captain. I'm sure that if Maud Pelham had still been alive, she'd have found a suitable marriage partner for you by this time.'

He pulled a long face and shook his head. 'I must remember to send a prayer of thanks to whichever saint up there saved me from such a fate.'

She laughed again, then sat up and reached for her flask of juice. It was empty. 'Oh, do you have any left, Andrew?'

'Yes. Here, let me pour it into yours.'

'It's all right, I'll just have a sip from that one.'

He unscrewed the top and passed his flask to her, then watched as she placed her lips where his had touched, then threw back her head and drained the last drops. His eyes followed the graceful line of her neck and the way she ran her tongue over her bottom lip as she replaced the cap. 'Ah! How good that was.'

He felt his blood pumping faster, stirred by the playful intimacy that had grown between them during their time together today. Never before had he found someone like this to confide in. Someone he could permit to come close enough to see the void that was there behind the façade he displayed to the world.

She smiled at him, a smile warm with uncomplicated affection. His eyes drank her in. His throat tightened and he realized that this moment would be caught in time like a fly in amber, to stay with him forever.

Somehow, the day that had started off so miserably with the news of Ishana's death had lost the edge of its savage pain. Today he had discovered someone who could provide him with a fixed point of emotional safety.

Being with Victoria Latham was like finding a lifeline.

11

Andrew was increasingly irritated by the constant tardiness of Lady Phillips's guests.

Lady Marchant and Miss Eloise Marchant were running late again this evening. It hadn't taken him long to realize that they did this deliberately in order to make an *entrance* at every gathering, though why the ill-favoured pair would wish to draw attention to themselves remained a puzzle to him.

Lady Marchant's long bones were bereft of flesh, though she seemed to be endowed with more teeth than her tight mouth could accommodate. In view of that, he supposed it was fortunate for them all that she looked on the world with perpetual disdain and seldom smiled.

Miss Eloise Marchant, on the other hand, rarely stopped smiling as she looked about. Despite her family's standing in London society, she'd apparently had no success in attracting any suitable offer of marriage, and India offered a fresh hunting ground.

Tonight, the cast of *The Scarlet Cloak* was left behind stage in a fidget of nerves for fifteen minutes while they waited for the curtain to be raised, just as soon as the Resident and his party arrived to take their places in the front row. The clubhouse ballroom had been converted into a theatre for the evening, and the packed audience was growing increasingly restless at the late start of the performance.

With all the grace he could muster, Andrew ushered Lady Marchant and Eloise into the theatre behind Sir Ian and Lady Phillips who bustled down the centre aisle giving little smiles and nods of apology to the left and right for their late arrival.

Lady Marchant and Eloise refused to be hurried, seemingly determined to allow everyone in the hall ample opportunity to study their London fashions. Eloise swivelled her head from side to side, smiling at men who caught her eye. But her expression changed to one of astonishment when she glimpsed Victoria sitting in the audience. She stopped and blinked.

'Oh, Mama, do look! I can see Victoria Shelford! Hello, Victoria.' She gave a giggle. 'So this is where you've been hiding!'

Lady Marchant quickly scanned the faces turning towards them in surprise and, on recognizing Victoria, her eyes narrowed and her expression tightened. The audience stirred and people strained to catch a better view of whatever was happening.

Andrew noted how quickly Victoria covered her surprise and acknowledged Miss Marchant and her mother with a cool tilt of her head before turning away. For some reason, the sight of the two ladies seemed to have unsettled her, and that heated his own anger towards them. He took the mother and daughter each by an elbow and propelled them down the aisle to their seats beside Sir Ian and Lady Phillips. Damn women! What was their connection with Victoria?

And now as he settled into his own seat, he could sense trouble of some kind brewing for her in the looks that Eloise Marchant exchanged with her mother, and in their whisperings to Lady Phillips throughout the performance.

The high melodrama performed by the Amateur Dramatic Society would have been a disaster if the audience hadn't perceived *The Scarlet Cloak* as a splendid farce and laughed all the way through. While the audience was giving the cast an enthusiastic round of applause, Andrew looked around for Victoria. Her chair was empty.

The next performance that evening was given by Lady Marchant and Eloise at the supper party arranged by Colonel and Mrs Moncrief at their bungalow for the cast of the play and selected other guests.

'When did Victoria Shelford arrive in Srinagar? I was most surprised to see her here.' Miss Marchant posed the question loudly to the crowded room, but it was the colonel's wife who answered.

'Do you mean Mrs Victoria Latham? Mrs Latham has been staying here for several months now.'

'Mrs Latham? Are you telling me that Victoria Shelford is actually calling herself *Mrs Latham*?' Lady Marchant's voice could have cut glass. 'My dear Mrs Moncrief, that girl ran away to sea with a common sailor, and it broke her poor mother's heart when she discovered that there had been no marriage!'

Eloise smirked as she looked around the room to assess the degree of shock generated by her mother's revelation.

'I've always found Mrs Latham to be a very pleasant, refined young lady,' Lady Phillips said, flustered. 'Besides, she wears a wedding ring.'

Miss Marchant's neck appeared to stretch even further as she turned her head and gave the Resident's wife a patronizing smile. 'Well, *we* know that she is *not* married because Mama had an investigator search every parish register for twenty miles around the place where she was staying in Devon at that time. I can assure you that there was no wedding recorded in any of them.'

Andrew balled his fists until the nails bit into his palms. Dear God! If Eloise Marchant had been a man he'd be aiming a blow right now at that long jaw. The group around the Marchant women grew thicker.

'Victoria Shelford's wayward behaviour was the ruin of her whole family, I can assure you.' The way that Lady Marchant's thin lips drew back to reveal her huge teeth reminded Andrew of a killer shark about to attack. 'Poor Mr Shelford lost his seat in Parliament when the scandal became known, and her parents were forced to leave London and move to the south of France because of the disgrace their daughter brought to their doorstep.'

The enormity of the wreckage left by Victoria's misconduct left the audience clamouring for more detail. Andrew boiled. The vitriolic performance of these two witches was clearly no spontaneous act this evening. How many times had they rehearsed this slander? Would Victoria thank him if he went in now to defend her? Did he have the right to announce to the company that her marriage had taken place at sea and was perfectly legal?

He backed out of the room and sat in the garden to smoke a cheroot, trying to ignore the unstoppable torrent of gossip floating out to him through the open window.

'And, Mama, don't forget what happened to the older girl, too! The wild one, Caroline, who was named in court during Countess Overton's divorce hearing.'

'Ooooh!' The pain in Lady Marchant's voice sounded almost sincere. 'I have no words to describe what a picture of her wanton behaviour emerged from the evidence presented by the servants during the trial. It was in all the newspapers, but she and her husband had run off to America. They went on the stage over there, singing and dancing — and she even shows her legs, so I've learned.' She clicked her tongue and looked around at her audience. 'There was obviously something sadly lacking in the way Lady Mary raised her daughters.'

★　★　★

The next morning Andrew rode to Nigel's house to talk to Victoria, and met her as she was stepping through the front door. He could see that she hadn't slept well and that she was very angry.

'Well, Captain Wyndham, are you sure that

you want to be seen speaking to a woman like me?'

He hadn't slept well, either. 'Don't be ridiculous, Victoria. Those of us who know you will never believe the lies that those women are spreading. Perhaps you should sue them for slander — or I'll cheerfully strangle them both, if you'd like me to.'

She couldn't help but smile at his ferocious expression. 'I do appreciate the offer, Andrew, but there was probably a grain of truth in whatever they were saying about me. It's their misinterpretation of everything that's so cruel and wrong and I've been tossing all night thinking about what I should do about it.'

'Are you going to have it out with them? I'll come down to the residency with you now, if you like.'

'That's brave of you, my friend! Yes, when I got out of bed this morning that's exactly what I thought I'd do. I wanted to face the Marchants and tell them that they'd been grossly misinformed about the matter and to — and to — ' The corners of her mouth took a downwards turn. 'And that's exactly the way my mother would have responded, so I know that an argument with the Marchants would resolve nothing. It's all a game with them. They thrive on petty spats and they'd soon find some way to distort the facts of my case even further.'

She gave a long sigh. 'Of course, my mother played exactly the same game and she went out of her way to humiliate Lady Marchant and Eloise whenever she found an opportunity. Last night's little drama, I'm sure, was their chance to retaliate after my mother publicly snubbed them one day in Hyde Park after my sister's engagement had been announced.'

'Victoria, I'm completely lost. What has that — ?'

'Sorry. It would take a month to unravel the tit-for-tat nonsense that has been going on for thirty years between Lady Marchant and Lady Mary Woolcott, so let's not try. No, I think it best if I simply turn my back on them and try to walk away with my dignity intact.'

He gave a grunt. 'Well, I've made it clear to Lady Phillips that, of course, your marriage wouldn't be recorded in any parish church because it took place at sea — '

'Please, please, Andrew, don't become involved in this ridiculous situation. I've learned exactly how this community thrives on fresh gossip and that's why I'm packing up to leave tomorrow. I'm just on my way now to see if Thakur has finished the work on my elephant.'

'Oh, Lord! Victoria, don't let those witches drive you away. You have friends here who'll stand by you. I can assure you that Sir Ian and Lady Phillips are quite disgusted with the Marchants' gossip. And everything else about them.'

She shrugged. 'Perhaps, but the Colonel and Mrs Moncrief — and probably every man in the officers' mess will be sniggering about me this morning.'

'But you mustn't go yet! What about Nigel's wedding?'

'Can't you see that it's Nigel and Kitty I'm thinking about? I've tried to warn Nigel about what he's likely to hear today, but I don't think he realizes just how damaging his connection to me could prove to be if I stay in Srinagar. No, Andrew, the sooner I go, the quicker the gossip will fade and dear, loyal Nigel and Kitty won't have to go into battle every time my name is mentioned.'

He continued to frown down at her and, when she tried to step past him, he put a restraining hand on her arm. 'Wait. Stay here and go on with your packing while I ride down to collect the elephant. Wait for me, Victoria. Please just go back inside and *wait*.'

Kitty, with her boys and their *ayah* in tow, arrived shortly after he'd ridden away, and she was shocked to hear Victoria's decision to leave.

'Please don't be so hasty, Vicky. You must stay here for our wedding. Yes, I've heard what some people are saying this morning, but I don't believe a word of those lies.'

'Thank you, Kitty, I know it's all very petty and ridiculous, but I don't want anything to spoil your wedding day. I really think it's best for me to slip away and let all the nonsense simmer down as quickly as possible.'

'Vicky, it won't be the same if you're not there in church. It's just not fair. Besides, where will you go? Do you have friends to stay with — wherever it is that you're going?'

At this point Victoria had given no clear thought about where she might go when she left Kashmir. The spectre of that unknown frightened her, so she pushed it out of her mind and went on with her packing.

By mid-afternoon, Andrew had still not returned with her elephant.

Nigel arrived home early from his office, puffing with indignation at the gossip about his cousin that was being magnified by speculation as it flew around the community. 'How dare those women spread such lies — '

Nigel's fighting spirit, once roused, was not easy to douse, and Victoria was still trying to explain the running feud between her mother and Lady Marchant, when Duleep announced the arrival of Captain Wyndham. He was carrying no box or parcel, and she was hit hard by a childish disappointment that brought her to the edge of tears.

'Don't worry, Thakur has finished the elephant and I know you're anxious to see it. But I'll deal with all that tomorrow, I promise. Sorry, but I had a more important errand to attend to today.' From his pocket, he produced an envelope addressed to her in a bold, elegant script. 'I'd like you to read this, Victoria.'

My Dear Mrs Latham
Please give me the pleasure of sharing your company on my houseboat before you depart from Srinagar. Come this evening with Captain Wyndham and join us for dinner. I will send my carriage to bring you around the lake to the Nagim Basin where I am at present moored.

It was signed *Yolande, Begum Raziid Khan*.

'Oh, Andrew! This is — I know that this is all your doing. Thank you so much.'

He smiled at the relief in her expression. 'The begum's invitation is perfectly genuine, I assure you. She looks forward to making your acquaintance, and it will be simple enough to arrange for you to be brought across to the church on the day of the wedding.'

'Oh, thank you! This is a wonderful solution.' She beamed at him. 'And you're wonderful for arranging it.' For one moment he thought that she was going to embrace him, but she turned away and threw her arms around Kitty instead.

★ ★ ★

The setting sun was painting the sky with a glorious salmon-pink glow as the melon-seller paddled away from the begum's houseboat. He'd sold an extra melon there today. An English lady might be coming to stay, the cook had told him. He found that good news, indeed, for strict routines grew slack when visitors joined the household. The melon-seller was a patient man and his sack was waiting.

Each day he observed the girl-child playing under the canopy on the top deck of the houseboat, and sometimes saw her taken to the Shalimar Gardens in the begum's *shikara*. Sometimes they drove off in the begum's open carriage to visit the fort on the hill. And wherever they went they were escorted by the

Sikh bodyguard with the black pistol in his belt.

The girl-child was flawless and would fetch a high price from the beggar-master in Calcutta, especially as she carried European blood. Now was the perfect age for such a child to be taken — not too young — for children of very tender years were likely to die before they reached their destination. Older ones could become difficult to handle on the journey south. The little blue bottle of sleeping magic lay ready in his sack, and he would be watching for the one chance he needed to succeed.

★ ★ ★

'Papa! Papa!' Annabelle squealed as she saw him approaching with Victoria sitting beside him in a *shikara*. She ran from the roof deck and, by the time they had pulled in to the steps leading up from the water, she was there on the top one, skipping with excitement while the Sikh kept a tight hold on the wide pink satin sash around the waist of her spotted muslin dress. 'Papa! Papa!'

Andrew helped Victoria aboard the house-boat, before opening his arms to the child. 'Belle!' She flung herself at him and he scooped her up into a bear hug, then kissed her cheek. 'Sweetheart, I'd like you to say hello to Mrs Latham.'

Annabelle looked at Victoria with little enthusiasm, mumbled her greeting, then threw her arms possessively around Andrew's neck.

The begum was waiting to receive them in an opulent drawing room which ran across the width of the boat and was furnished with a triumphant blend of oriental and European tastes. Even the cobalt blue silk dress she wore today seemed an amalgamation of Indian and Parisian styles.

'I am so happy that you are able to accept my invitation, Mrs Latham — or may I call you Victoria?' the begum said, speaking English with a strong French accent. She came forward with her hands outstretched, even before Andrew had made the introductions.

'The pleasure is all mine, madame,' Victoria said, as the begum took her fingers firmly. 'It's most kind of you to offer me this sanctuary. I know that Andrew has told you about the awkward situation I've found myself in.'

'Oh, my dear Victoria, you speak to one who has frequently been in awkward situations.' Her voice was deep and melodious, her chuckle warm. 'I live very quietly here on the lake, and I'd be delighted if you would stay as long as you wish.'

'That's very kind of you, madame. I have no fixed plans.'

'Splendid! Andrew tells me that you've found no opportunity to understand the true ways of Kashmiri life so, perhaps, while you are here I could introduce you to some of my friends? I have a horse and vehicle stabled not far away on the shore, so we could pay some calls and perhaps make a few excursions to see a few of the interesting sights in this region.'

'Thank you madame. I'm keen to see as much as I can before I leave.'

The begum turned to Andrew. 'My dear, do take Annabelle up to the roof deck to eat her supper, while I show Victoria to her room.'

* * *

Later, when Andrew was rowed back to the city, he carried away a rare feeling of harmony. Victoria and the begum had taken to each other straight away, as he was sure they would. Annabelle? He grinned. Did a little jealousy lie behind the tantrum she'd thrown at bedtime?

Once home, he slipped off his jacket and

glanced at the papers on his desk. A telegram lay on the top and his heart leapt as his eyes flew over the message from General Roberts in Mardan. It had come already! It was the offer of a post with the Guides, and if Captain Wyndham wished to accept the offer, he should apply for his transfer to the Northwest Frontier without delay.

He gave a groan. This was just the news that he'd wanted to hear, yet he'd been dreading its arrival before he reached some decision about Annabelle's care.

He swore. What the devil was he going to do now? It had been his father's scathing words that had goaded him into writing prematurely to General Roberts, but this prompt reply was something he certainly hadn't expected.

And neither had he expected any transfer to take effect *immediately*. It usually took time for these moves to be approved.

'Oh, Lord!' He groaned again and ran his fingers through his hair. If he took up the Guides' offer he must find someone to be a mother to his daughter, a lady who'd be prepared to share a soldier's life on the frontier. Damnit!

Images of the women he'd known during his misspent youth flew wildly around in his head, and after he'd deleted all those with a colourful reputation, or those already married or downright stupid, ill-humoured, opinionated, timid or weepy, he could think of only one lady of his acquaintance who'd be up to the task: Victoria Latham.

Oh Lord! Refined, elegant Victoria was the last woman in the world he could invite to share his uncertain life on the frontier. Anyhow, she'd be a fool to accept an offer from a man like Andrew Wyndham who had so little to recommend him. Until Annabelle's arrival had brought him down to earth, he'd lived his life as if there was no tomorrow.

He drank a brandy and went to bed, but while he lay hovering on the brink of sleep, images of Victoria's pink, smiling lips and supple body danced again and again through his mind. It didn't take long for those thoughts to drift into the erotic, and that was a mistake which cost him a great deal of much needed sleep.

Ah, Victoria! If only — oh, dear God! If only he had more than just himself to offer her.

★ ★ ★

When the begum received a message from Andrew next morning to say that he was likely to be late arriving for dinner that evening, she suggested that they take a drive to an outlying village to watch the *Lhori* festival taking place.

'I've never really understood what the celebration is all about, but on this day each year, young boys dress up as spirits, then form a long line and perform a *chhajja* dance as they wind their way around the houses to visit elders and newly-wed couples, hoping to be given sweets. It's a very cheerful and rather noisy day, and I'm sure that Annabelle will enjoy it, too.'

Indeed she did, and when Andrew arrived that evening he was met by a tired little girl who refused to go to bed until she had attempted to tell him about all the exciting, noisy and confusing things she'd seen at the festival.

The rambling report of the three year old, was made even more incoherent because the child spoke to her father in a mixture of French-accented English, interspersed with what Victoria assumed must be Urdu.

Andrew himself seemed to be weary. His patience started to grow thin and several times he interrupted the child's flow and asked Annabelle to repeat certain words, using his own standard English accent. It was an exercise that didn't go at all well and before long cross tears were spilling onto the rosy cheeks. Andrew took her to her room and read to her until she fell asleep.

'My apologies,' he said stiffly when he joined the ladies waiting at the dinner table.

'Not at all, my dear.' The begum spoke matter-of-factly. 'We all know that children are like little parrots who pick up the words they hear spoken around them, and Annabelle listens to far more Urdu being used by my servants than she hears English being spoken here.' She picked up her soup spoon and kept her eyes on the bowl. 'But now that Victoria has come to stay, I'm certain that will start to change.'

Andrew nodded to Victoria. 'Thanks, I'd appreciate your help.'

★ ★ ★

The following day the begum suggested that they drive into the city to pay a call on her good friend, Vashti, the senior wife of a carpet merchant. 'Annabelle loves playing with her grandchildren, and I know that Vashti will be delighted to show you how Kashmiri ladies run their houses.'

★ ★ ★

The dark eyes of the melon-seller narrowed as he peered across the lake to watch the begum set out in her grand *shikara* and head to the bank where her horse and carriage stood harnessed. The child was with her and she was accompanied only by the lady who'd arrived yesterday. No bodyguard travelled with her. The man smiled. His prediction had been correct: already the presence of a guest in the household was causing a crack to appear in the usual ring of protection around the English child. The sack lay ready on the floor of his craft.

★ ★ ★

The begum's carriage set out for the city next day and, once there, ran along a lane leading behind a row of shops. Here, they entered the gates of a sprawling, two-storeyed brick and timber house with carved shutters on the windows, where they were welcomed effusively by a handsome, middle-aged woman. When the begum introduced Victoria, Vashti's brown eyes lit up.

'You are the very first British lady whom I have ever had the honour of meeting.' The begum translated the Urdu and Victoria coloured.

'In that case, I hope we may have many more meetings,' she said to the woman, and held out her hand.

Vashti introduced her husband's second

wife, who was somewhat younger, and then the six daughters of the house. She insisted that the visitors must stay and join them for a meal of spiced lamb and lentils, which the ladies ate after the men of the household had been served.

Later, while Annabelle and Vashti's small grandchildren played through the house and chased each other up and downstairs, she and the daughters led Victoria through the rooms. They proudly showed her the number of servants they employed, as well as the splendid carpets that had been woven in the family's factory, as well as their collection of carved ivories, and tables inlaid with semi-precious stones. Hanging on the walls were the skins of tigers and leopards shot by the menfolk of the family.

The ladies opened jewel boxes for Victoria to admire their treasures, and displayed their chests full of fine silk saris.

Giggling, the daughters took out several saris and draped them, one after the other, across Victoria's shoulder. Each seemed more vibrant than the last, and it wasn't long before they'd persuaded her to remove the tight-waisted English dress she was wearing and replace it with a sari the colour of a golden-pink summer dawn.

When the yards of silk were draped and

folded around Victoria's body, the next step in her transformation was to pull the pins and combs from her dark hair and dress it in Indian style — parted in the middle with a jewelled ornament suspended in the centre of her forehead and ear-rings that almost touched her shoulders.

The younger wife slipped a gold bangle from her own wrist, one which was fashioned in the shape of a coiled snake, and placed it on Victoria's

As she stood gazing at her reflection in a long looking-glass, she was swept by a sensation of having stepped into an unknown world. The begum smiled her approval.

'Oh, madame, can you imagine the stir it would cause if I found the courage to appear in the cantonment dressed like this?' She gave a giggle. 'Lady Marchant would have a fit!'

When it came time for the begum's party to leave the house, Victoria was once again dressed as a respectable English lady. And she was deeply touched by the insistence of Vashti's family that she accept their gifts of the dawn-pink sari and the gold snake bangle.

'Madame, would I be permitted to thank these ladies as I would do if they were my English friends? With a kiss on the cheek?'

When the begum translated her request to the merchant's wives, their eyes widened in astonishment. 'The ladies would be honoured, my dear,' she said and Victoria stepped forward to take Vashti's hands and touch her lips lightly to one cheek.

'I am delighted to have made your acquaintance, and I thank you for the lovely gifts. I will treasure them always.' Then she did the same to the younger wife, while Vashti quickly urged all the daughters to come forward one by one and share in the unique experience of being kissed by a memsahib.

'This has been a most remarkable day,' Victoria said, as they set out in the carriage, with Annabelle sitting on her lap and struggling to keep her eyelids open. 'Thank you so much for introducing me to your friends, madame. Isn't it disappointing that such a gulf exists between those ladies and the ladies of the cantonment?'

'It's called prejudice. I've felt it' — she nodded towards Annabelle — 'and she's likely to know it too, despite Andrew's determination to present her as a little English memsahib.'

Victoria frowned. 'Do you think he's making a mistake?'

The begum avoided an answer. 'Let me show you another aspect of Indian life tomorrow. It's time to visit the fort up there on the hill and pay a call on the maharaja.'

12

The begum, Victoria and Annabelle were all dressed in their best next day when they set out to visit the massive Hari Parbut Fort standing on its high hill a few miles from the city.

The iron gates of the fort swung open as the begum's carriage approached and, when the guards threw a salute to the party as they passed through, Annabelle waved to them. Clearly she was no stranger to this place.

They entered a courtyard lined with cannon, and then through the next gateway that led into a garden where a domed pleasure-pavilion stood beside a water channel and peacocks strutted, dragging their long, iridescent tails across the grass.

When the carriage halted at the steps of the palace, a servant dressed in purple and gold, ran down to escort them to the entrance where one of the maharaja's officials received the begum with due ceremony and acknowledged Victoria with a deep bow when she was presented.

Annabelle skipped off happily with an attendant who arrived to take her straight up to play with the children in the women's quarters.

'The maharaja has agreed to grant us an audience,' the begum said quietly when she and Victoria were shown into a decorated chamber, where servants came with silver basins and ewers of rosewater to pour over their hands. For the next hour they sat alone in the room while sweetmeats were served, and musicians entertained them on a durkra, sitar and drums until they at last received a summons into the royal presence.

'What do I do?' Victoria whispered. 'Curtsy?'

'No, simply bow low. But not *too* low.'

They were led through an empty, echoing marble chamber towards the heavy, beaten silver doors of the durbar hall. As they were flung open, Andrew was striding away from His Highness Maharaja Ranbir Singh who was seated at the far end of the hall on a raised marble platform. From the tight-lipped expression on Andrew's face, Victoria suspected that his meeting with the maharaja had not been a productive one.

He was astonished to see them, and slowed his pace, though there was no opportunity to do more than exchange a few muttered words as their paths crossed. 'Annabelle is somewhere playing with the children,' Victoria whispered.

'I'll come this evening,' he said under his

breath. His eyes told her that there was more he wanted to add, but already a courtier was approaching to escort the ladies to their audience and an attendant was hurrying to place two carved and gilded chairs for them at the foot of the steps leading up to the *gadi*.

Flanked by a courtier on either side, the overweight maharaja sat looking down on them from his cushions. He was splendidly dressed in yellow brocade and wearing an emerald green turban fronted by an aigrette with a ruby as big as a bird's egg. Behind His Highness stood his fan-bearer waving a large peacock-feather fan on its thick ebony stick, though there was no heat in the day. The tableau was meant to impress. And it succeeded.

At the foot of the steps, the begum bowed and Victoria followed her lead. His Highness waved a signal for them to sit in his presence, before he launched into a personal eulogy which the begum initially tried to translate, then gave it up as a hopeless task.

That didn't concern Victoria. There was much to observe around her on the painted and gilded walls and columns, the colours of the brocades and the gleam of jewels worn by the courtiers. She smuggled a yawn into her gloved hand and spent the time mentally listing all the new images to include in her next letter to Emily and Martin.

After an hour had passed, the royal hands clapped to signal that the ladies' audience had concluded and, after making their bows, they were escorted through the winding hallways of the palace to the eunuch guards who lounged at the foot of the staircase leading to the Pearl Tower, home of the maharaja's two queens, the princesses, and his concubines.

'When we enter the *zenana*, it's most important for us to present ourselves immediately to *First* Her Highness before speaking with *Second* Her Highness, or any of the other daughters and women in there.'

The begum was no stranger to the ladies, but Victoria's arrival raised a hum of interest when they walked into a long room where the delicately fretted windows threw patterned shadows across the white marble floor. A dozen maidservants and eunuchs were moving about, removing dishes and platters with the remains of a meal, while thirty or more ladies remained sitting on cushions with their greasy fingers held away from their clothes, waiting for rosewater to be brought and poured over each pair of soft hands.

When the women had dried their fingers, they began to drift across the hall to inspect the visitors. Victoria noted an amount of ill-humoured jostling amongst the maharaja's ladies before she and the begum were summoned into a curtained alcove by First Her Highness who became increasingly agitated as she talked rapidly in a low voice. Again, Victoria was handicapped by not understanding the language, but when the begum was at last able to ease the conversation to an end, she slipped an arm through Victoria's and drew her aside.

'There's much resentment in the air today because one of the daughters of First Her Highness had been chosen last month to marry a son of the great Raja of Jaipur. But they've just been informed that the prince now desires the youngest daughter of *Second* Her Highness instead. As you might imagine, that news has not been received here with universal delight!'

'Oh dear!'

'Yes, so now, while I spend a little time with Second Her Highness and listen to her crowing over the coup, why don't you take a stroll in the garden? In their present mood, I doubt the ladies will put themselves out to entertain any visitor here today.'

Simply by watching how little clusters of women were forming and turning their backs on others, Victoria found it impossible to ignore the tension running high within these walls. It was there in the sullen looks exchanged, in the tone of petulance injected into spoken words, in the act of a cup being hurled across the chamber and a serving woman slapped hard on the cheek for not sweeping up the shards quickly enough.

And throughout it all, Annabelle played in the gardens and pavilions with the girls and smaller boys. No sons remained in the ladies' domain past the age of six, and Victoria noticed how the girls were now beginning to align themselves with one or other of the currently warring parties. Several had begun to spit what sounded like insults towards each other across the courtyard.

Victoria cringed inwardly at the thought that Annabelle's mother would have lived this life of pampered confinement in the *zenana* of the palace at Gwalinpore — a place where the future held nothing but the past. It was chilling to think that this would have been Annabelle's fate, too, if she'd not been rescued and sent to be raised by an English father.

Victoria strolled to the far end of the garden and sat alone on a marble bench to watch Andrew's child playing with the water in a fountain and wetting her dress as she chattered in Urdu to a little boy about her own age. Suddenly she noticed Victoria, and ran to tell her something.

'Belle, please speak to me in English. I can't understand what you're saying otherwise.'

The little chin lifted and the child regarded her crossly. 'Is my papa coming to see me tonight?' The words might have been spoken in English but Annabelle delivered them in the sing-song tone used by her Indian *ayah*.

'Thank you, Annabelle. Yes, I'm sure you'll see your papa this evening.'

The child skipped back to her playmate, and appeared to be translating her good news back into Urdu for him.

Later, when they were all driving back to the lake in the carriage, Victoria recounted the episode to the begum.

'Yes, it's Andrew's plan to raise her as an English-speaking child, but, as you see, she's already beginning to walk a difficult tightrope between two cultures. I was brought up to speak French and Persian, and I'm afraid that our little parrot hears the servants talking to each other far more often than she hears her father's language.'

Victoria took the tired little girl onto her lap. 'Tell me, Belle, has your papa taught you to say some nursery rhymes? Do you know Humpty Dumpty, or Jack and Jill?'

Annabelle sat up straight and her weariness faded as she began to recite 'Little Miss

Muffet', 'The old woman who lived in a shoe . . . ' and others that Victoria had almost forgotten.

She exchanged an amused glance with the begum as the child babbled on. 'What did we say about little parrots?' She hid the laughter in her voice as Annabelle repeated each rhyme in her father's crisp, well-modulated accent.

'I think Annabelle would have few problems with pronunciation if Andrew was able to spend more time with her.' The begum raised an eyebrow. 'And I'm sure that you will be of great help to her also, my dear.'

'Of course, I'll gladly do what I can while I'm here, madame.' Nigel's wedding was less than two weeks away now, and she was still undecided about where to go after that. Where was the direction — that *purpose* — she needed to find in her own life?

The begum's voice cut across her ruminations. 'I think that Annabelle has had sufficient excitement this week, don't you? We'll have a quiet picnic tomorrow in the Shalimar Gardens. She always enjoys our visits there.'

* * *

As soon as the begum's party stepped ashore at the gardens next morning, Annabelle demanded to be given her pull-along elephant and instantly ran off with it along the central path beside the water channel leading up to the pleasure-pavilion.

'I'll go with her,' Victoria called, as the *ayah* began unfolding canvas chairs and arranging rugs and cushions under the trees.

Once inside the pavilion, Annabelle stepped straight into her own make-believe world, taking the little wooden dolls from their *howdah* on the elephant's back and sitting them on a marble bench. And chattering to them in Urdu. 'Please tell me about your game.' Victoria spoke slowly and distinctly, using her most persuasive tone.

Annabelle shook her head and stubbornly continued to chatter in Urdu, excluding Victoria while the long game developed into one that involved a great deal of running to and fro with the dolls playing hide-and-seek. Or that was how it seemed to Victoria.

But eventually Annabelle grew tired of it all, announced clearly that she was hungry, and made a bolt for the door.

Victoria picked up the toys and followed her back to where the begum was lounging in a canvas chair, reading a French novel. Bowls of chicken, sweetmeats and fruits had by now been delivered from the houseboat, and were laid out on a white linen cloth.

Victoria sat beside Annabelle on embroidered cushions while they ate, and sent an unspoken signal to the begum that her efforts to communicate in English with the child had so far met with no success today.

It wasn't long before Annabelle began to lose the struggle to keep her eyelids open and, once she'd put her head on the cushion, she was soon asleep. Victoria reached across her to lift a wayward strand of hair from her cheek, then allowed her fingers to play with a long brown curl falling over one shoulder. Her mother must have been truly exquisite, she thought. No wonder Andrew had fallen so desperately in love with Ishana.

But her unspeakable ending on the pyre seemed something from a nightmare. Was it really possible for any woman to bring herself to do that without heavy persuasion? Would any of the ladies she'd seen yesterday in the *zenana* wish to throw themselves into the funeral pyre of the Maharaja of Kashmir when he died? If Annabelle hadn't been rescued from a life in a *zenana*, might she one day — ?

Victoria gave an involuntary shudder and looked up quickly to see the begum smiling at her enquiringly.

'I find her a most delightful child, Victoria, don't you? Yes, she's strong-willed and needs a firm rein at times, but can't you see how desperately she needs a mother? And don't you agree that her father would make a fine husband?'

'No, no, madame — *please* say nothing more! I have not the faintest notion of marrying Andrew. Besides, he's not in love with me, any more than I am with him. We share a friendship that's uncomplicated and undemanding, with absolutely no element of passion. And that's the way I'd be happy for it to remain.'

The begum raised her brows. 'Really? I must confess that a long time ago I had a rather passionate affair with Gordon Wyndham, until I came to understand the full measure of his disregard for anyone but himself.' She smiled archly. 'However, my dear, if I was thirty or forty years younger now, I could easily fall in love with a man like Andrew Wyndham. Life with him would be filled with surprises.'

Victoria shook her head slowly. 'No, I've been in love and I know exactly how it feels, madame. From the moment I met Peter Latham — my late husband — I was gripped by a sensation that set my heart racing every time I thought of him. I could hardly breathe, and every part of me ached for him. I couldn't bear for us to be apart. And that's why I *know* that what I feel for Andrew is *not* love, although I do feel a real fondness towards him.'

The begum raised her brows. 'And nothing more than that?'

'Of course, I enjoy his company, I respect his judgement, I'd trust him with my life, and I admire his devotion to his daughter. And yes, I find him quite an attractive man when he's not scowling.'

For a moment the begum regarded her sceptically. 'Are you being honest with yourself, my dear?'

Victoria blushed. 'Yes, I am.'

'Don't be too hasty in deciding to close the door on the prospect of marriage to Andrew. I know from experience that love arrives in many guises — sometimes quickly, sometimes not. You see, like Annabelle, I grew up between two cultures. My father was French — a diplomat who spent much of his career in this part of the world — and my mother was the daughter of a Persian nobleman.

'Theirs was a true love match and I was their only child. We often travelled to visit relatives in Paris, and I still do, but this country became my homeland when I married Raziid Khan. Although I was just seventeen at the time and he was a man more than twice that age, my parents permitted the marriage even though he had two other wives at the time. However he'd fathered no children.'

Victoria wasn't sure what to say, so didn't try.

'I hardly knew him at all when we were married — and I was terrified — but I discovered that he was wise and tender, and it wasn't long before I came to love him deeply. I, too, desperately wanted to give him children, but it didn't happen, and I wept when I — we three wives — were widowed ten years later.' She looked directly into Victoria's eyes.

'The other ladies and I were fond of each other, though we chose not to continue living together when our husband had gone. But life does move on, old wounds heal, and I'm glad to say that I've been able to love again.'

It took Victoria a little time to digest the begum's story. 'Well, madame, I'm twenty-six now and, yes, I'd like to share my life with a man who truly loves me. But I have to tread warily because when Peter died he left me with something that inevitably changes the way people perceive me — if they hear about it.'

The begum raised her brows questioningly.

'Peter left me his share of a trading vessel named *Fortitude*, and I'm growing increasingly wealthy with every voyage it makes.'

'And you consider this to be a difficulty?'

'Yes, I certainly do, because once a whiff of *wealth* is sniffed in the air around a woman, every fawning, worthless fortune-hunter in the country is drawn to the honey-pot. I've seen that happen to young ladies in London. But what's even worse, I know that a woman's wealth can frighten away a good man who has little money himself.'

The begum looked at her keenly. 'Surely you're not suggesting that Andrew Wyndham — ?

'I'm suggesting nothing at all,' she answered, more sharply than she'd intended. 'I'm simply saying that if I do meet a gentleman and fond feelings start to develop between us, I need to be sure that it's *Victoria* who stirs his heart, and not Peter Latham's wealthy widow.'

Unexpectedly, thoughts of Peter slipped into her mind throughout the day. Her black ocean of grief had calmed, but she was still carrying the old sense of emptiness and lack of purpose in her life. The augury had told her to look into her heart to find her destiny. *It is waiting all around you. Search for it with your heart.*

Well, she *was* searching, and so far nothing had appeared, apart from visions of the nameless girl who'd died giving birth on the floor of a filthy tenement, and the orphaned Molly Collins whose future might have been similarly grim without the generosity of Martin and Emily and the good people at Cloudhill.

She prayed regularly that Molly would learn a useful trade, or train in some skill that would enable her to earn a decent wage and keep the wolf of poverty — or worse — from her door. Molly might even achieve her dream of becoming a milliner and one day have her own little shop, or perhaps Mrs Dobson would teach her to cook in the Cloudhill kitchen. Or maybe Mrs Frost would train her in the secrets of running a fine household. Would she make a good nursemaid?

The important thing was that Molly had now been given a chance to find a better life. Might that nameless girl in the East End tenement still be alive today if she'd learned a skill which enabled her to earn a wage and become independent? How many more girls would be trapped and misused because they had nobody to turn to?

While the begum dozed in her chair and Annabelle slept soundly on a cushion, Victoria narrowed her eyes and stared into the mesmerizing glare shimmering across the surface of the lake. Cloudhill could offer a new direction for Molly Collins's life, but how many other girls — like those she used to walk past on the streets of London — would ever find a chance like Molly?

Apart from working in the hell of a factory or a mill, where could an uneducated girl turn if she wanted to earn a living? Alone in the world without a skill or a trade, what chance did life offer a female who had no one to protect her?

As Victoria sprawled in the canvas chair and continued to stare across the shimmering lake, a scene began to swim before her eyes, like a far-off mirage in the desert.

She screwed up her eyes tightly against the glare. *Close your eyes and see your destiny with your heart.* The old soothsayer's words shot into her head, and when she looked across the water again, she saw a line of girls who seemed to be moving towards a doorway. One of them was wearing a shabby patchwork skirt. Another was in a soiled petticoat with a few remnants of fine lace clinging to the hem.

Victoria blinked. Was she hallucinating? Where did the doorway lead to?

13

'You've been in a very pensive mood this afternoon, my dear,' the begum said gently, as she and Victoria sat on the roof deck, sipping sherry while they waited for Andrew to arrive for dinner. 'Is there something worrying you?'

'Oh, no, on the contrary, madame.' She leaned forward in her chair. 'I'm sorry to have been so distracted, but a very exciting thought suddenly popped into my head this afternoon and it's triggered an avalanche of ideas about what I might be able to *do* with the rest of my life.'

'That sounds very profound, Victoria.' The begum seemed decidedly sceptical. 'And you say that this idea suddenly came to you in the Shalimar Gardens?'

'Don't laugh, madame. If Peter had lived, I'd now be sailing the world with him and he would have taught me to be his navigator. Instead, I've become a useless, tea-drinking, game-playing creature who's still looking for some new direction in her life. Now I think I might have just found it.'

'Today? In the gardens?'

'Don't look so surprised, madame. Yes, the

details are still swirling around in my mind, but I can see a great need for a place in London where penniless, unschooled and unprotected girls could come to be trained in useful skills like needlework, or dressmaking and millinery — perhaps cooking, or nursemaiding — even book-keeping. Some girls might even learn to be governesses. Or teachers.'

By now her cheeks were flushed and she was sitting on the edge of her chair. 'I want to use Peter's money to establish such a place in London. To be run as a charitable foundation. I know that's just the kind of thing that he'd approve of.'

For a moment, the begum remained speechless. 'That would be a huge undertaking, my dear Victoria! Have you really given it sufficient thought?'

'Indeed, I have, madame, though the details are going to take some time to work out. But I know how much an establishment of that kind is needed.' She painted a picture of the girl she'd seen die on the floor of the tenement and the plight of an orphaned child alone in the world.

'The streets are full of girls like that, girls who have nothing ahead of them but misery or exploitation. Perhaps a foundation would be able to help only ten or twenty girls a year, but I'm going to make a start and do whatever I possibly can.'

She reached into a pocket, pulled out a notebook and pencil, and added another thought to the list of ideas already there.

'I'll write straight away to my London attorney, Mr Bartley-Symes, and ask him to set up a trust with the money that the *Fortitude* has already earned for me, and will keep on earning, I'm certain. Of course, we'll need to form a committee to get the establishment up and running and I know some ladies who are excellent at that kind of thing.' Another name was added to her list. 'I'll write to them immediately.'

She drew breath for a moment and reined in her galloping thoughts. 'My name won't be associated in any way with this trust. I want it to be known as the *Fortitude Foundation*, and the late Captain Peter Latham will be announced as the benefactor.'

She was forced to swallow hard. 'I'm perfectly sure that this is absolutely the right thing to do, but I'm not ready yet to discuss my plans with anyone, apart from you, madame.'

'Not Andrew?'

'No, certainly not Andrew! Not yet — not until everything is settled.' She could see that the begum was about to question her decision. 'I'll know when the right time comes to tell Andrew about it, madame.'

Their conversation was interrupted when they heard the sound of a *shikara* at the steps, followed by a deep male voice speaking in angry tones.

'Oh, he's early — ' Victoria began, but she was stopped by the begum's expression.

'That's not Andrew! Quickly, please come down to the drawing room with me, Victoria. If that's who I think it is, I have no wish for him to linger.' She left her chair as she was speaking and smoothed a hand over her hair as they walked downstairs.

The begum was closer to being flustered than Victoria had ever seen her, but by the time they entered the drawing room, she was ready to face General Wyndham who was standing on the doorstep and venting his fury on the Sikh for refusing to announce his arrival.

'Gordon, do please calm yourself!' the begum said, sweeping into the room. 'Even after all these years you should have remembered that I do not like to be disturbed at this hour.'

She gave him a limp hand and, as he raised it to his lips, his glance drifted to Victoria. That knowing, lingering look made her suspect that Lady Marchant's gossip might have reached his ears and that *she* could well be the reason for this visit.

'A thousand apologies for this unannounced arrival,' Wyndham's deep voice purred, 'but I've been away shooting up in the mountains with Mr and Mrs Cooke. We returned only last night.' Neither the begum nor Victoria showed interest.

'Yes, we had a most *delightful* camp set up near Sonamarg. It was a hugely successful hunt — good weather, good shooting and *very* good company.' He raised his eyebrows meaningfully.

Victoria felt compassion for the mountain wildlife shot by this man, but little for the lady whom he seemed to be implying was also in his trophy bag.

He rubbed his palms together. 'Sadly, I must set off for Delhi soon, so I had to take this opportunity to call on you — and *Mrs Latham*, of course.' He smiled at her in a way that left Victoria in no doubt that he'd heard Lady Marchant's gossip and had probably come to see this notorious woman for himself.

The begum capitulated and signalled for him to sit. 'So tell me, Gordon, what parts of the country have you been hammering into submission recently?'

The general settled his heavy frame into a

chair and looked from the begum to Victoria. 'Yes, Yolande, I've had some victories here and there, but the one that gives me most satisfaction is — at last — winning the battle I've been having with my son. Do you remember young Andrew? Well, I'm afraid he's not quite so young any more, but I've just heard that he's found the backbone to join the Guides.' He made a guffaw. 'Not that he told me himself, of course! Colonel Moncrief mentioned it at lunch today.'

The begum and Victoria exchanged a swift glance. If Andrew was to leave Srinagar, what plans had he made for Annabelle?

'Ah, yes, he'll find plenty of action out there on the North-west Frontier, and if he uses his head, he should do well. Luckily for him I just happen to be here to cut across the administrative queue and have his transfer pushed through without any delays.'

'How . . . convenient,' the begum said as she let out a breath.

Victoria clamped her jaws and felt a sharp stab of disappointment. This was too sudden. She would miss Andrew very much. And their conversations. Perhaps they'd correspond? But what arrangement had he made for Annabelle? Her mind raced and she turned a deaf ear to the general's long-winded monologue, until —

'Papa! Papa!' Annabelle's piping voice carried through the boat. Victoria swallowed her gasp and saw the begum tense. They had not expected Andrew's arrival for another hour, but Annabelle had obviously been watching for him through her window. 'Papa is coming!'

There was a soft thud as a *shikara* nudged the steps and, at that moment, the child burst into the drawing room. Victoria's heart lurched: Andrew's secret was about to be revealed to the last person in the world he'd want to know about his daughter.

Without a clear thought to direct her movements, she sprang from her chair and opened her arms, catching the little figure in flight as she passed, and swinging the child off her feet in a full circle. 'General, I'd like to introduce my daughter, Annabelle. Darling, do say hello to the general.'

Annabelle stiffened and her cheeks grew pink with fury. She put her hands against Victoria's shoulders and pushed hard, wriggling to escape the hold, kicking with her bare feet. 'Papa! Papa!'

Andrew appeared in the doorway and stood there, thunderstruck as he surveyed the scene.

'Oh, General, just listen to my adorable little matchmaker!' Victoria forced a smile and ignored Andrew. 'I'm afraid that my daughter has quite lost her heart to your son! She makes me blush, don't you, sweetheart?'

She tightened her grip even further around the squirming, kicking child. 'Sadly, my husband died before Annabelle was born, you see, and she's been letting me know in no uncertain terms that it's high time I found a father for her. And Captain Wyndham has been so very kind to my poor little darling.'

She clamped her tongue between her teeth and walked unsteadily towards Andrew. His chin was braced for trouble, but as soon as he opened his arms to Annabelle, she flung herself into them and snuggled her face against his neck.

'Well, there you have it, Gordon. Victoria's daughter has certainly lost her heart to your son.' The begum threw Andrew a speaking look. He frowned and kept his mouth closed.

The general was nonplussed. 'I had no idea, Mrs Latham — the child, I mean. I heard no mention — '

Her cheeks heated. 'But, General Wyndham, why should you have any interest in the fact that I have a daughter, when the matter can be of absolutely no concern of yours? I would like to make it clear to you that I am accountable to no one regarding what I do, or don't do, in my private life.'

Her waspish tone took them all by surprise and, for a long moment, nobody spoke. But Gordon Wyndham was never a man to let matters lie.

'Well, come along now, Andrew, here's your opportunity. Can't you see that it's high time you began to woo this lovely young mother as well as the daughter?' He laughed. 'And if you're quick off the mark, there might be time to arrange a wedding before you leave for Mardan, eh?'

Resentment burned in Andrew's eyes and he took a step towards his father. 'Whatever Mrs Latham and I decide to do is the business of neither you nor any other person on God's earth, and I'd be obliged if you kept right out of it.' His jaw tightened. 'In fact, as from this moment, I'd prefer it if you kept right out of my life altogether. Forget you ever had a son. I'm sure that won't present any difficulty for you.'

His father's neck coloured. 'Damnit, boy, I'm your father! Where do you think you'd be now if I'd not been there to steer your course?'

'Don't make me laugh! When have you ever been a father to me? For all the fatherly concern you've shown, I could have been one of the stray dogs the servants fed on the kitchen doorstep.'

The general seemed ready to explode. His eyes bulged and his chest heaved. 'And that's the thanks I get for giving you all the opportunities that you were quick to squander? What do you have to say about that trouble you got yourself into in Agra? You certainly needed my influence to get you out of that! And the time in Lahore when you were court-martialled for disobeying orders?'

'I'll be the first to admit that I'm not proud of some of the things I did ten years ago. But that was then, and this is now. And besides, aren't you forgetting that I was exonerated by that court martial?'

Victoria's insides were churning at the family implosion she'd triggered, and the raised voices in the room alarmed Annabelle. She whimpered and looked around at the adults. Andrew stroked his hand to and fro across her back. 'Hush, sweetheart, hush.'

The begum stood and faced the general. She was almost as tall as he. 'As you can see, I have guests, General Wyndham, and I would like you to leave. We have absolutely nothing more to say to each other.'

'Yolande! You can't — '

She clapped her hands and the Sikh instantly came into the room to open the door for the general while the begum signalled to Victoria and Andrew, carrying

Annabelle, to follow her up to the roof deck.

'The devil take the man!' he spat, as they saw his father's hired *shikara* moving off towards the shore. 'Of all the times for him to arrive! I'm so dreadfully sorry about this, Victoria, but — why in heaven's name did you tell him that Annabelle was *your* daughter? He's going to spread that news as soon as he steps into the officers' mess — and it's going to provide those damn Marchant women with even more fuel to work up into a fresh frenzy of lies.'

She sat motionless, white-faced. Why *had* she done it? Why had she been so ready to bring down another avalanche of gossip on her own head in order to protect Andrew Wyndham's secret? Just like a warhorse, she'd charged in to battle at the first bugle call. It was an odd feeling, but she was rather proud that she'd done so. And, if she had to, she knew that she'd do it again.

'Andrew, what does it matter if people here are gossiping about me? I can pack my bags and leave at any time. Your career is in this country. *Somewhere.*'

He looked thoroughly wretched. 'Well, first of all let me give my apologies to you both. I wanted to be the one to give you the news about this offer I've had from Mardan.'

They listened quietly as he told them about

the enquiry he'd sent to General Roberts. 'I didn't imagine that things would move so speedily. I thought I'd find time to work out a happy solution for my dilemma.' He cast a significant glance down at Annabelle. 'Quite frankly, I don't have any alternative now but to stop all this damn procrastination and decline the offer. I've got to bite the bullet and resign from the regiment immediately, then make a serious attempt to find some position in a place where Annabelle will be welcome.' He kept his voice flat and spoke quickly in an attempt to smother the emotion boiling inside him.

As Victoria gazed at him, her breasts rose and fell. Her own father, who'd always claimed to love her, had turned his back on her at the very first hurdle. And here was Andrew Wyndham willing to throw aside his whole career for the sake of his child. Her admiration for him swelled and she sensed a rising tide of urgency within herself to join him in his fight against whatever forces were aligning against him.

Strong feelings were drawing her to him: Andrew was a unique man.

14

When Andrew rode through the gates of the residency later that evening, Victoria Latham's extraordinary claim to be Annabelle's mother was still creating fantasies in his mind, and his thoughts were far away when Miss Eloise Marchant ran out across his path. She was being chased from the shrubbery by a large, golden-haired gentleman, and Andrew had to quickly swing his horse off the drive to avoid a collision.

Though he pulled the grey wide of her, Eloise fell into a fit of hysterics and swayed, seemingly about to collapse from shock, as the fellow ran up to fling his arms around her in a knightly fashion.

'Ho, sir!' he bawled at Andrew, as he dismounted to make his apologies for the near mishap. 'I should deal with you for such reckless riding! Miss Marchant could have been killed!' Eloise gave a little moan and seemed to sag further against her hero. It was an invitation for the big man to scoop her up in his arms.

It was an effort for him to lift her, but he was determined and, after Andrew had uttered the appropriate words to Miss Marchant, he and her champion exchanged a fleeting look that acknowledged their acquaintance. While Eloise Marchant was carried into the house, Andrew remounted and rode to the stables, grinning to himself.

So, Rufus Alexander, the womanizing prince of rogues, had arrived in Srinagar and had apparently set his sights on Lady Marchant's heiress. How delightful! Andrew chuckled aloud as he left his horse with the syce and walked to his quarters. Victoria would be amused when he told her about the notorious Rufus Alexander and their meeting years ago in Madras when Mr Alexander had hidden for days in the attic of a house where Andrew had been a guest.

Rufus — using one of his other names at the time — had been caught in a compromising situation with the wife of a Dutch merchant who'd quickly sent his band of cutthroats to find Mr Alexander, along with the lady's ruby brooch that he'd slipped into his pocket. But Rufus had remained undetected, and eventually managed to escape from the city with both the brooch and his skin intact. Andrew later heard that he'd gone on to woo a woman in Lahore.

Victoria would laugh when he told her that story, Andrew thought as he slipped out of his jacket. What if he could find some way to help the handsome scoundrel bait a hook to snare the awful Eloise? Yes, indeed, if she became entangled with him, it would cost Lady Marchant dearly to buy him off. And she'd have little hope of smothering the scandal that would explode around her ears. What a delightful revenge that would be for the hurt that the Marchants' vicious tongues had dealt to Victoria.

* * *

Both the Resident and his wife were showing signs of strain and counting the days until the Marchants' visit came to its end. 'Oh, Andrew, never have I known such difficult guests,' Lady Phillips said shakily. 'Absolutely *nothing* pleases them.'

Sir Ian looked at him over the top of his glasses. 'Do stay and join us for lunch today,' he said, a shade anxiously. 'Lady Marchant has persuaded me to invite a gentleman — Mr Rufus Alexander. Do you know of him? He arrived up here only a week ago with a rather strange letter of introduction from the Governor-General, and he seems to have gone out of his way to ingratiate himself with our guests.'

'Has he indeed?' Andrew murmured.

Lady Phillips sniffed and sat forward. 'I find him a little too, er — Mr Alexander is a most entertaining gentleman, but we know absolutely nothing about the fellow and Eloise Marchant has become quite sickeningly besotted with him.'

'Well, I'm sure that neither you nor Sir Ian could be held accountable for any stupidity displayed by that young lady — and I don't see how I can be of any help.'

'Well, you're a man of the world, Andrew, and I'd like to hear your impression of the chap.' Sir Ian's forehead furrowed. 'Of course Lady Marchant tried at first to discourage the relationship with Eloise, but Mr Alexander has quite won her over now by inviting them both to sail down the Ganges with him on his yacht.'

Andrew was forced to turn his head quickly, cover his mouth, and pretend to cough.

'It has all been so very sudden,' Lady Phillips added, 'and while I'll be delighted to see the Marchants pack up and leave as soon as possible, I feel a certain degree of responsibility for having been the one to introduce this unknown gentleman to my sister's friends.'

Andrew kept a straight face when he walked into the dining room and was introduced to Rufus. Initially there was a flash of panic in the fellow's eyes but it disappeared when they shook hands and no reference was made to their previous acquaintance. Though Rufus had gained a little weight over the last ten years, his golden hair was still thick and waved to perfection, and he was expensively dressed.

Actually, a more handsome man would be hard to find, Andrew thought, as they sat around the table and he watched the two Marchant women falling under the spell of Mr Alexander's silver-tongued tales about his adventures around the world. And his description of the yacht that he had moored at Benares.

Lady Marchant smiled frequently at his eloquence, and Eloise squealed with excitement when Rufus reached into his breast pocket and produced a photograph of a sleek steam yacht. 'What a beauty,' Andrew murmured, wondering which photographer's shop had sold him the picture. 'Are you planning to sail soon?'

* * *

The storm of gossip in Srinagar about Victoria Latham's secret child was immediately dampened by Nigel's outrage at the

287

suggestion. 'Utter, vicious nonsense! Who could have suggested such a thing? Obviously someone who doesn't know my cousin at all!'

But all that quickly took second place to the news of Eloise Marchant's engagement, and the cantonment buzzed all week with receptions and farewell dinners for the Marchants and Mr Alexander. But there were no tears at the residency when the trio finally departed for Benares.

But there were tears of laughter in Victoria's eyes when Andrew described the whole charade as they sat alone on the upper deck that evening. 'Oh, Andrew! You are a wicked, wicked man. There's no yacht, is there? Should I feel sorry for Eloise and Lady Marchant? How long will it be before they discover that Rufus is a fraud?'

'Well, it will have to be before they reach the Ganges.' Andrew's grin grew wider. 'Rufus is sure to choose a night for Lady Marchant to discover her daughter in a compromising situation — and there'll be witnesses, too, of course. Her ladyship will demand that they marry immediately, at which point I imagine that Mr Alexander will announce — most apologetically — that he already has a wife.' He gave a hoot of laughter. 'Oh, yes, Lady Marchant will be expected to dig deep into her purse to keep that scandal quiet.'

Victoria shook her head. 'To think she couldn't see through all his lies! Well, let's hope she'll learn a lesson and put that malicious tongue of hers to rest at long last.'

He raised an eyebrow at her. 'Clearly, my nature is not as forgiving as yours, Victoria. After their attack on your good character, it will give me enormous satisfaction to speak to Lady Phillips while she's writing her next Saturday letter to her sister in London — the sister who arranged the invitation for the Marchants' visit.'

'You're going to tell her the whole truth about Rufus?'

'Absolutely! Once they've left Srinagar, I'll say that I've just uncovered some very unpleasant news regarding the background of Eloise Marchant's fiancé, and I *know* that we can then rely on her to send every detail straight to her sister.' He winked. 'How long will it take for the gossip mill of Mayfair to grind that pair of witches into the dust? I'm sure you'll soon be able to enjoy the sweet taste of revenge, Victoria.'

She blew a long breath between her lips and shook her head slowly at him. 'I'm very glad to have you as a friend and not as a foe, Andrew Wyndham.'

He hesitated before he reached into his

breast pocket and pulled out an envelope. 'Well, I've done it, Victoria. This is it — my resignation from the regiment. I'll give it to Colonel Moncrief in the morning, though I'll have to stay on here until another man arrives to take on the job. And then I'll head off with Annabelle and her *ayah* for Delhi or perhaps Bombay.'

Victoria stared at him wordlessly. Her fists clenched tighter as she listened.

'Once I'm down there I'm sure to find a position in business somewhere. Perhaps in a merchant house, or with a shipping line. And the railway companies are expanding — '

She began to breathe fast. 'Stop it, Andrew! Stop it! I know that you don't want to leave the army. You *can't*. You *mustn't!*' She gripped the arms of her chair. 'Look, two things are crystal clear to me. In the first place, your dearest wish is to go out to Mardan and join the Guides. And secondly, you have a daughter who should not be separated from her father.'

She stopped and ran her tongue over her bottom lip, waiting for him to acknowledge her statement. But he made no comment and his frown deepened. She saw herself standing on the edge of a high cliff with this man whom she'd come to care for very deeply. Yes, she was willing to admit it! Her feelings for him were strong. And decidedly warm. Now she thought that she could hear Aunt Honoria chuckling.

She drew in a deep breath. 'Andrew, don't you see that there's a perfectly simple answer to your dilemma? If you joined the Guides in Mardan as a married man, you'd have a wife to care for your daughter while you were busy doing — well, whatever it is that you'd be required to do out there.' She watched him expectantly, but he remained tight lipped.

Her impatience mounted.

'Oh, Andrew! Open your eyes and look at me. Don't you see that you'd only have to ask me to marry you and my answer would be yes?'

For a long moment he stared at her incredulously. But no words came. Should she have mentioned that she'd grown to love him?

'Come along, Andrew, just think about it! Our marriage would solve your problem instantly, and I'm positive that we'd get along well together wherever we go. We already know that we can trust each other, and I'm sure many couples start out in marriage with much less than that.'

His frown deepened. Perhaps he'd understand her message more clearly if she went to him now and pressed her open lips against his tightly clenched ones. Yes, and when they opened, she'd slip her tongue into his mouth to play warm, velvety games with his. She wanted very much to do that. She felt her cheeks heating. She wanted him to hold her close so he could feel the pace of her racing heart and then he'd understand how much she wanted him to love her.

He didn't move, and she remained sitting where she was, though her tone became softer, more persuasive.

'I'm ready to go wherever you're sent, Andrew, though you'd have to teach me how to be a proper army wife. I mean, I'll need your help to understand the regiment's rules and regulations, but I promise I would never let you down.'

'Oh, for God's sake, stop it, Victoria! What you're suggesting is absolutely out of the question. I couldn't ask you to — You have no idea what the isolation is like. You could never — '

She sighed, stood slowly and walked to his chair, crouched at his feet and placed her hands on his knees. 'Don't make the mistake of underestimating me, Andrew. I'd soon learn to be a *useful* officer's wife, though I'm afraid that cooking is a complete mystery to me at the moment. But would I have to cook? No? Well, hopefully, I wouldn't be expected to attend endless tea parties and play croquet. Anyhow, while you were away I could certainly teach Annabelle to read and write, sew — and draw rather badly. And to speak the Queen's English. We'd always be there waiting whenever you returned from . . . wherever.'

She hesitated for a moment. 'I admit that your daughter and I are not yet the very best of friends. I think she looks on me as a rival for your time and attention, but that would change once we were all living under the one roof.'

He shook his head at her, knowing full well that he was mad to reject her perfect solution. He should feel gratitude. Was it simply male pride that refused to let him even consider the idea? He didn't know whether to laugh or cry.

'Victoria, you haven't given this nearly enough thought. Marriage is for men and woman who feel — I mean, you can't really be serious!'

'Oh, but I'm being perfectly serious, Andrew.'

'No. Believe me, it's best for you to forget about the whole thing. I'm not the easiest man to live with and you're likely to find that you hate it out there on the frontier. Wives always have a difficult time when a husband's duty has to take precedence over anything else, and — and accommodation is often Spartan. Sometimes families are left on their own for weeks at a time. No, Victoria, I would never ask you to share that kind of life, though I do thank you for your very charitable offer.'

She held his gaze. 'All your talk of isolation and discomfort out there doesn't frighten me. And besides, Andrew, what I'm suggesting is certainly not *charity*. Indeed, far from it. I think I've come to understand you very well now, and my feelings for you have grown extremely warm. I *want* to become your wife. I want *you* to become my husband for better or worse.'

He saw the expression in her eyes and words eluded him. Was he imagining it, or was this delightful, intelligent woman prepared to open the door of her heart and invite him to enter? He stood slowly and took her hands in his, drawing her to her feet. A warm feeling of something like hope came rushing through his veins, urging him to drop his feeble resistance. 'Victoria, do you really understand what kind of life you'd be stepping into?'

She gripped his fingers tightly and lifted her face. 'No, Andrew, at this moment I probably don't know much at all, but I promise to learn quickly. As I've said, don't ever under-estimate me.' When he looked into her eyes, he could no longer doubt her resolve; he could only wonder at it.

Emotion threatened to overwhelm him, so he mastered it by becoming pragmatic. 'Of course, if I do go out there and join the Guides, I'll gain a promotion — which means I'll be earning more than I do now. So, if I was to be — I mean if anything should happen, you'd find that living on a major's pension —'

'Yes, I hear what you're saying, Andrew.' She recognized his oblique acceptance of the marriage idea, and took care to speak matter-of-factly. 'I think it's good for us to talk openly about these things, because I want to assure you that if something dreadful did happen to you, my sister and her family would always welcome Annabelle and me into their home.' She smiled reassuringly. 'And, by the way, I'm not a penniless widow, you know. Peter left me something in his will.' Although she tried to make light of it, he bristled.

'No, Victoria, that money is yours and I will *not* have a penny of it touched for either Annabelle's needs or mine! We should be able to do well enough on what I'll earn and I've probably got sufficient set by now to establish a household wherever we're posted.'

'Splendid.' It dawned on Victoria that this was the second time that she'd been the one to propose marriage to a man. How very different this tall, lonely man was from her handsome, ebullient Peter. But again she had no doubt that the decision to join her life with his was the right one. She *wanted* to become part of him. She *wanted* him to show his love.

As they sat facing each other, listing the practicalities of setting up married life together in a frontier outpost, she thought how Aunt Honoria must be chuckling now if she was looking down from her cloud!

Yes, my dearest aunt, I'm going to share the life of this reserved, complex man who is in desperate need of the love that I've come to feel for him. It's not at all the wild, glorious excitement I shared with Peter. But I do love and admire Andrew for his strength and devotion, and the tenderness he tries so hard to hide.

Suddenly she stood and held out her arms. 'Oh, for goodness sake, Andrew Wyndham, please stop talking this instant, and kiss me.'

He heard her words through the ocean roar of his own blood pounding. Scarcely breathing, he stood slowly and reached out to hold her. She gave a little gasp when their lips touched, tentatively at first, but as if it had set flame to tinder, the kiss swiftly became ravenous and the shameless splendour of desire carried him on. He held her closer and felt her tremble as she twined her arms around his neck and returned each kiss with a heartfelt response that rocked him to his soul.

This lovely woman truly desired him! As he desired her. He had no wealth, no glory for her to bask in, no proud family tree, yet by some miracle, she was prepared to become his wife, his companion through life. There must be a God in Heaven after all!

Slowly, reluctantly they steadied their headlong rush into passion and pulled apart, both breathing raggedly, both smiling. 'Oh, yes, Andrew. I'm sure we'll do very well together out there on the frontier or anywhere else.' She held out her hand. 'Now, please show me the resignation that you were going to present to Colonel Moncrief in the morning. I want to watch you tear it up.'

He did as she asked, and felt as if a weight had been lifted from his shoulders. When he'd reduced the page to shreds, she gathered them up in her hands and threw them all into the lake.

'Now, your first duty tomorrow, Captain Wyndham, will be to send a telegram to the Guides accepting the post they've offered.

And please don't neglect to advise them that your wife and child will be accompanying you out there.' She beamed with triumph. 'I'll tell the begum that we're engaged the moment she wakes in the morning. And will you call on Nigel tomorrow to give him our news?'

★ ★ ★

The melon-seller, sitting in the dark under the branches of a willow growing on the bank, nodded knowingly as he watched the English officer and the begum's lady guest embrace on the houseboat. More change was coming. The augury he'd consulted last month had warned him that impatience would be the undoing of his enterprise. Wait, and watch for that one moment to act, the man had said. Be prepared to strike like a cobra. Fast and silent. The man pulled his rough cloak around himself as mist drifted across the lake. He waited and watched the houseboat. His patience was being tested.

★ ★ ★

'You and Victoria are engaged? Andrew, my dear chap, this is wonderful news, indeed!' Nigel pumped Andrew's hand when he called the following morning. 'And have you set the wedding date?'

'No, we've made no announcement yet. Actually, it's a long story, but we're waiting to do so after my father leaves Srinagar in the next day or so. Then I'll speak with the vicar. But I have other good news, too: I've been accepted into the Guides and Victoria will be coming out to Mardan with me. Along with *my* daughter. I have a three year old who's being looked after by the begum.'

'Aaaah!' Nigel was stunned for a moment, then he nodded sagely. 'So this was the root of the recent gossip about my cousin?'

'I'm afraid so.' As briefly and simply as he could, Andrew explained the whole extraordinary story of his child. 'I was on the verge of tossing in my commission and taking Annabelle away, until Victoria came to my rescue. I can still scarcely believe that she's prepared to help me bring up Annabelle — and travel so far away from the comfortable life she's always known.'

Nigel gave a chuckle. 'Do you really imagine that she's going with you all the way to Mardan simply to help you bring up your daughter? Clearly, old chap, you still have a great deal to learn about your fiancée. By the way, do I have permission to whisper your news to Kitty?'

15

No more than two dozen close friends, including the Resident and Lady Phillips, had been invited to Nigel and Kitty's wedding.

Andrew paced up and down like a nervous schoolboy while he waited outside the church for Victoria to arrive in the begum's carriage.

Dear God how he loved her, this woman of beauty, charm and wit, who was willing to marry him and bring up his daughter. And, wherever they went, he'd be called a lucky man, and envied for having such a wife at his side. Was it too much to hope that there might be other children as well in the years to come?

He prayed that the engagement ring in the gold silk pouch he had in his pocket would meet with her approval. It was a small diamond, but he'd chosen a setting that he thought would sit prettily on her finger. Lord, how he wished that his finances could have been stretched to afford the brilliant diamond cluster that the merchant had been tempting him with.

Of course, if he sold the ruby from Gwalinpore — but he could never do that.

The ring had been Ishana's, and one day it would be Annabelle's — her one link with her own mother.

Victoria reached the church a few minutes before the bride's arrival, and Andrew missed his opportunity to hand her down from the vehicle when one of Nigel's old friends hurried forward to greet her.

'Your timing is perfect, my dear Mrs Latham,' the fellow said. 'Look, I can see Kitty's carriage coming up the hill now, right on time! Nigel has been waiting in the church for thirty minutes already! What a splendid day this is, and it does my heart good to see you, looking so well. It's been far too long since we've seen you in Srinagar. Been away in the hills? Come, m'dear, I think it's time to take our places.'

She looked across to Andrew and smiled apologetically. 'Good morning, Captain Wyndham.' He returned her greeting and followed her into the church, taking the pew directly behind hers.

The scent of massed flowers filled the air and the notes of the organ swelled as Kitty, radiating happiness, walked down the aisle on the arm of her cousin, the forestry officer.

When she left the church as the wife of Nigel Pelham, the guests formed a semi-circle to watch while her dimpled smiles and

Nigel's proud stance were captured by the photographer he'd engaged. Victoria thought how delighted the family at Cloudhill would be to see this new version of the cousin they'd once called *dreary*.

A small reception was waiting for the wedding party at the forestry officer's house half a mile away and, as soon as Kitty and Nigel had cut the cake, Victoria and Andrew quietly excused themselves and slipped away. He helped her into the carriage, tied the reins of his horse onto the back of it, and climbed in beside her.

'I'm afraid I must dash back to the fort and play more games with the maharaja this afternoon, but right now you and I need a little time to ourselves. I have something important to say to you.'

He called for the driver to pull over in a shady spot beside the lake, then reached into his pocket for the gold embroidered silk pouch. He heard her sharp intake of breath when he opened it and held the ring gingerly in his fingers.

'Oh, Andrew!' When she slipped off her gloves, he saw that she was no longer wearing her wedding ring.

'Victoria Latham, will you — would you — ?' Until five minutes ago he'd had an impressively romantic proposal rehearsed in his mind, but now the drumbeat of his heart drowned out the gallant words he'd stored in his head.

'Oh, Andrew! Yes, yes, yes, of course I'll marry you.' She held out her left hand and he slipped the pretty little diamond onto her finger. 'It's lovely.' Her voice caught. 'It's absolutely perfect.'

'I hope the day will come when I'm in a position to give you something more impressive but — '

'Stop this minute! You could give me the crown jewels, but they would never mean as much to me as this ring does.' She held up her hand to examine it. 'I love it. I love you.' She reached behind his neck and pulled his head towards hers, to kiss him full on the lips.

'Yes, Andrew, let's marry very soon — just a private little ceremony with Nigel and Kitty there as our witnesses — though I'm sure you'd like to invite Sir Ian and Lady Phillips, too? Good. We don't need flowers, or the organist, or the photographer — just the vicar, our signatures in the parish register, and a marriage certificate to show to my parents when they come to call.'

She gave a giggle at the thought of such an unlikely event ever taking place. 'But, wait, actually, I do believe that they would approve of my marriage to you! After all, you are the son of a famous military hero General Gordon Wyndham!'

They both laughed at that and kissed again. And again.

★ ★ ★

Two days later, General Wyndham led his company from Srinagar with Mrs Beatrice Cooke looking very superior as she rode beside him. Mr Cooke had gone back to kill more mountain animals, but Mrs Cooke had suddenly discovered urgent business down on the plains that required her immediate attention, so she'd said. Gordon Wyndham offered to escort her all the way to Delhi. It would be no trouble — no trouble at all.

When Andrew visited the houseboat that evening, he gave an amusing description of his father's departure. 'Actually, I went to see him last night — to say farewell, and also to inform him of our engagement.'

When she winced, he gave a grin. 'Don't worry, Vicky, you'll find that I can be quite civil at times. Besides, I wanted to brag, didn't I? And until now I've never had much to brag about.'

'So, what was his reaction to our engagement?'

'Oddly, my father seemed to be singularly

unimpressed by my visit and everything I told him. All he wanted to talk about was his latest trophy, Beatrice Cooke. Anyhow, the good news is that a telegram arrived today from Mardan, confirming my posting, as well as our family arrangements.'

She threw her arms around him. 'Splendid! But how do we get there? Do we have to ride the whole way? How long will it take? When will we leave? And when can we be married?'

'Well, the answer is — yes, we ride through the mountains and over the Indus River. It's about a hundred and fifty miles as the crow flies, but once we get around Nanga Parbat, the country gets higher, so make sure you have a thick coat to wear. We should be there in two or three weeks, depending on the weather and the pack animals.'

'Oh dear! How my poor body will ache after all that riding.'

'Never fear, I'll find a sturdy mountain horse for you and have it brought down to the begum's coach house so you can learn to ride it before we set out.' He cupped her face in his hands and kissed her forehead. 'And, tomorrow, I'll see the vicar about marrying us just before we set out for the Frontier. Perhaps two Saturdays from now?'

* * *

Annabelle, sensing that some change beyond her comprehension was in the air, became increasingly restless in the days that followed.

'Sweetheart, very, *very* soon, you and I and your papa, and *ayah*, too, are all going to set off on a long ride over the mountains, so we must pack up all the things we want to take with us. Along the way, we'll eat our dinners beside a camp-fire, and sleep in tents — you and *ayah* will have one tent, and Papa and I will have another. And when we get to Papa's new fort, we'll set up house with all the lovely rugs and cushions and pretty things that the begum is giving us.'

The begum also presented Victoria with a length of ivory silk and yards of lace for her wedding gown, and set her tailor to work on a design that she, herself, had drawn. Victoria wrote a long letter to Emily, describing every detail.

My only disappointment is that you and Martin can't be here to see me wearing this utterly beautiful gown when Andrew and I are married. Oh, Emmie, I do love him so very much, and I know that you and Martin will love him, too, when we come home on leave in five years' time. He's like no man I've ever known. There's a goodness about Andrew Wyndham that he either can't or won't reveal to the world at large, but I can see it, and so can Annabelle. I know that we're going to be a truly happy family, wherever we are.

Andrew sent a message to Victoria saying that he'd found a well-behaved horse for her, though he warned that the mare was no great beauty. But she was a sure-footed animal, he said, and bred for rough mountain travel. He added that if Victoria had no objection to riding astride, he thought the saddle coming with it would suit her well.

When the begum heard that, she had her tailor make a divided skirt in a serviceable twill fabric, and the shoemaker was asked to stitch a pair of riding boots for both the memsahib and the baba-memsahib.

'Come quickly, Annabelle, my new horse has arrived, so let's go ashore to meet her,' Victoria called, when word came that the animal was waiting. 'We have to give her a name, too. Can you think of a pretty one?'

She took a small cake from a plate in the drawing room and, accompanied only by the Sikh, they were paddled to the bank where the begum's *syce* was standing with the reins of the saddled mare in his hands.

'Is it a lady horse?' Annabelle asked, as the shaggy-coated brown mare turned her head to inspect them. 'Then her name is *Ladyhorse*.'

'Thank you, that's a lovely name.' Victoria held out the cake and the mare's velvet lips scooped it delicately from her palm. 'Now, Ladyhorse, I know very little about riding you, so will you be very gentle with me when I'm on your back?'

The Sikh and Annabelle stood side by side, watching the *syce* hold the stirrup while the memsahib put her foot into it and heaved her right leg over the saddle. She felt balanced once astride the horse, and comfortable in her new divided skirt. Then, taking a nervous breath, she gathered the reins, touched her heels to the mare's flanks, and it set off at a fast trot along the grassy bank.

The unfamiliar motion bounced her uncomfortably on the saddle, causing her to wobble precariously, and several times she came close to losing her balance and slipping off.

Both the Sikh and the *syce* began to run after the horse, calling directions which Victoria had no hope of comprehending. But she pulled on the reins and when the horse slowed, the men eventually caught up to her. They continued to run beside the saddle, using gestures to encourage her to rise to the trot and try to match the mare's rhythm. It was some time before she began to master the movement, but by the end of the lesson, she had sufficient confidence to urge the mare into a gentle canter backwards and forwards along the bank, though she kept one hand clutched nervously onto the pommel.

★   ★   ★

The melon-seller sitting under the screen of willow tree branches lining the bank watched it all and readied himself. The child had been left unattended by the foolish servant while he ran off after the memsahib on the horse. The girl-child had been left to wander alone, and she was stopping every few steps to pluck something that caught her interest growing in the grass. Now she was coming in his direction and he felt his excitement rising. He looked quickly at the floor of the boat where the sack was waiting.

The memsahib had turned the animal back along the bank; the servants were still running beside her, and the moment to snatch the child and escape with her this day had vanished. But it was all happening as he knew it would. Those who guarded the child were growing careless, and his patience would soon be rewarded.

Andrew came as often as he could to help Victoria gain confidence on the horse. 'Try to put in a little practice every day, if you can.'

'Yes, I promise I will.' He didn't need to remind her that long days in the saddle were going to be torture if she didn't prepare her body for the ordeal ahead.

The bustle on board the houseboat mounted as the time of departure drew closer. Boxes packed with rugs and furnishings which the begum insisted would brighten Victoria's life on the frontier were nailed down and stacked to await the arrival of the pack horses.

The begum was also preparing to leave Srinagar after Victoria and Annabelle had gone.

'It's been more than four years since I last visited my cousins in Paris and for some time they've been urging me to come. Of course, it's been a pleasure to have watched Annabelle growing up, but now that fortune has smiled on Andrew, little Miss Annabelle Wyndham will have you to guide her. I'm delighted for all three of you.'

16

The day of the wedding was bright and cloudless, and the begum insisted that she, herself, would dress the bride in the glorious new ivory gown, and brush her hair into a soft, upswept style to display the sapphire ear-rings that were her gift to Victoria.

'Think of me each time you wear these, my dear, and know that all my blessings go with you.'

Victoria kissed her cheek. 'Thank you, madame — for everything. Oh, how I wish that I could have loved my own mother as I've come to love you. Do, please, write to me often, and I'll send you news about all our adventures.'

The begum had declined their invitation to the wedding. 'Thank you, but I made a vow forty years ago never again to set foot in that cantonment.' Though she said it with a laugh, she remained adamant.

This morning, a string of pack horses had arrived on the bank, led by porters wearing the thick brown cloaks and caps of mountain tribes, with each man carrying a long-barrelled jezail musket slung over one shoulder.

Victoria's impatience mounted as the hands of the clock continued to slide around the dial with agonizing slowness towards the time that she was due to stand beside Andrew in the church. Her smile became unstoppable. Every inch of her body was filled with the joy of anticipation.

Andrew was a man whom few people truly understood, and when she'd first come to know him, it had been hard to label the feelings he stirred in her. He was not a man to woo a lady with tender words or shallow flattery. But he'd permitted her to see beyond the uncompromising façade he presented to the world, and what she'd recognized deep inside him was love, pure and simple. A whole, untapped lifetime of it was now waiting for her, and tonight when they lay together she'd show him the first of the pleasures that she had in store for him.

Several *shikaras* were now plying to and fro between the houseboat and the shore with boxes of goods and provisions to be loaded onto the pack horses. They would go on ahead to set up the first camp in readiness for the sahib's group when they rode in this evening.

The begum placed a veil of the finest lace over Victoria's head. The moment for departure was drawing near, and in the midst of the bustle, a letter from England arrived. It was from the London solicitor, Mr Bartley-Symes, and contained the most recent statement of her growing fortune.

She tapped her foot in frustration. Obviously, her plans regarding the *Fortitude Foundation* hadn't yet reached London when he wrote this to her. It was essential for everyone concerned to be perfectly clear about her intentions so that there would be no misunderstandings and delays. Her simple instructions had been for everything from Peter's bequest — as well as every penny of future profit — to go straight into the Foundation.

There was no time now to sit down and send off a reply confirming this with Mr Bartley-Symes when she was shortly to walk down the aisle with Andrew. He still knew nothing about her plans, and she felt guilty to admit that. Time and again she'd considered discussing her ideas for the Foundation with him, but he'd always been so busy. And, besides, the legalities were still to be finalized and a committee hadn't yet been formed to assess all the practicalities of finding a building —

Stop it! she scolded herself. It was nothing but pure cowardice that had stopped her from confiding in Andrew. Frankly, she did feel concern about his reaction if he should discover the current disparity in their fortunes. But once Peter's money had been put to use by the Foundation and was no longer *hers*, of course, she'd have no hesitation in explaining everything about it to him.

She folded the attorney's letter tightly and stuffed it into the little purse she was carrying on her wrist. Kitty had arranged a small reception at their house to toast the newlyweds after the wedding ceremony and she was sure to find a moment there to speak privately with Nigel and ask him to respond to the letter on her behalf.

When the time came for Victoria to leave for the church, the begum handed her a bouquet of cream roses that had been picked in the Shalimar Gardens at sunrise, and therefore — so legend said — carried a mystical significance.

Annabelle let everybody know how cross she was when she realized that she was not being taken to the wedding. The adults had discussed it, but in the end it had been Andrew who'd decided against it.

'No, I want this to be *our* day, Victoria,' he'd whispered into the warm curve of her neck. 'We'll have many other special days to share with Annabelle in the years ahead.'

She'd been incredibly touched by that.

Annabelle's tantrum quickly ran its course when Victoria pulled a few blossoms from her bouquet and found a lace shawl to throw over the child's head. 'There you are, see, now you're a bride, too. Give me a goodbye kiss, because I'm going off to find your papa, and I promise to bring him straight back here, along with your new mama. And do you know who that will be?'

Annabelle shook her head.

'Belle, it's going to be me! I'm going to be your new mama.'

'My forever and forever mama?' Her face broke into a smile.

'Yes, my sweet. Forever and forever you'll be my little girl and I'll be your mama.' She opened her arms and the child ran to be hugged. 'We'll play, and draw, and read books — and we must always talk to each other in English because that's the only language I know.'

They waved to each other when Victoria boarded the begum's *shikara* to be rowed to the steps on the shore where the beaming Sikh was waiting for her beside the carriage. The begum had decided that he should be the one to drive the bride to and from her wedding — and that he should be dressed for the grand occasion in a dazzling white uniform with an embroidered yellow silk sash across his chest. His huge moustache was heavily waxed to curl at each end, and just for this special occasion, he'd permitted a sparkling aigrette with tall feathers to be pinned to the front of his turban.

* * *

Annabelle and the begum continued to wave until the carriage carrying Victoria had gone from view. Then, while Annabelle and her *ayah* played with her dolls on the deck, the begum went to her writing table, smiling to herself as she took out a sheet of mono-grammed paper and began a letter to Andrew.

This was something she had been planning to write for the last two years — a surprise that she wanted him to have before he set out to start a new life with Victoria as his wife — and mother to his daughter.

My dear Andrew
It has been my great joy to have had Annabelle as part of my life for the last three years, and I thank you for the privilege. From the day she came into my arms, I have loved your beautiful little daughter as my own, and I write this now to tell you that on her first birthday I made

changes to my will to include Annabelle Wyndham amongst my beneficiaries.

When I am gone, she is to inherit one-fifth of my estate, the remainder of which will go to my nephews in France.

Andrew, my dear friend, I must insist that until then you say nothing about this matter to her, nor to any other person — apart from Victoria, of course. Actually, it was she who reminded me not long ago that society in general, and gentlemen in particular, have a distorted perception of a woman who is known to have wealth. Worthless fortune-hunters are likely to come flocking for her hand, and pride can turn away a worthy candidate who has no fortune of his own. That is why I beg you to disclose nothing of this inheritance to the world at large, nor to Annabelle herself, until she reaches the age of twenty-one. Allow your beautiful daughter to grow up being loved for herself alone.

The letter went on to express her deep affection for both himself and Victoria, and her fond wishes for their future together. After signing it with a flourish, the begum sealed it in an envelope and took it to the bedroom where Andrew's travelling clothes had been laid out, ready for him change into when he and Victoria returned from the wedding. She slipped her letter into a pocket of his brown jacket.

⋆ ⋆ ⋆

All along the route to the cantonment, heads turned to stare at the sight of the magnificently dressed Sikh driving an open carriage carrying a veiled lady as it clopped past hamlets and farms scattered around the lake. It travelled through the crowded lanes of the old town, and around the corner where the ancient augury had seen Victoria's future in his hot oil. There was no sign of the old man there today.

Soon they were heading up the hill towards the neat gardens and bungalows of the British cantonment with its steepled church looking as if it had been plucked straight from a village in Kent.

Nigel was waiting for her on the church porch and, as he handed her down the carriage step, she was surprised to hear the notes of the organ coming from within.

'Yes, I know that you chose to have a very simple wedding, but Kitty decided that we couldn't let you walk down the aisle on this special day without music to accompany you. So come along now, take my arm. Andrew and the rector are waiting in there for you. Ready?'

'Yes, I am. Very, very ready, thank you Nigel. But, afterwards, I need to find a brief moment to speak with you privately about a letter that I must ask you to write to my lawyer.'

Kitty had decided also that the church should be filled with flowers, though apart from Sir Ian and Lady Phillips, along with their daughter, Lucy, the only other people in there were a few of Andrew's friends from the regiment.

The notes of the organ swelled as Victoria and Nigel entered. Andrew was waiting with the vicar at the end of the aisle, looking tall and striking in his full dress uniform, and facing her with an expression of longing that struck up an anthem of joy on her heartstrings. The light slanting in through the stained glass windows touched the gleaming brass ornaments and the massed blooms filling the church, creating a dream-like atmosphere.

But, as she walked slowly down the aisle with Nigel and came to stand beside the man at the altar, she knew that this was no dream. Andrew Wyndham was very real, and with all her heart she made her vows to love, honour and obey this man. His hand was a little unsteady as he slipped a simple gold band on to her finger, and when the rector declared them to be husband and wife, he lifted the veil and touched his lips to hers in a kiss that held a thousand promises.

Her happiness soared. She was loved. She was no longer alone. She and Andrew had become one, and tonight she would sleep in his arms, knowing that she would always be safe and cherished. Her heart overflowed with love and she held his arm tightly as they walked from the church to the accompaniment of the organ.

Kitty had also arranged for a photographer to record the day, and when Victoria and Andrew stepped from the church, he was waiting for them. He positioned them to stand side by side while they smiled into his camera lens and were dazzled time and again by his flash.

'There!' Kitty said. 'Now we'll have pictures of your wedding for Nigel to send to your sisters. Everyone will want to see what a distinguished husband you've brought into the family.'

With the photographs taken, Andrew kissed her again and they sat closely side by side in the carriage with their legs pressed tightly against each other's for the short drive to Nigel's house. When he put a hand on her thigh, she could feel the heat of his palm through the silk.

'Vicky, I want to say so much more than simply thank you, but I can never find the right words when I need them.' Her hand touched his and their fingers interlocked. 'I do love you, Mrs Wyndham, and I'll never cease to be amazed at your astonishing ability to love a man like me.'

'Actually, I find it rather easy, sir. I like the tone of your voice, I like the scent of you, and especially the shape of your mouth on those occasions when you decide to smile.' She turned her head with an unspoken invitation to kiss her again. He was quick to oblige, and she felt a twinge of disappointment when the horse pulled up at Nigel's house and there was no opportunity to exchange more than one more fleeting embrace.

Duleep was waiting at the door, bowing low and grinning widely. Kitty ushered the guests into the dining room where an elegant little reception was waiting with sandwiches, pastries and jellies, set out on the dining room table, as well as a magnificently decorated three-tiered cake that the cook had copied from one of the new Pelham-memsahib's books.

Lady Phillips and Kitty each presented the newlyweds with a gift. Her ladyship's box contained a dozen silver dessert spoons. 'I feel that one can never have enough spoons,' she said, and Victoria agreed.

Kitty and Nigel's gift was a set of three Mogul miniatures painted on ivory — which Victoria knew that Nigel himself must have chosen. They weren't at all Kitty's taste. 'Thank you, both,' she said. 'We'll treasure these.'

When the toasts had been made and the cake had been cut, Victoria noticed Andrew glance several times at the hands of the long-case clock. She gave him a nod of understanding and began to push her chair back from the table.

'Ladies and gentlemen, Andrew and I have a long journey ahead of us today, so please forgive us for leaving you so soon. But first, Nigel, I wonder if you and I could have a moment alone? Something arrived from London just as I was to leave this morning and I didn't have time to reply to it myself.'

He held her chair as she stood. 'Perhaps, Kitty, m'love, while Vicky and I go into my study, our guests might like to be taken upstairs to see some of the changes we've made up there.'

Once alone with Nigel in his study, Victoria handed him the lawyer's letter. 'As I mentioned, this reached me this morning, and I'd be most grateful if you'd reply to Mr Bartley-Symes on my behalf. I simply want to make absolutely sure that there can be no confusion about where all the profits from Peter's ship are to be sent. Please tell him that I will require no part of it to come to me from now on. Everything is to go straight into the *Fortitude Foundation*.'

'Yes, very well, Vicky. I'll write to him and clarify the matter this evening.' He pursed his lips and looked at her thoughtfully. 'Of course, I applaud the worthy cause you're sponsoring, though I can't help wondering if you might be a little rash in refusing to accept even a small percentage of profit from the ship's future trading ventures.'

She shook her head firmly. 'I have a husband who will provide for me now.'

'Very well, and you know that I couldn't be happier for you both, my dear.' He folded the letter and put it to one side. 'Forgive me, Vicky, but do you mind telling me just how much have you given to set up this foundation?'

'Sufficient.'

'Sufficient for what?'

'Sufficient to buy a building and modify it for our requirements; sufficient to engage suitable staff to train the girls; sufficient to buy the equipment needed to run the establishment; sufficient to provide good food — and medicines if they're needed — and I'd also like the foundation to have a fund that could help some girls establish themselves in their own little business, when they're ready.'

'Good Lord! Vicky you must have laid out a fortune!'

She tapped her finger on the latest statement of profits. 'Well, — with this added, I think that there will now be close to twenty-two thousand in the trust.'

Nigel gaped at her. 'You have donated *twenty-two thousand pounds*? No! Oh, my! Does Andrew know about this?'

'No! And please don't mention it — to anyone. Ever. Peter — the late Captain Peter Latham — will be known as the Foundation's benefactor, which is perfectly right and proper. Andrew will understand it when I explain the scheme.'

★ ★ ★

It hadn't taken long for Andrew's interest to wane as Kitty led them through the upstairs rooms to admire the woven French silk fringes edging every curtain, chair and table-cover throughout. Sir Ian and Lady Phillips, on the other hand, were engrossed with it all, and continued to follow Kitty from room to room.

Andrew was impatient to be on the way to Mardan. He excused himself and walked downstairs. The door to Nigel's study stood ajar and, when he reached the bottom step, it was impossible for him not to hear the voices coming from within, and to catch the gist of their conversation.

For a moment, Victoria's words held him rooted to the spot. He couldn't believe he'd just heard her saying that in one stroke she'd given away more money than he himself had earned in his whole career! Of course, she'd mentioned to him once that she'd not been left penniless when her husband died, but he'd assumed that she'd been referring to a few hundred pounds.

Anger slammed him in the solar-plexus; his chest heaved. A girl with that kind of money could have bought any man. Why in God's name had she insisted on marriage to Andrew Wyndham? She'd even been able to look straight into his eyes and lie to him about her situation — admittedly a lie of omission — but as they were to exchange marriage vows, why couldn't she have told him frankly about her fortune? He ground his teeth. Had she no trust at all in him?

His fists clenched and he was almost

overwhelmed by the need to smash them into something — anything. God! Twenty-two thousand pounds! Would he have married her if she'd been open with him about her wealth? Like hell he would. Never! So what the devil was he going to do about it now?

Twenty-two thousand bloody pounds! Tightening his jaw, he strode to the front porch and called for the begum's carriage to be brought to the steps.

What excuse could he find to send the new Mrs Wyndham straight back to England? Back to a privileged life with her wealthy family. Back to — ? Damn! Now what the devil was he going to do about Annabelle?

The Sikh's colourful feathers fluttered on his turban and he was grinning as he pulled up and sprang from the driver's seat to open the vehicle's door.

As he waited for his bride to emerge from the house, Andrew's white-hot anger drove him beyond reason and his mind raced as he tried to convince himself that he had no need to produce a wife to raise a daughter on his own in Mardan. He could simply arrive out there with Annabelle and her *ayah*, and lie to the regiment that his wife had been called back to England. For a few years. Indefinitely. After all, he had a marriage certificate now to confirm that his wife, Annabelle's mother, was as English . . .

So what answer could he concoct when people asked why Annabelle's mother had not taken her child home to England with her?

Victoria came out of the house with the others, laughing, looking radiantly happy. There was much hand-shaking and affectionate kissing as the party escorted the bride to the carriage. Then another flurry of goodbyes were exchanged, and handfuls of rose petals were strewn over the newlyweds before the horse clopped out through the gates.

Victoria gave a long sigh of contentment and sat back against the seat. 'Wasn't that just the loveliest wedding? And our signatures are there in the parish register for the whole world to come and see. I'm sure that Emily will write to Mama and Papa and tell them that I've become a respectable woman at last, thanks to you!'

Andrew made no answer, though he wondered what his new bride would say if she could to read his mind at this moment.

'It won't take me long at all to change into my travelling outfit when we get back and say farewell to the begum. I won't keep you waiting. I think Annabelle has been dressed and ready since dawn. And the clothes that you had sent over this morning are all laid out waiting for you.'

Andrew remained silent while he attacked the rose petals that had landed on him as they left Nigel's house. When the last one had been banished from his shoulders and trouser legs, he sat mutely, and as far away from Victoria as possible, with his fingers tightly laced together on his lap.

'Annabelle looks so sweet in her new little riding boots. I think she'll be asking for a pony of her own soon. And I've had big straw hats made for us both.'

When her chatter brought no response from him, she clamped her lips. Obviously, he had a great deal on his mind at this time. The long journey ahead of them, the new responsibilities waiting in Mardan.

From the corner of her eye, she slanted a glance at the man who would sleep close beside her tonight. It had been years since she'd felt as happy as she did today. And when she remembered his kiss on the steps of the church less than two hours ago, a small glow began to warm the core of her being. She was impatient to feel the touch of his hands on her skin — her breasts, her stomach, her thighs. Her toes curled inside her shoes as she anticipated the taste of his tongue invading her mouth, and of her legs parting as he stretched his body full length over hers. Would they be able to leave the door of the tent open tonight and watch the mountain stars blazing above them?

He ignored her sigh and she was left to wonder what thoughts were chasing each other behind the frown on his forehead.

When they came closer to the lake's edge, she saw that the pack horses had gone on their way, and the riding horses were waiting to be saddled near the coach house. Nearby, two mountain guides had arrived and stood waiting for them with another pack animal to carry the remainder of their luggage.

The Sikh continued to drive around the shore until they reached the begum's landing stage where her *shikara* would be waiting to collect them. He looked around at Andrew with a frown: There was no sign of the craft, either beside the houseboat, or coming for them across the lake.

As soon as the carriage came to halt, Andrew sprang to the ground, took two steps, then spun on his heel and looked up, frowning hard at his new wife.

'Victoria, are you ready to admit that this marriage has been one hell of a mistake for us both? It's perfectly clear to me that you have no real wish to spend the rest of your life in some isolated place out there on frontier with me. And I know damn well that I can never be the sort of husband you expect. You'll soon come to regret the whole thing. For God's sake, just accept the fact that it would be better for us both if you went straight back to England. Or stay in Srinagar. I really don't care — one way or the other.'

His words sent her reeling with disbelief; her head seemed full of moths that were fluttering away with her sanity. Was she in Kashmir or some madhouse? She stood up in the carriage and looked down squarely into his face.

'What in heaven's name are you talking about? Only a short time ago we stood in church and you gave a solemn vow to love and cherish me, Andrew Wyndham. Till death us do part, actually.' Her voice quaked and her mind raced to pinpoint the source of his outburst. It escaped her.

'I'm your wife now, may I remind you? I do love you, I will honour you, and I'll even do my very best to obey you.' Hurt and anger balled in her throat and brought her close to tears. 'I have no intention of going back to England without you — either now or in the future. I'm coming with you — to the ends of the world, if necessary. And I do advise you to discover a little more about the woman you married today before discarding her so rashly.'

The Sikh, looked from one to the other,

distraught. He had no understanding of the English words being hurled to and fro, any more than he could guess what had ignited this sudden conflict between the pair. And where was the begum's *shikara*?

'Victoria, if you — '

The sound of two pistol shots coming from the houseboat instantly silenced him. The Sikh reached for his weapon, then stood floundering. The begum had instructed him not to carry his gun to the wedding today.

Victoria remained standing in the carriage while Andrew, with the Sikh at his heels, ran down the steps to the water's edge and called to the begum whom they could now see standing on the top deck, waving a pistol. She raised her arm and let off another shot into the air while several agitated servants milled around her.

The houseboat was too far out on the lake for even raised voices to be heard distinctly, but the begum's high-pitched screams lanced the distance and they were able to catch a few intelligible words. Annabelle . . . gone. *Shikara* . . . sunk.

Victoria's heart plunged. Her breath caught. The unthinkable had happened: the child had been kidnapped!

Andrew and the Sikh rushed back up to the top step of the landing and stood looking about them wildly, but there was nobody in sight. Andrew barked an order to the Sikh and they ran off in opposite directions along the bank. Victoria remained standing in the carriage, and this slightly higher position gave her a wider view over their surroundings. She looked around desperately, unclear of exactly who or what she was searching for.

Suddenly, a movement caught her eye and she glimpsed a stooped man darting furtively from under one willow tree and into the next. He was more than 200 yards away and within the blink of an eye he vanished again into the green branches.

Was she right in thinking that he appeared to have been carrying something over his shoulder?

She shouted across to Andrew with all her might and signalled the direction she had seen the man taking. Whipping the wedding veil from her head, she hitched up her skirt, then sprang from the carriage and began to run hard towards the place where the figure had disappeared into the tangle of overhanging trees.

From far behind, she heard Andrew roaring at her to stop, but terror lent strength to her legs and she ran faster into the willows, brushing aside the low branches that slapped at her face. Suddenly, she burst into the open and found herself stumbling across an empty hillside field ploughed for planting. Andrew and the Sikh were closing in behind her now but there was no sign of the figure she was trying to chase.

'A man!' she panted when they caught up to her. 'I saw a man — and I think he was carrying something. Where could he have been going?'

Andrew and the Sikh looked around, then pointed towards a hamlet lying on higher ground beyond the ploughed field. They began to run in that direction, with Andrew veering to the right, the Sikh to the left. She had no hope of keeping up with either of them but, panting hard, she continued to follow until her attention was caught by something on her right. From the corner of her eye she glimpsed what appeared to be a hut lying near a fold in the hillside across a distant meadow.

Some instinct drove her to turn in that direction and, as she ran, she cried out to Andrew repeatedly until she had caught his attention. He saw her frantic gestures, though from his own position it would have been impossible for him to see the almost-hidden thatched-roofed hovel nestled close into the fold of the hill that she was racing towards.

The man inside the hut was ready for her.

The thin little melon-seller had either seen or heard her approach and he burst from the low entrance, uttering a throaty hiss and brandishing a curved knife in one hand. Victoria could hear Annabelle's muffled screams coming from the dim, stinking interior and, ignoring the talons of terror tearing into her, she thrust her way inside, dodging the man's lunge in her direction.

How could she defend herself? She snatched up a stool that was standing against a wall and, as he came at her again, she swung it wildly with all the force she could muster.

It caught him on the shoulder and, as he staggered sideways, she saw Annabelle fighting to scramble from a sack on the earthen floor. The child's eyes were wide, her cheeks drenched with tears and in one hand she was grasping a little wooden doll from the painted elephant's *howdah*.

'Out, out, out, quickly, Belle, run outside as fast as you can. Now!' she shouted over the child's screams. 'Papa is coming. Run to him now! Run, run, run.'

The man made an attempt to snatch the child as she fled screaming from the hut, but his fingers missed their mark when Victoria held the legs of the stool and struck out at his wrist. His face twisted in a mask of fury and his eyes burned into hers as he spun towards her. Saliva pooled in the corners of his mouth, and with a snarl, he raised the knife high and swung it downwards.

Victoria could see the flashing blade coming towards her throat and heaved the stool at him. It missed, but it was enough to unbalance him and change the knife's trajectory. From that moment, everything around her began to happen very slowly, as if in a dream.

The blade missed her throat and sliced through the right shoulder of her gown, embedding itself in her flesh. She cried out. Staggered. The pain was sharp. Blood gushed and a red stain spread over the lace front of her beautiful wedding gown. The wretch had ruined it! It seemed odd to be feeling this rush of anger when she was just about to die.

She didn't want to die! 'Oh, Andrew! Andrew!'

Her legs gave way; she felt herself falling backwards — down, down — and when her head struck the hard floor, she became aware of nothing more.

17

Victoria lay lost in a thick, black cloud of nothingness. There was no memory of how she came to be here. No memory of who she was. The pain was returning. Her head. Her shoulder. Why did she feel this pain?

Somebody was close beside her. So close she could feel warm breath on her cheek. A deep, husky voice began to speak softly, and she felt herself floating in the flow of his words. Such tender words.

> She walks in beauty, like the night
> Of cloudless climes and starry skies;
> And all that's best of dark and bright
> Meet in her aspect and her eyes:
> Thus mellow'd to that tender light
> Which heaven to gaudy day denies.

Running footsteps approached. 'Mama! Mama! Is Mama awake now?'

'Hush, Belle. Not yet, but soon, sweetheart. I'll lift you up so you can kiss her cheek. There — very gently now.'

A childish voice had called her *Mama*. Who was the man so close to her pillow? His scent

— it was his scent that began to stir faint memories. His voice — the soothing words he spoke. She wanted to hear more. He lifted her hand and touched his lips to each finger and, somehow, she knew that this was how it should be. There was something she must tell him, but she had no memory of what it was.

The black nothingness began pulling her down into itself again when a different scent came to her side. She tensed. This man, who wafted the aroma of herbs and strange unguents and mumbled words she couldn't understand, lifted her head and placed a sip of something vile on her lips.

She gave a little moan when he touched the source of her pain. But after he'd placed a pungent substance there, the pain faded.

'Vicky, my darling, it's going well,' the husky voice close beside her whispered. 'You're getting stronger. Keep hold of my hand. There! I won't let you go. I'll never let you go.'

'I don't know who I am.'

'Oh, Victoria! You are my love and my strength.' His voice broke. 'You are the mirror that shows me my soul. You are the angel who saved our daughter's life.'

There was a tenderness in his tone that brought a smile to her lips, though she still struggled to recall what it was that she must tell him. The nothingness began to swallow her again, but she caught another waft of his scent and the blackness lightened.

She struggled to open her eyes. 'I saw a man — !'

'He's gone, my dearest, and I promise that he'll never again trouble us — or anyone else for that matter.'

Again and again, the blackness washed over her like an incoming tide, which rose and then retreated. She saw Peter smiling at her. Emily and Martin. Aunt Honoria. The begum. Her parents. Nigel and Kitty. They all came and went, and in the fleeting moments of awareness, fragments of memory started to return.

'Where am I?' Her lips barely moved. Her voice was a whisper. 'There's something I must do . . . '

'You're safe. We're here on the begum's houseboat and her Healer will make you well again.'

'Who are you?'

He gave a long sigh. 'Who am I? I'm Andrew, the man who had the honour of becoming your husband three days ago.'

She lifted her eyelids, struggling to focus her gaze on the features of this man who said he was her husband. It was a strong face with a thin white scar down one cheek, but she seemed to be looking at him through the wrong end of a telescope. He was far away. Andrew?

'And also, Vicky, I'm the fool who is bitterly ashamed of the harsh words he spoke to you, and who wants you to know how desperately he regrets those lies. Can you forgive my stupidity?'

The image of an irate face drifted into her mind's eye. Andrew? What had caused him to be so angry. 'There's something that I must tell you, but I can't recall what it can be.'

She felt herself floating again and fought to keep her eyelids from closing in order to bring his face back into focus. And when she did, she saw the moisture gathering in his eyes.

'Vicky, I want you to know that I love you with all my heart and nothing means more to me than the future we're going to share. When you're strong enough, we'll make our way to Mardan, but until then the whole world will have to wait until you're ready to travel.'

'I can't stay awake any longer. Please, lie here beside me and put your head next to mine on the pillow. I need to feel you close.' His lips touched her forehead and the scent of him stirred fresh fragments of memory.

But, as she lay beside him with her eyes

closed and her hand held tightly in his, images began tumbling over each other in her mind, all struggling to find a foothold on the slippery mountain of some misunderstanding that had come between herself and this gentle, possessive man at her side. How could she make sense of everything that had happened when her head ached so?

She slipped into sleep again and when she woke, the clouds had lifted further, allowing other images to line themselves up in her mind and start to form a chain of recollections.

Yes, of course — as soon as possible, Andrew must be told all about her plans to establish the *Fortitude Foundation* in Peter's name. There must be no more delay. She parted her lips, drew in a breath, but when she began, her tongue seemed to be incapable of forming the words she wanted.

'Hush, sweetheart. Just lie quietly here with me and don't try to speak. Give yourself a little time and soon you'll be able to recall everything.'

But did she need to recall everything? Did she *want* to recall everything? Memory can have a way of being selective, and at that point Victoria chose *not* to remember the scene at the lakeside when her new husband had hurled bitter, incomprehensible words at her in the carriage. If ever he raised the topic again she would look at him blankly and shake her head.

Whatever it was that had upset him so much that day could no longer be pertinent, so she wiped that image from her mind with the ease of a child cleaning a schoolroom slate with a damp sponge.

Andrew was here close beside her now, Annabelle was safe, and waiting ahead for them was a lifetime of fresh memories to be made.

We do hope that you have enjoyed reading this large print book.

Did you know that all of our titles are available for purchase?

We publish a wide range of high quality large print books including:
**Romances, Mysteries, Classics
General Fiction
Non Fiction and Westerns**

Special interest titles available in large print are:
**The Little Oxford Dictionary
Music Book
Song Book
Hymn Book
Service Book**

Also available from us courtesy of Oxford University Press:
**Young Readers' Dictionary
(large print edition)
Young Readers' Thesaurus
(large print edition)**

For further information or a free brochure, please contact us at:
**Ulverscroft Large Print Books Ltd.,
The Green, Bradgate Road, Anstey,
Leicester, LE7 7FU, England.
Tel:** (00 44) 0116 236 4325
Fax: (00 44) 0116 234 0205

THE WAYWARD WIND

Ashleigh Bingham

It's 1867, and when Tom Sinclair learns that his sister has run away, he sails from London, confident of finding her. The trail leads him to Morocco where his fears for her safety are confirmed. Stranded in a country, understanding neither the language nor the culture, his quest seems at a dead end. But help is thrust upon him: Francesca, a sharp-tongued Spanish governess, has spent years in North Africa, and learns of Tom's need for a translator. She snatches the opportunity to join the search for his missing sister — while hiding her own grim agenda in the enterprise . . .

WINDS OF HONOUR

Ashleigh Bingham

The Honourable Phoebe Pemberton is beautiful and wealthy, but is the daughter of the late, disgraceful Lord Pemberton and Harriet Buckley . . . Phoebe escapes her mother's plans to teach her the family business of wringing profits from the mills. She dreams of running away, and, when she learns of her mother's schemes for Phoebe's marriage as part of a business transaction, she calls on her friend Toby Grantham for help . . . But Harriet's vengeful fury is aroused, leaving Phoebe tangled in a dark and desperate venture.

SCANDAL AT THE DOWER HOUSE

Marina Oliver

When Catarina's elderly husband dies, she moves to the Dower House where things are about to change dramatically with the arrival of Catarina's young sister Joanna. Tricked by her cousin Matthew into a sham marriage, Joanna is now pregnant and alone. Catarina has a plan to hide her sister's disgrace, but then tragedy strikes suddenly at the Dower House. What will be the fate of Joanna's unwanted child?

CHEF

Jaspreet Singh

Kip Singh is timorous and barely twenty when he arrives for the first time at General Kumar's camp, nestled in the shadow of the mighty Siachen Glacier that claimed his father's life. He is placed under the supervision of Chef Kishen, a fiery, anarchic mentor who guides Kip towards the heady spheres of food and women. As a Sikh, Kip feels secure in his allegiance to India, the right side of this interminable conflict. Until, one oppressively close day, a Pakistani 'terrorist' with long, flowing hair is swept up on the banks of the river and changes everything.